DEADLINED

DANIEL D. BAUMER

Copyright

deadline - To remove a vehicle or piece of equipment from operation of use for one of the following reasons: a. is inoperative due to damage, malfunctioning, or necessary repairs (the term does not include items temporarily removed from use by reasons of routine maintenance and repairs that do not affect the combat capability of the item): b. is unsafe: and c. would be damaged by further use.

US Department of Defense

With silent lips. "Give me your tired, your poor,
Your huddled masses yearning to breathe free,
The wretched refuse of your teeming shore.
Send these, the homeless, tempest-tost to me,
I lift my lamp beside the golden door!"

From 'The New Colossus' by Emma Lazarus

Prologue

Jonathan Robert Scotts was going to die tonight. He settled into his comfortable camping spot beneath the eaves of the South Hayward BART station tracks for the last time, his impending death by gunshot coming within minutes. This wasn't something Jonathan, JR to his friends, had anticipated, but he wasn't one to live a calendared life. Having lived on the streets for the better part of two years, his social activities didn't call for much planning.

Luckier than most of his peers, he got a modest disability pension from the VA. It wasn't much, just enough each month to get drunk a few times before the money ran out. Apart from that, Scotts depended on donations from the churches on Tennyson Road. Sometimes, he scavenged in the dumpsters behind the markets, but there was often too much competition from his fellow street dwellers for whatever treasures they might contain.

He wanted to be around his family, but he'd burned those bridges. They still lived down the road in Fremont, but they'd grown tired of his bullshit. They'd grown tired of his lies, and they'd grown weary of him stealing from them when he needed some kind of fix. There were only so many times they wanted to retrieve JR from the county lockup.

The day arrived when they no longer came, and he could only manage a ride to Hayward. Then Hayward became home. JR tried downtown around the bus and BART station but found it crowded with too many hardcore drug users. The industrial areas lacked food or booze sources, and the prime foraging spots along Mission Boulevard were already occupied. After a few weeks of exploring and experimenting, he found his way to the Tennyson corridor and made it his home—for what that was worth. Sure, he had to break camp every night, but that didn't take long, and it was easy to pack with him on the bike he had stolen. He'd never been robbed, the BART police never rousted him, and only the strongest of winds would bother him in the faux cave beneath the tracks.

Tucked away under his blue tarp, sipping the last of his malt liquor, he weighed whether to take a piss now or hold it in through the night. He wanted a better life, and he had a plan for it. He wanted his disabilities reevaluated to see if he was eligible for a better pension. He'd qualify for VA medical care if he had a high enough rating. If he could do that, he would get to rehab. With rehab, JR almost teared up at the thought that he might get his family back.

He'd fucked up so much, so many times. He knew his family would never forgive him, but he'd wanted to try. He had no idea how to get sober and had every excuse and opportunity to keep drinking as things were now.

Sleep approached as he thought of his ex-wife, Debra. She hadn't remarried, so maybe he had a chance. He recalled their first dates, how they met, how they kissed and made love. It made him sad.

He turned in his blanket to face the concrete wall, took a heavy breath, and eventually slipped into slumber.

JR wasn't aware how much time had passed, but he woke with a jolt when his tarp and blanket were jerked away. Was he being robbed? For a moment, he felt relieved, knowing he had nothing to steal.

That comfort ended with two quick spits of light from the gun barrel pointed at him. For the briefest of instances, images of Debra passed through his mind before the final shot entered his brain, and he slipped to the other side.

* * *

Oscar Braga looked forward to the killing on this night. It was an idea a long time coming, and that time was now.

While traversing this busy corridor, commuting to and from work sites, he had observed the patterns of people in this area and kept mental notes of their activities. He'd seen where the homeless gathered, where they hid and nested. A few weeks back, he'd parked his truck and scouted this area to get a more intimate feel for which dark corners held his targets. He had found the alleys and corners that gave shelter to those he despised.

Tonight, he would clean the streets and make a better world for those remaining.

Tennyson Road ran east-west and crossed Hayward just south of downtown. Lower-middle-class neighborhoods saddled its length up and down with a few strip malls, churches, and schools thrown in. Once gentrification took hold, the area's glory days were behind it and, if lucky, ahead of it. For now, though, it had more than its share of homeless souls seeking refuge from the world's economic woes where and when and how they could.

The South Hayward Bay Area Rapid Transit station was the site of his first planned contact. Braga didn't know if it was a male or female, only that this silhouetted figure would be in its usual spot, as it had been every time he'd checked in the past few weeks.

Braga had been keeping himself calm during the roundabout walk from his truck to this starting point, but knowing he was about to commence his wave of cleansing, he was both scared and excited beyond words. His breathing was quick, and his heart rate elevated like he was about to begin a trip on a roller coaster. But he was ready.

He walked westward along the north side of Tennyson, dipping low to avoid the BART tracks in a half-underpass. Braga shone his flashlight into the dark corners to check for anyone unaccounted for. Had there been occupants in that dry area, he'd have to skip this first kill, but he already knew from his weeks of prep work that no one had taken up shelter there. Braga wanted a clean start with no potential witnesses. At other spots, he'd easily be able to kill anyone who saw him, but not at the beginning. Too open, too busy with traffic, too well-lit.

Head on a swivel, he reminded himself while keeping one of the massive concrete support pillars between him and his target. One flickering light cast his shadow intermittently upon the stone. It was a short path and worth the risk. Traffic was clear.

Once on the other side, he steeled himself, pulling a suppressed 9mm pistol out from the front pouch of his black hoodie. It was an old military surplus Beretta 9mm and probably had a few thousand rounds sent through its barrel—maybe even a few in anger. It would work for tonight's mission.

With one final glance over his shoulder to the street behind, Braga turned and hustled up the concrete incline toward the eave, where it met the underside of the BART track overpass. There it was, in the same spot it had been every time. Reaching his target, Braga seized the edge of the tarp and blanket the person had used for protection from the world and whipped them away, rousing him with a start. It was a man, after all. Before the man made a sound and while staring into his rheumy eyes, Braga overcame the rapid rise of the man's stench and placed three quick rounds into him: two in the chest and one in his face. No time to enjoy the victory. He had more to do.

Three blocks west, someone had made a home of tarps against the tall noise-abatement wall, partially protecting the adjacent neighborhood from the sounds of passing trains. The wall kept him safe from the elements but not from predators.

Braga grabbed the tarp that served as the man's home and ripped it away. Held in place by ropes and bungee cords, it didn't get torn down altogether, but it did expose the alarmed occupant to the cool Hayward night.

The man's panic didn't last long. Two quick shots to his chest, with another well-aimed shot to his forehead, ended any possible emotion or commotion.

Braga crossed over Tennyson again to a small camp in the shadow of overgrown oleanders near the corner of the recently refurbished strip mall two blocks west. There were the usual businesses, all closed: a laundromat, bar, liquor store, taqueria, check cashing store, and a doughnut shop—minimal illumination at this hour.

As soon as the lights from a passing van faded, Braga used the noise to cover his movements as he headed toward the far side of the lot and oleanders. Walking a slow arc to avoid making a straight line to the bushes, he noticed movement to his far right while focusing on his target area. A man shuffled toward him. No, not toward him, but in the direction of the shade and shadow and safety of the overgrown plants. The approaching man carried a bundle, probably sleeping gear.

Braga took a chance to see if anyone inside was sleeping. He looked around in the gloom while adjusting his eyes to the darkness. Two, no, three people were sleeping in their blanket cocoons. The suppressed 9mm had nine rounds remaining, ready to go in Braga's grip.

The homeless man, his belongings in hand, stepped between two overgrown oleanders. As the shadows of the heavy branches embraced him, blocking the light, Braga greeted him with two quick shots to the chest. Only one of the three vagrants inside the impromptu camping spot stirred from the muffled gunshots. Though they were in the shadows, Braga saw his dark Central American features and greeted the man's shocked appearance by placing two rounds into his forehead. Neither other camper stirred.

Five rounds left. He put one into each man's heart and followed it with another into where their heads would be. He gave the second man an extra round in his skull just for fun.

Motionless and silent, he absorbed all the sights, scents, or sensations from the scene: spent propellant from the multiple rounds, the metallic tinge of blood, human filth of the routinely homeless, the wash of noise from the rare passing car, and a distant train. Nothing close enough to pose a threat.

He reloaded his pistol and surveyed his latest kills for signs of life, satisfied they were all ex-homeless and would no longer be a burden on society. As at the other scenes, he left his spent shell casings behind. He had stolen all the ammo, making it untraceable to him, and wiped down each round before loading it into the magazine—no chance of leaving a print behind.

The next kill site was two blocks west on the other side of the street. An auto repair shop sat on the opposite corner from a brightly lit 7-Eleven, its lights a blanket of hope and a sense of security for those ensconced inside for the time it took to buy a late-night pack of cigarettes or a Slurpee.

Braga walked to the kill site, the shadowed side lot of the shop, and played this stop differently, knowing he had a full magazine. He quickly placed two rounds in the chest of each of the three sleeping victims he knew frequented the place, short Latino men who appeared to be in their forties. Then, taking a few more seconds, he put a final round in each skull.

He had no more attacks planned out. His truck waited a few blocks away, and if the night's killing ended here, he'd be okay with the body count. Nine. About as he expected. Naturally, he wanted more, but prudence demanded he take precautions. If he really wanted, more targets could be found in the dark alleyways behind nearby businesses or tucked under bushes at parks. He'd learned in his many trips up and down Tennyson that no matter the hour, there were always stragglers lurking about in the landscaped to add to the count. The fat one without shoes who often stopped traffic by walking right into the middle of the street, regardless of how busy it was. There was the gal who slept in front of the Mexican market and changed her clothes on the sidewalk. He also knew of an old man who pushed his two shopping carts up and down Tennyson and made his home wherever he felt like it.

There was always more.

Between here and his truck, the most likely spots to find safe prey were behind the Life Church community center, outside the 24-hour Jack in the Box, or near the park library. They all looked busy. Too busy. Braga knew already, but he triple-checked his ammo count. Loaded with a new magazine and two more ready, he had one other quiet spot to check.

Ruus River was the local name for the cement creek that ran perpendicular to Tennyson. It was part of the city's rainfall-runoff abatement that gathered all the rainwater from the Tennyson Basin. It brought the water to the shoreline during the rare storms that dumped so much rain and runoff that the regular drains and gutters couldn't handle it. During the drier seasons, like now, the river served as a pathway for those trying to stay out of the streetlights. The county fenced off the area where Tennyson and the river met, but the chain link fencing wasn't enough to stop the natural flow of humans on this primate game trail. Braga found a place where someone had cut through to make a path. There'd been no rain, so the concrete river was dry except for a bare trickle down the center of the channel. The tunnels under the road proved too dark to see anything, but the stench of human filth was thick. He gave his eyes a moment to adapt, then noticed a motionless human silhouette at the far side of the street leaning against a pillar. Braga made an arc around and behind the man, walking past the target with about ten feet between them, making side glances in his peripheral vision. He couldn't tell if the homeless man was asleep or unconscious.

He'd seen this man several times shuffling up and down the street, wrapped in his old blanket, looking as bad as he smelled. *Probably smelled worse than that fucking donkey*, Braga thought. Whatever alcohol or drugs he had gotten hold of had incapacitated him enough that no matter what noise Braga made, he wouldn't have roused. *This wouldn't be a killing. It would be euthanization.*

He changed his mind about how he wanted this kill to play out and slipped his Beretta away. He pulled out the five-inch lock blade from the rear pocket of his pants and used his thumb to bring the blade into position.

Taking a quick step toward the target, he dropped to one knee, clasped a gloved hand over the homeless man's mouth, and slid the blade with ease directly into his eye, dead center of the socket. The man's body convulsed violently, his upper torso lurching toward Braga before flopping into stillness. He kept the pressure on the knife until the man's body relaxed completely and then pulled it free, not bothering to check for a pulse, but he didn't get up immediately.

Braga wiped the bulk of the gore from the blade onto the homeless man's blanket and stood. He was concerned there may be blood on his face or hoodie, but there was nothing much more for that than a quick, cursory wipe with his sleeve. He retraced his steps back to the cut in the fence to see if anything was different, any new people, or maybe someone *not* there who was before. No. All looked smooth and clear.

Passing back through the fence, he noticed a slight uptick in traffic, which meant more eyeballs on him, but mostly it meant more noise and movement in which to remain concealed. Several parking spaces were empty on the side street where he parked. A few locals headed out to work, he assumed.

On his walk, he pulled out his cell phone and turned on the camera to check for any splatters on his face. There were none, but there was some blood near the right cuff of his hoodie. He'd have to get rid of it, but that's why he bought cheap ones.

Approaching his truck, he unlocked the passenger side with the fob he had secreted inside the wheel well and got to work. He removed his hoodie, placing it along with his pistol, gloves, shoes, and knife inside a plastic bag. He put his regular sneakers back on. Next, he pulled a package of baby wipes from the glove box, then cleaned his face and hands. Those dirty wipes went into the plastic bag, too. He brought out a small bottle of hand sanitizer, the kind with a substantial alcohol percentage. If he missed any blood, the sanitizer would destroy any DNA value it held. Lastly, he switched out of his "work" shoes, stuffing them in the bag as well.

Braga gave himself a final visual inspection before climbing into the driver's seat, feeling good about his appearance. He pulled from his spot, headed northward along smaller streets, and reviewed his after-action checklist. Moreso, he thought about the drain on society caused by his ten victims and the incalculable gain to the community because of their deaths. No one gave out medals for this sort of thing—but he felt they ought to.

1

It wasn't any particular sound that stirred me, nor was it the gaining daylight of the late summer morning. It was more the slight increase of the urban symphony in the air. Traffic on the freeway above had picked up; a few delivery trucks were near the produce warehouses, either picking up or dropping off their wares, and the gulls were overhead, letting the world know they were there. Plus, a few feet away, Xtra's gentle snoring joined as part of the morning chorus, not loud enough to wake me, but enough to let me know he was still sleeping.

I stayed motionless on the cool sidewalk for two reasons. First, I didn't want to disturb my friend yet; more importantly, any movement took more effort than I cared to invest. The bourbon and beer hadn't cleared out of my head yet, and the awkward sleep position had tightened my lower back into a series of knots. It didn't hurt too badly at the moment, but getting out of this position and back onto my feet would be a chore I wasn't looking forward to.

I'd never seen Xtra sleep. I've seen the man motionless but never actually in slumber, but there he was, resting as gently as a butterfly on a flower. This morning was the first time, but it lasted only the briefest moment. Shortly after I roused and let the morning come into focus, I saw his dark brown eyes open and blink the sleep fairies away. No telling how long he'd been there.

Thinking back over the early morning, I left my bar, The Golden Door, around 1 am. It was Tuesday now. I didn't like that day. My ex left me on a Tuesday. Laura. I remembered stopping at the convenience store on Webster to grab a few cans of beer, but the rest seemed a blur. It was 5:30 am when I woke, so I may have stumbled around for a couple of hours before I plopped down here. Who the hell knew how Xtra came into the picture, but he was a welcome sight.

Xavier Travers, Xtra or X informally, spent several years in the US Army, and, like many vets, Xtra had a rough time after he departed from service: money troubles, inability to re-acclimate to civilian life, and, worst of all, nagging injuries that led him down a path to addiction. He'd been clean for the year I'd known him, but he'd hinted before it damn near killed him in the past.

We sat silently for a few minutes, enjoying the blue and orange hues swirling in the morning light. The sounds of the waking city were still only a dull roar. No noise spikes, merely a simple wash from the traffic on Interstate 880 above and an occasional delivery truck on the nearby streets.

The longer I sat, the more I recognized how filthy I was. I reeked of old sweat mixed with the sleep drool of a drunk man dripped in for good measure. I wasn't proud of my drinking, but it's where I was in my life.

"Good morning, Young Sergeant," Xtra said. "Looks like you had a fun night."

"Good morning, Old Sergeant. If it was fun, I don't remember. How long you been here?" I asked.

"I'd guess around two hours. It's been a peaceful morning so far," he said. "No one messin' with us. No one except the birds. I was out doin' my thing and damn near tripped over you. Figured I'd sit with you and hang out before the seagulls and crows got ya."

"Well, I appreciate the hell outta that, friend. Those gulls can be a handful when they're hungry."

He wasn't worried about the local avian foes. The crows hadn't made their presence known yet, and the gulls rested on the nearby rooftops, ignoring us. Like every sensible, homeless person in the East Bay, he was concerned about me becoming yet another statistic, another nameless, faceless soul on the street whose life ended mysteriously without concern from the wider world.

A part of me knew better than to fall asleep out here, yet another part wouldn't complain too much about two quick bullets to the head. Knowing what I've done in the recent past, I had probably earned some cosmic retribution.

Shame washed over me, so I shifted gears quickly. "X," I said. "Wanna come over to my place for some tea?"

"Got anything to eat?" he asked, knowing full well I did.

Xtra had been over before. This wasn't the first time he kept me company when my walks home from the bar got sidetracked by more alcohol and my drunken wanderlust. I didn't invite him into my warehouse home the first time I saw him, a rare midday sighting. We enjoyed several conversations and, over a few visits, built up our

Young Sergeant/Old Sergeant routine. He'd had a colorful life on the streets, but clearly had a good soul. I liked him.

The first time I offered to let him use my place to shower and wash his clothes, he politely declined. A sense of honor or pride, I suspected. Or, maybe he thought I was some kind of lunatic. The second time, I threw in the offer of a good meal and some coffee, and he accepted graciously. That's when he told me, to my surprise, he was a tea drinker. That a long-time soldier would drink tea instead of coffee shocked the hell out of me.

My home sat a stone's throw from the underpass, and he'd seen me there several times; in fact, I suspected he'd seen far more than casual passers-by ever do. On this morning's trip home, we noticed the crew working the produce distribution warehouse in my building was already up and busy. A couple of vans unloaded goods, and two staff gathered the various vegetables to build up the orders awaiting completion and delivery. They spoke a mixture of English and Chinese. The man who drove the forklift spoke exclusively Chinese, except for the occasional use of the word "fuck" or "fucking" thrown in. Multiculturalism at its best.

I didn't have the wherewithal to stop and chat like I often did, so we slipped through my little side door and up the stairs to my loft. The climb was more challenging than I'd expected. Still swirl-headed from the drink, I felt my stomach churn. I needed water, some aspirin, and more sleep.

"X," I said, closing the curtains in my too-bright living space, "I'm gonna go pass out some more. You know where all the stuff is. Help yourself."

I trusted him at my place. He had a sense of honor and gratitude I hadn't seen nearly enough of lately. It's why I liked and trusted him. While I managed my hangover, I knew Xtra would strip down and wash a load of laundry in the downstairs washer; whatever he was wearing and whatever was in his backpack that needed attention. He'd shower in the downstairs bathroom and come upstairs, wearing clean sweatpants or shorts to help himself to whatever I had in the kitchen. I won't pretend my cabinets were bursting with supplies, but I had enough there that he'd be fine.

My cash was stashed in the safe in my room, so there wasn't much he could swipe of great value. I regretted the thought as soon as it passed through my head, wrestled with my guilt for a moment, and then wiped it from my mind. Sleep came quickly after, and soon after that, the ghosts of dead cops visited.

Adrian Husted from up in Westwood, Idaho. That shiny ginger fuck stumbled his way into the path of death and probably had no clue about how until it was too late. Sergeant Lewis Leonard died on a patrol that didn't need to happen. Killed by an IED. Officer Sheila Black. Dead. Walked into a domestic violence situation too soon, without backup, and became a statistic.

They didn't haunt me as spooky ghouls would. They just visited my memories as the forms in which I remembered them in life. In Husted's case, I only met him a few times in passing, a goofy rookie, always making jokes, trying to cover up his awkwardness and how green he was. Leonard. As solid as they get, his spectral presence reminded me that I had never become the person I wanted to be. Black's ghost was the worst and a harbinger of a rough time for me.

She was the best of us. Her visits were a reminder that goodness fails, and kindness can be a weakness. Sheila's death was the hardest of them all.

I was glad the alcohol still had a hold over me so I could eventually crash for a few more hours, but it was a fitful sleep. Waking from a night of drinking had both its benefits and its drawbacks. There were rare days when I woke refreshed and ready to face the world, but more often, I'd begin the day with regret for last night's actions. Sometimes, I'd wake to visions from the past, but I've been fucking up enough lately that there are plenty of new sins for which to feel guilt.

Through the fog of memory, it took me a few moments to recall that Xtra had been here earlier. Without moving, I listened for any sounds of activity or snoring. Nothing. He was either still asleep or had slipped away while I was still out.

My space was a safe one. All mine, sort of. When the time came, I had to leave the Westwood farm, so I looked for a new place to roost. With an influx of cash from the Kansas City deal, I had options I didn't have before. Doc Bradley engineered more financial voodoo to hide the transactions and even had me lose money by selling the farm at a loss. He and his assistant had earned their higher-than-normal fee.

My property had to be sold for less than market value because I had placed an Idaho land trust and a conservation easement on the place. Eighteen of the twenty acres would never be used for agriculture ever again. Harvesting the dead bodies last season made the decision easy. The next owner, a retired California firefighter, and his partner had no problem with that. They got a huge barn and house, a burgeoning meadow around them, and enough space for their garden.

And chickens, too. I couldn't handle the specter of dead women anymore, but the girls and Big Red were oblivious. They stayed.

The new home in Oakland's Jack London Square was a warehouse for a family-owned produce distributor who had come through some hard times. They had owned the building and the business for decades, but the arrears on ever-rising property taxes had become too substantial and too backdated for the state, county, and city to ignore. As a result, the reality of running a fresh produce business specializing in niche vegetables and imported products from China was tenuous.

Ronald Man, the third-generation owner of Hub Produce, had some decisions to make. He could sell the property for a good profit, but he'd have to uproot his business. There would be nowhere to go in Oakland or the surrounding areas with the space and freeway access they'd had up until now. He could find something affordable in the Tri-Valley, but that would cut off access to many of his farmer-wholesalers. The added time and cost of distribution would wreck him.

Doc, who had been looking for such an opportunity, ran the idea past me, and it all made sense. I, or rather one of the LLCs Doc created, took ownership of building a lump-sum deposit and paying off back taxes. Hub Produce would stay with a modest but fair rent.

Man did have to give up some space for me, though. Of the five large bays making up the width of the thirty-two-foot-tall building, I took over the one on the far left side, added a partition wall and a living loft, and spruced up the ample floor area. The loft has an outside set of stairs that lead to the side street, and it has its own address, separate from the warehouse. Downstairs, I added another small living space with a kitchenette in case I ever had visitors. So far, there has been only Xtra.

The warehouse was a significant investment, even though I had to put up a hefty amount of my liquid assets. The rent I took from Man was more than enough to pay off the monthlies and provided additional income from a legitimate source. That was a good thing, a safe way to launder the money from the Idaho mill.

By the angle of the sun's rays peeking through my dark curtains, I guessed it to be early afternoon, not that I felt like reaching for my phone to check the time. The clock didn't dictate a single thing in my life, so I had no great urge to move or get up. I listened for any sound of X. Still nothing. A light sleeper, I assumed he'd taken care of his laundry, showered, swiped a bite to eat, and took off again.

That guy was a machine. I could learn from him regarding personal discipline and minimalism. He knew his place in the world, set his goals, gathered the resources he needed, and moved off with a quickness. No baggage other than the shame and humility he seemed to carry with him. He didn't tell me much about his family, but it sounded like in the dark days after leaving the Army, he stayed in the depths of addiction long enough to break the bonds of his family's love.

Except for my desire for caffeine, the bed would have been a safe space to stay for a few more hours, but I became restless, and the want for a hot cuppa kicked in hard. Assuming X had departed, I rose from the bed naked, stretched for the heavens to release the joints, and padded my way to the kitchen. Like the Idaho prairie, this space in Oakland's Jack London Square didn't provide any errant views from neighbors into my home, so I lived as I pleased. I spent most of my alone time naked. The winter chill in both Kansas City and Idaho made that more prohibitive. Although not always hot, California provided a year-round comfort I hadn't experienced before.

Decorating wasn't my strongest skill. I had enough money to hire a fancy designer or buy trendy furniture, but I preferred minimalism and simplicity, so like my space in Idaho, I'd kept my Oakland loft clean and sleek. Sterile, some might say: white walls with very little artwork of any kind save a variety of pictures of my hens I had made, a light birch hardwood floor, white kitchen cabinets, two matching blue couches, a bookshelf, and a recliner. Not much more. The California sun shone brightly most days, so I kept the thick curtains closed to dim the light in the great room. They were perpetually closed in my bedroom. My cave.

The kitchen counter held a note for me.

Karl,

Thank you again for the kindness of a hot meal and a safe rack. I'm grateful but I must say that I've seen better men than both of us drink themselves to death so maybe you should take it easy on the booze.

Come out with me some night to keep an eye on others. Lots of folks been getting killed

and disappearing lately. An extra
set of eyes watching out would
help a lot.

X

Message aside, his penmanship was flawless. Not cursive. Neat, self-contained block letters in a personal font of a type I'd seen before, used by engineers and orderly thinkers. Xtra's artful use of the characters was impressive as hell.

The content, though, that's what got me worried. I knew what he referred to when he mentioned the disappearances and killings. I'd read the news about them, but had been part of bad news and misery too much in the past few years, and had no desire to jump into another fire. The main reason I moved down here was to separate myself from that type of experience. Perhaps it was heartless of me, but I immediately dismissed the idea of these safety patrols. I'd worked hard to avoid responsibility, and I sure as hell would try to enjoy it.

Xtra was a good soul tossed around by life and his demons. Hell, he left the kitchen spotless, so how bad of a guy could he be? I envisioned him out there, watching over his fellow man. Why couldn't I? The pot of coffee he made for me was still warm, which meant he left only within the last two hours. I hoped he'd rested well and prepped himself for another circuit of his spots in the less-seen parts of the Bay Area. I was tempted to put a GPS tracker on him to see how many miles he puts in.

My main living space had a large east-facing window and a west-facing skylight. This gave me natural light all day long, and the colors, brightness, and contrast shifted as the sun made its way across the skyline. My coffee perch wasn't as free and natural as my porch on Westwood, but it provided a wonderful slice of the day's light.

Sitting and sipping, the realization hit me as it had almost every day in the past few years: now what?

2

The Binh family wasn't happy, and when the Binhs weren't happy, the Tran family couldn't be happy. Roger and Aaron Tran were two people who could do something to make things right.

In 1975, as Saigon was falling to the Vietcong, the elder Tran made a devil's bargain with Quyen Binh, a minor Saigon warlord with a vision for the future, to get his family out of Vietnam and into the United States. During the conflict, the warlord made connections with the American CIA and used them to secure passage to the US for several family members. Binh held plenty of evidence of grossly unlawful conduct by various CIA officers, so it was just a matter of finding the right CIA officer to bribe and blackmail to get the Trans on a cargo plane.

The paperwork was fake, the connections tenuous, and the passage dangerous—but it worked. Binh arranged immigration for several grateful Trans into the US. All the emigrants who still had family in Vietnam agreed to work for Binh in the US in exchange for their emigration expenses. Implicit in the deal were reprisals against the remaining family members if the new Americans reneged on their end.

In return for the transportation and fake visas, the Binhs profited from the prostitution networks the Trans had set up in the States and the money made from all the willing couriers they had in a dozen places across the new nation. The Trans weren't the only family they had helped enter the new land. All in all, it was a good deal for everyone involved. Most family members in the US lived their lives to the fullest, occasionally doing small jobs for the puppet masters back in Saigon.

When Quyen Binh passed, his son, Dang, assumed control of the family business and, as he had become accustomed to the steady flow of income from his father's investments, wasn't of a mind to let the whole operation slip away simply because the elders were dying off. Instead, he doubled his effort. A few culled fingers and ears from family members remaining in Vietnam were sent to their American members, letting all involved know the old deals held. The arrangements couldn't last much longer. His children didn't have the heart to continue, and the American family members grew distant enough from the old family that a third cousin getting stabbed in an alley wouldn't be a heartbreaking loss. He had to pull the strings while he still could.

The Binh family needed to find more young girls to work in the massage parlors of Oakland, Long Beach, San Diego, and Las Vegas. These businesses had a high profit margin as long as you didn't have to pay for the girls working there. They'd sleep in dorms at or near the business, lived on thin soup, and knew any sustained complaining was met with harshness. As masseuses or prostitutes, each girl had a useful life of only a few years, so turnover was high. There were always ways to obtain new girls, but in the past decade, Vietnam's economy had been doing well enough that fewer people wanted to escape. Dang Binh had branched out to include Laotian and Malay girls, but now faced new difficulties. Language differences could be overcome, but the price of bribes to Vietnamese customs officials at the border was higher than he wanted to pay.

The economic changes in the US provided Dang with both problems and answers. While container ships often remained backed up at West Coast seaports for weeks, their human cargo sometimes perished, confined in the hot metal cargo boxes for so long that food and water eventually ran out. For the Binhs, this put a considerable hitch in their primary source of sex trade bodies. Conversely, in the past few years, the American economy and the Bay Area's ridiculous real estate costs have pushed many of the already poor into homelessness. Additionally, those hapless immigrants who made it to the area without family waiting for them found it almost impossible to source affordable housing, leading to even more souls out on the streets.

For almost two years, the Tran family, now led by the eldest of the new generation, brothers Roger and Aaron Tran, scoured the Bay Area's homeless shelters and encampments in search of new talent. To satisfy the most popular niche and secure the greatest value from any investment, they needed girls aged eleven to fourteen. They'd grab a young boy occasionally, but the pickings for girls in their target range were usually good. The best hunting grounds were Richmond, South San Francisco, Fruitvale, and West Oakland.

It was a week before they were scheduled to transfer the girls to their buyer, and they still needed more product to meet their target. The harvests were yielding less and less fruit as time passed. The underground buzz about missing girls and their murdered mothers spread throughout the homeless communities. Rumors and fears of the serial killer of homeless people didn't help. This made the Trans have to work harder.

As they drove along the darkened streets, they spotted the camper trailer that one of their street sources mentioned. It was two blocks from where they were told, but it was in a safe, dark spot and matched all the other descriptions. The brothers parked and watched it for a while, hoping to catch sight of any inhabitants. Nothing yet, but they had time, so they waited.

Sometimes, they convinced young runaways into the lifestyle with promises of steady work, income, and a chance at freedom, but more often, they'd have to go on the hunts—*harvests*, the young men would call them—where they'd snatch the girls away from their homeless families. They'd often have to kill the homeless mother, but that was an unfortunate part of the task they were willing to do. The police didn't seem to care about a few extra dead homeless victims.

Tonight, the young men had chosen East Oakland as their scouting area. Two shelters and two other churches operated food programs there, so the homeless population knew this was an excellent area to set up temporary homes. Moreover, with all the freeway overpasses, train tracks, warehouses, and abandoned houses, East Oakland, near the Oakland Coliseum, was theoretically safe. Several homeless camps and informal RV parks had sprung up along the sides of back streets and industrial cul-de-sacs.

On their previous recon trips, the Tran boys had seen a few families in the area with girls who might fit their needs, but tonight was just another scouting mission. They'd drive past the two soup kitchens and the homeless camps to see if there were any girls they could harvest. The Trans paid several homeless men to watch for new girls. If they spotted their spies, they'd check in to see if they had found anyone new who might fit their needs.

They detested this part of their life, but they did their duty to honor their family's agreements and keep their distant family members in Vietnam safe. Plus, it was profitable. Hurting women and children was unpleasant for both young men, but, as they told themselves, these were wasted people living miserable lives. Getting them out of there, either through death or kidnapping, was an improvement upon their shitty lives. Besides, who would bother even looking for them once they'd gone?

3

The Golden Door was a restaurant and bar well past its prime, but still a popular, well-regarded place a few blocks from my home. It had been in the same space since 1949, and though it had a few owners, all of them were Taiwanese or Chinese.

My preferred spot was the far end of the bar with only two stools and the game machine, an ancient device that occupied most of the counter space where people only sat while playing the thing. Its programming had few games. Picture Match, Music Trivia, and Movie Trivia were the most popular, but that word was subjective. Since the content hadn't been updated since 2010, only the older crowd knew the movies and music referenced. That whittled down the potential user base and meant few folks ever sat there. That suited me just fine.

The current owner of the Door was Shirley Chu. She was approaching seventy-five, but visited each and every day. Her daughter, Carol, managed the business on a daily basis, and Shirley's younger sister, Su Wen-Je, ruled over the bar. Everyone knew Su as "Ma." Only the family called her by her given name, and most of the regular patrons didn't even know it. Ma wasn't young, but she was young enough to run the bar on even the busiest nights easily. During those busy times, another family member would often be present, doing the bulk of the work so she could chat peacefully with regular patrons and handle the to-go orders. The entire scene was a frenetic ballet I often watched for hours on end, leaning on the laminate bar top and sipping my poison.

During my year here, I had come to know, or at least recognize, many of the regulars. Some were distant family or close friends of the owners, but most were old-school barflies from the area. I suppose the frequency of my visits made me a barfly, too.

Ma and her family had been in the US since 1982, but her English was barely above a functional level. We all understood her, and she understood us, but it was an effort to follow along. I'd be looking right at her as she spoke about one thing or another, and I had to work to comprehend everything she said. Most of the time, I would smile and nod as she would throw out a story, interrupted by an occasional "You unnerstan?" It was entertaining, but sometimes a chore to pretend I actually understood. All the regulars, me included, knew when to laugh, nod, and say back to her, "Yes. I understand."

As the dinner wave came, crested, and faded, the bar crowd settled to the few regulars: me, Victor and his partner, Troy, Ma's Mexican "friend," Fred, and Duke. In the time I'd known him, Duke had rarely said a sentence of over four words and seldom made eye contact with anyone. Ma told me he was an Army vet. He certainly had that air about him and had the age to match. The 'Gulf War Veteran' inscription on the blue hat served as another piece of evidence. I tried to chat him up a few times with limited success, so I mostly left him alone with his Budweiser and double shot of Wild Turkey 101. He seemed a peaceful sort, and we didn't talk much. Well, except for that one time I got a little too drunk and shared a story with him about an old dog of mine.

I told him about Pearly, the old white German Shepard and Husky mix that had adopted us after we found her wandering the back roads near our house, half-dead from starvation and dehydration. I was eight when my mother, Belle, gave in after my brothers' begging became too much for her to fend off. My father wasn't pleased with the decision, but this was when he came home for only brief periods, so it wasn't his problem. Pearly was everything young boys would want in a dog: she was a ball chaser, a hiking companion, and a keeper of secrets. When my brothers, those young demi-gods five and six years older than me, died in a glorious back roads fireball, I was more bereft and alone than mere words can describe. The dog was the one solid soul in my life, my mother having been absorbed by her grief and loss. When Pearly passed away in her sleep during the last week of my senior year of high school, I was so inconsolable that I skipped the graduation ceremony. My father wouldn't be there, nor would the brothers. Mother would be in her chemical torpor, and worst of all, there would be no Pearly to come home to. I haven't had a dog since then.

I don't know why I told him that story, but I did. He bought me a drink, and we toasted to old dogs.

Victor and Troy, both always fantastically dressed, were the counter to Duke's stoicism. In fact, if ever there was a conversational debt anywhere in the world, these two could make up for it. The pair were never seen apart and shared information and observations on all manner of topics. Never at a loss for an opinion on any matter that may arise, they spoke at the same volume, whether chatting with each other on neighboring barstools or with someone on the far side of the bar. Tonight, they were in fine form, talking about local happenings and current events: the closing of the import store, the new easement for a condo building's back parking lot, and the latest killing of an undocumented guy living in an alleyway. When they were expended, I mentioned I had hung out with Xtra, a known entity in these parts and well-liked by all.

Duke's eyes lifted from his glass at the mention of him. The old, stoic veteran had survived a homeless phase a few years ago, and Xtra had befriended him, their shared military backgrounds forming the basis of their friendship.

"How's Xtra these days?" Duke drawled.

"He looks and sounds well," I said.

"Still doing safety patrols?"

I was struck by the obvious; Xtra had found me on one of his safety patrols. What could have happened if he hadn't been there to watch over me?

"Yeah. He's still putting in his miles. Not sure where he goes, but he gets around."

The conversation quickly lulled, and I returned my attention to the last of my drink. I stared at the ice as the colored lights of the Door bounced in and around the glass. Xtra's invitation to walk and patrol with him had bothered me all day. It wasn't like I didn't get out and about often, but I didn't have the same size of territory that X did. His offer to go for walks with him was easy to dismiss at first, but the idea kept returning throughout the day.

I truly didn't want to do it, to leave my comfort zone. My late-night walks were all the adventure I wanted and all the patrolling I needed to keep up with the vibe in the area. I liked my walks. They allowed me time to let my mind wander about how my life could be or could have been. They were my private time, my quiet time. X wanted me to help him keep watch over his community and keep it safe from the uncivilized among us. Public service was in my DNA throughout my years in the Army and at the department. These past few years, I have enjoyed my selfish isolation from responsibility to anyone but myself.

Yet, something about the idea enticed me. There was an appeal to the notion of being an alpha predator patrolling its territory. Or maybe the image would be more like a working dog keeping its flock safe. Maybe an owl flying through the dark forest, surveying the land for anything amiss. All silly ideas. All part of the old me. It all took more effort than just walking, drinking, and thinking.

Regardless of how inebriated I was, I preferred leaving the bar before closing, so I could say I, indeed, left the bar before closing. By 1 am, Jack, Stella, and the Jägermeister had me in fine spirits, so I figured I would cut my losses and call it a night while the going was good. I managed to leave with some of my original $100, even after a sizable tip for Ma.

4

Surprisingly, the nights can get crisp along Oakland's waterside, even during the late summer. The wind coming through the Golden Gate from the Pacific Ocean carried a coolness to match the salt air. Any storm in the ocean's western or northern expanses brought winds rushing down and around the Pacific Rim, becoming increasingly chilled with every mile. By the time that cooled air reached the Farallon Islands or the Marin Headlands in the evening, heat from the day had dissipated, and the cold Pacific gave the breeze an extra briskness before funneling it through the Golden Gate. This natural feature, the three-mile strait connecting the Pacific Ocean and the San Francisco Bay, was the weak link in the defenses of the Coastal Ranges and gave San Francisco and the greater Bay Area a unique microclimate. Mark Twain once famously commented that the coldest winter he had ever spent was a summer in San Francisco. Those same climate factors that made for such an astute comment back in his time still applied to the cool nights in Oakland after a warm day.

As I made my way from the Door to my convenience store of choice a few blocks away, I noticed more tents in the underbrush and alleyways than had been there in recent weeks, a sign that the cooler weather and even cooler economy were coming to the area. The scents in the air were changing, too. There were the ever-present odors of urban life: car exhaust, asphalt, loose refuse, and the combined stench of a city after a warm day. The air had something different tonight, something unpleasant. The wind and water, brought across the bay in the form of marine-layer clouds and night mist, dragged with them an unknown tinge. Salt? Metal? Decay? I couldn't put my finger on it, and my time along the water hadn't been long enough to allow me to learn all the vocabulary for the senses of the seasonal changes.

Tonight's shopping location was an old standalone store. It may have been a 7-Eleven way back in the day, but that must have been several owners ago. Its signage had been altered as often as its windows had been broken and replaced. The steel poles set into the concrete in a semi-circle, a few feet outside the front doors, showed they were the best investments the owners had ever made. The many large and small dents showed direct evidence that some type of vehicle had been stopped from ramming through the front on more than one occasion.

Steel and concrete. Classic security tools. Seeing them and their efficacy at this store made me think of all the bases I'd been posted to throughout the years. Of course, the ones in Iraq and Afghanistan were buttoned up with as much steel, concrete, sandbags, HESCO barriers, and T-walls as possible. During times of threat, even the bases back home and abroad in Allied nations took firmer footing and used more of these practical steel-and-concrete tools. My two tours in the sand acquainted me with plenty of security devices, not the least important of which was my M4, but all that concrete and steel was more than welcome. Here, though, I knew where to stand if a car headed my way.

Outside the shop flitted the regular coterie of night flies. Some were homeless or vagrant types avoiding going back into the shadows, some were locals living their best lives by drinking and joking with their buddies, and others were working at either selling their chemical product or their own flesh. It's a tough world, and I wasn't one to judge. I'd usually nod, say hello, and pass by without a problem. My size and demeanor gave off a vibe that suggested further contact would be unwelcome and possibly unhealthy for them. It usually worked. Until it didn't.

The store's late hours and proximity to a dense, mixed population provided a revolving cast of faces and cliques who hung around the place. Most were either harmless or too wrapped up in their bubble to be of concern to anyone else, but once in a while, someone or something caught my eye. Such was the case tonight.

On my way in, I noticed a trio of young men chatting amongst themselves. They were loitering at the edge of the parking lot near the outer circle of weak light put out by the one lonely light post. Young, in their late teens or early twenties. Hispanic, though perhaps not Mexican. One wore a silver Raiders jacket that caught and reflected the streetlights. They weren't tall, but even so, I didn't like the math of three against one. The only thing they were doing that caught my eye was trying to appear like they weren't looking at people. There are few things more suspicious than trying not to look suspicious.

After purchasing a twelve-pack of Stella Artois, I headed back out. Taking a quick census, I noticed the three men had moved closer to the area under 880, across the street from the path I had taken to reach the store. They stood ominously quiet, the guy with the shiny jacket shuffling from one foot to another. None of them glanced back my way. I'd seen this behavior before, both in Afghanistan and in wildlife videos. There were enough worrisome indicators for me to become alert and, unfortunately, slightly more sober.

Since my time with the Kansas City PD, I've done my best to avoid trouble. I moved to Idaho to escape the evil humans do to each other, only to end up directly in the middle of what turned out to be a burial ground for Charles Baker's evil. All those dead girls buried on my farm made it impossible for me to stay there, so I moved off again—this time to sunny California. I could have chosen a beach house, a mountaintop cabin, or a trailer in the desert. No. I chose a warehouse in the middle of where a hundred different demographics intersect, a place where all manner of ecosystems vie for dominance. Here, in this pool of crime, poverty, self-abuse, gluttony, and malice, I'd so far done a good job of avoiding the world and adult responsibilities. I'd seen what was around me, and I'd so far been able to blink it or drink it away, but something about these three men activated an animal part of me.

I grew up near goats and chickens, but I was by no means a farm kid. We always lived near cities, and we had cable and trash service. I didn't have to scrounge for food or fight my way through school. My young life wasn't a primer for being an adventurer or extreme athlete. We were a mostly boring family with a mostly absent military father with mostly normal lives. He kept us in a steady home, at least, instead of dragging us all over the world.

With my training and experience in the military and law enforcement, and despite all my time away, it was almost impressive how small things could trigger the cave-dweller part of my brain. These three guys moving into their hunting formation did it for me. Like all other triggers, I'd figure out the why and how later. Now, my chemistry spiked, and my mind reverted to old patterns of defensive thought. There would be emotional consequences later, but that would be later.

Based on what little I'd gathered in the few seconds I'd observed them, I made some big leaps of logic. I had to. If my suspicions were correct, I was their target. They only hoped for the few dollars I might possess and whatever I had bought from the store. They were amateurs with only fists or, probably, knives to use in their attack. Still, a dedicated man with a knife and a big-dog attitude can be a problem, no matter the size of the obstacle. I was their obstacle, and I'd have to be careful.

Broadway lay dark and silent as I crossed toward the far side to make my way home. I didn't turn my head to look at them as I passed, but I managed to grab quick side glances as I moved. They were looking my way, but one, the tallest and roughest looking of the bunch, had crossed the street to the same side I was on, while the other two slowly walked in the same direction on the other side.

The lights of Jack London Square dimmed after midnight, but compared to the darkness of the underpass, they provided all that I needed. The many streetlights caught every pedestrian. As a person walked, they were handed off from one light to another, their shadow starting behind them, then swinging around as they passed the light and continued ahead until they were picked up by the next. I had a brief image of a monkey swinging through the trees, hand over hand, not letting loose of one branch until the next was firmly grasped.

My mind split in two, half focused on the three men behind, while the other half wandered and reminisced. So far, my life in

Oakland has been simple. Coffee, lunch, reading, some modest attempts at fitness, long walks, lots of alcohol, and grand efforts at making my castle a safe haven where I pretended the wider world didn't exist except when I needed it to. The plan had been working wonderfully so far. It wasn't long ago that I was in a similar position, on the cusp of what other people call happiness or contentment. I had my twenty acres, a barn, and a modest home, ample coffee, and a whole mess of chickens. It was close, that contentment thing. Close, almost close enough that I let my guard down.

Broken glass crunched beneath the feet of one of my new friends. The noise was a gift as my mind had drifted away. My mental absence only lasted a moment, but during my stupor, I had walked past my street. Was it forgetfulness or instinct? I had already decided I didn't want to walk to my home, letting them know where I lived.

Instead, I walked another two blocks up Broadway, staying in the light. They wouldn't do anything if I were in the bright areas. They'd wait until I strayed into a darker space to attack, but sadly for them, that would work for me, too. Using a window on the angled front wall of a Chilean restaurant, I glimpsed the two across the street, the shiny jacket giving them away. The other one looked to be wearing a dark hoodie. They were twenty-five yards back and still on the other side of Broadway. I assumed the one on my side of the road would only attack once his compatriots were closer, and I took advantage of that.

As I approached the corner of 2nd Street, I stayed far from the buildings and closer to the street so they wouldn't think I was making that turn. Yet I did. I turned, and as soon as I walked out of their view, I sprinted fifty feet ahead down the sidewalk to a space lit poorly by the streetlights where a large delivery truck was parked along the sidewalk. The truck blocked out the light from the opposite side of the street. I stepped up onto the truck's running boards and was enveloped in darkness. Here, I would stand my ground.

Two of their heads comically poked around the corner to see if I was still walking. Perhaps there was a chance they would give up and go elsewhere if they did not see me. The animal part of me would have been disappointed had they done that, but at the same time, I'd prefer that option when looking at myself in the warm light of day. I didn't need the extra shame or guilt.

No such luck. In unison, they dashed around the corner. They couldn't have seen me on my perch, and they again tried to pick up my scent. My only available weapons were my small flashlight and a twelve-pack of Stella. They would do fine. As the men approached, I weighed the last-minute idea of letting them pass and avoiding them altogether, but my lizard brain weighed in with the convincing thought that these three would only find someone else to harm, someone less able to defend themselves. Besides, I wanted to lash out and release some anger as I'd grown weary of this peace and contentment bullshit.

The delivery truck's running board was a great place to watch them approach. I gripped the flashlight, a lightweight beast that put out 1400 lumens, my thumb resting on the power with two inches of its shaft extending beyond my palm. Using my right hand only to balance the weight of the beer, the twelve-pack rested on my chest, secured by my left hand in a manner that made the whole thing a heavy projectile.

Twelve feet away. Another moment, I thought of letting them pass.

Nah.

The man closest, shiny jacket guy, got the worst of it. The full impact of the beer case crashed against his head, directly on his right temple. As he fell, he lurched into the man to his left, and they both tumbled to the asphalt. Now, a lone man stood motionless, an easy target. Stepping down from the running boards, I took one long stride and gave him a Spartan kick to his chest that would have made Leonidas proud. He flew backward into the wall, his head thumping off the old brick, and bounced back toward me. Using his momentum, I grabbed the front of his hoodie, spun him wildly around, and released him in the path of his downed buddies. He tripped but scrambled quickly back to his feet, where he remained. Even in the dim light, I saw his trembling bottom lip, the knock on his head stunning him into inaction.

The first man I hit lay writhing on his back, and his mate had been in the process of untangling himself when the third man stumbled over him. I straddled the second man's chest, placing my knee squarely against his center to prevent any chance of escape. Clutching his neck firmly, I raised the flashlight, switched it on, and pointed it straight into his eyes.

1400 Lumens is enough to cause permanent damage if shone too long at a person's eyes, especially when already in the dark. The muscles and nerves that control the functions of the eyes can't work quickly enough to constrict the pupil, and even with closed eyelids, the power of so much light can cause significant harm. When applied for brief instances, it causes discomfort but no lasting damage. A quick flick of light across the eyes will activate anyone's primal desire for survival. In this man's case, he couldn't do much with someone eighty pounds his superior bearing down upon him.

I recalled the man I'd tossed away and flicked the beam toward him. If he were packing a gun, he'd reveal it now. If he reached for it, I'd have to rush him. Nothing. In his hesitation, he remained, waiting for one of the others to decide the next step.

But now, I was their alpha.

"Terminamos?" I said, using my lousy Spanish.

"Si!" the two said in unison.

Looking from one to the other to gauge their sincerity, I liked what I saw. I released my weight from the supine man and stood, quickly stepping aside to avoid a potential kick to the groin should his submission waver.

"Grab your boy and get the fuck out of here!" I growled. My Spanish had limits.

The two grabbed the third, groggy friend, headed toward Broadway, and disappeared into the night with the still unknown tinge.

Grabbing the dripping twelve-pack of Stella from the sidewalk and hoping they weren't too shaken up, I cracked one open as I made my way home. I'd pay for this. Even though my lizard brain wanted this to happen, I know I could have avoided it had I chosen. I *could* have done any number of things to prevent it, but the part of me that yearns for trouble or to punish the deserving outrationalized my gentler angels this time.

In a sense, I made the problem even worse. If any of those three needed expensive medical care, it would either harm them financially, making them even more of a criminal threat, or leave them a drain on the social system. Instead of some more deserving soul, all I'd done was add another young thug to the pile of those awaiting community services.

These past few years, I've tried my best to stay away from violence. Aside from tonight's activity, my meeting with the two Canadians at the bar in Westwood, and, well, executing Williamson, I'd been relatively non-violent. Come to think of it, that's not non-violent, is it?

I wasn't ready to go home. These fuckers had crashed my buzz, and there was no way I'd be sleeping anytime soon. I needed a bottle of something. It wasn't too late to make it back to the store with the safety ring of light, steel, and concrete.

5

The gulls were my alarm clock again. A big one sat perched above me, resting on the arm of a light post, looking down, casting its judgment upon me. *What are you doing, human? There's no wind down there to take you aloft.*

"Fuck off," I snarled at the bird with his attitude, but if the rest of the world heard me, they could do the same.

One of the many benefits of heavy drinking is that I tend to forget the details of my horrible behavior the previous night. When I wake up in random places downtown, under the freeway, or near the water, I usually don't have the details of what I did to fuck up and get myself into this position. Sure, there's the shame of not knowing, but that's pretty easy to deal with. Sometimes, the specifics of the night come dripping back to my memory throughout the day. Sometimes not.

The early morning's self-assessment found me leaning against the wheels of an unhitched truck trailer parked on the north end of Jack London Square, about five blocks from my house. Early morning delivery vans worked their routes, backed up at warehouses, filling their gullets with goods.

This area wasn't generally in my territory and wasn't part of my usual walking route. Didn't know how I got there, but there I was. I remembered the fight, and I remembered returning to the store because some of the Stella cans had busted open. After a fight like that, even a victory, I needed something to calm me down. That much adrenaline kept me up and at 'em for hours, and this one was no different. Beer and alcohol, for all of their negatives, had always been a wonderful remediator of anxiety and adrenaline for me.

I'm no saint, mind you, but I've been a part of more than my share of violence and wanted nothing other than to step away from any more of that stuff. I left my small Missouri town to get away from it. I left the Army to get away from it. I left Kansas City to get away from it. I left Idaho to get away from it. Now, here, I'm back into the groove again, back to the cycle of drinking, depression, and avoiding the real world, yet with an occasional bout of violence.

Perhaps I should have run and hidden last night, but my animal brain chose not to. The three attackers made the aggressive moves, and I'm not yet passive enough to cower or avoid a fight that's brought to me. That's probably why I'm hurting now. Though all the details escape me, my current injuries tell the tale of what may have happened afterward; amped up from the first fight, I got more beer and more booze from the shop and wandered around drunk until I stumbled across someone or a few folks that wanted my bottle and wouldn't take no for an answer. I wasn't in a condition to stop them, though apparently, I tried. I'm lucky I didn't get stabbed. Towards the end of the scuffle, some other men interceded on my behalf, and I recall some handcuffs being placed on the guys. That part is fuzzy, but if true, it means the police were involved, and I somehow avoided arrest for being drunk and disorderly.

My legs were weak. Both hips were bruised. I felt like I would shit and puke at any minute. My heart raced, its pace irregular. My eyes hurt, and they were hard to keep open. I couldn't focus, and the light hurt. In fact, thinking hurt me. All my cash was gone, but at least I still had my wallet.

Nothing broken. Well, maybe a rib. Maybe a concussion. I sat for a minute to gather my thoughts. My head felt like a jack-o-lantern kicked in by the neighborhood punk.

No. I had to get up. Sleep would find me again if I sat here any longer. If it were a concussion, I'd require attention sooner rather than later. An urgent care center stood only two blocks away, so I worked my way there and submitted myself for a good look-over.

Afterward, I slept, trying to catch up on the rest I should have taken instead of getting my drunk ass whooped. 1 pm seemed a perfectly normal time for a grown man to stagger out of bed, especially when convalescing from a recent injury. Even more so when still processing the remnants of the previous night's booze. It helped that I didn't have a job to get up for or chickens to deal with any longer. In that case, 1 pm sounded downright puritanical in its efficiency.

The clinic decided that I didn't have a concussion or cracked ribs, only some bruising. They gave me a few 800 mg acetaminophen to get me through the day and a prescription for more. I'd have to get up and head to a pharmacy to fill it, so I used what I already had at home instead. The dosage wasn't as strong, but I'd double up to get the same amount. Hauling my ass out of bed was enough of a challenge. I didn't have the energy for a trip to the pharmacy just yet. Making coffee and getting up to my roof patio would be enough adventure for the day.

When I bought and renovated this warehouse, I added a few extras. One of those extras was the roof patio, where I installed a water line for the plants and two electrical outlets. I had the contractors create a modest sound-abatement wall, which cut some of 880's din, but there was only so much the cedar, free-flowing fabric roof, and sun-friendly ornamental grass could do. Even with the noise, the place was a tiny oasis high above the dirty street I called home.

The stairs leading to it were steeper and narrower than one would typically see in a staircase. Since this entire patio wasn't allowed by code and would probably be torn down for the next buyer, the contractor and I didn't worry too much about adhering to building codes. It was safe and sturdy enough for my needs.

It had a great view but didn't afford a sight of the waterside itself. Several taller buildings were between mine and the waterside promenade, though I saw a little up and down the estuary. The best part of the vista lay to the north and west. I had a great view of the San Francisco-Oakland Bay Bridge as it joined the City by the Bay. On a clear night, I had a view of the lights and excitement of Oracle Park whenever the San Francisco Giants had a home game. I saw the massive Sutro Tower silhouetted against the distant clouds, and on most days, the cloudless ones, the tips of the city's more prominent buildings peeked above the bridge.

The sky was clear and robin egg blue, but the area's weather being what it was, you could often see a cloud front trying to push its way up the windward slope of the coastal range. It was one thing or the other: either clear sky with a band of clouds trying yet failing to push over, or the clouds would win, and a marine layer would cover the entire bay. Like my dark moods, always trying to take over or, in victory, covering everything, changing the flavor of all experiences.

Pretending to enjoy the sun, I sipped my cuppa and thought about Xtra and his request for me to go on his patrols or whatever he had in mind. I just didn't have it in me to do it, to put myself out there for anyone right now. The idea of doing anything except hiding and avoiding seemed dreadful to me.

6

Few areas in America are more of a melting pot than East Oakland. There are spices, colors, languages, crimes, odors, and sins of every imaginable kind found within the imaginary boundaries on the map.

While there had always been a flow of new faces from Mexico, and Black Americans had long been part of Oakland's history, the area's multicultural mix took on an even more diverse shape in the 1940s as a post-WWII bedroom community. In the 50s, East Oakland added flavor as a home to immigrants and castoffs from Asia and Central America as the United States opened its doors to refugees from troubled countries. In the 60s, Southeast Asia and South America added their people to the list. Decolonized African nationals immigrated to the US in the 70s, and the 80s were filled with thousands of new faces from India and Pakistan.

Driving today through any major street, you'd see cafes and shops with flags or signs of any country and with languages from anywhere in the world. You want a free Tibet? You got it! A dark beer from Peru? Yours! Need to send money to Lagos? Done! Between the internet, Amazon, local shipping ports, and three nearby airports, any home in this area can feel like home anywhere.

Massage parlors and churches were another way to ease the bodies and souls of all these new Americans. Many enjoyed visiting their own ethnicity's houses of worship, and others savored the variety and flavors of all the diversity found here. Sometimes, it was worship of the soul-based kind, or other times, of the flesh. There were often multiple denominations of churches for each nationality: First Presbyterian Laotian Church, Laotian Church of Christ, and Laotian Shepherd Society.

It was at one of these churches that Donald Vo worked, the First Vietnamese Baptist Church. An innocent-looking, bespectacled driver and handyman trusted by the elders because of his parents' and grandparents' longstanding good relationship with the church and community, the young Vo made all the right moves in the eyes of the church—in the daylight. He assisted the older congregants to their seats on Sundays. He'd run general errands for the pastor, go shopping for the widows and widowers in the congregation, and once, he even helped foster two kittens found abandoned in the parking lot. A good kid—mostly.

He was also a cousin of the Trans. This lone trait ruined him. On occasional nights, like this night, he would visit the dark spaces of the East Bay with his cousins and harvest a fresh crop of flesh to keep their supply line happy. A dirty trade that kept the cash flowing and the Binhs back home happy.

This night's mission was simple but messy. Aaron and Roger Tran had it all planned out: Vo needed to ready the van, drive to the site and the stash house, and then return home. They would be doing all the dirty work. And it would certainly get dirty.

Vo arrived at his church in his Hyundai Elantra a few minutes after midnight. He parked under the streetlights in front of the church and walked to the white van in the side lot. As usual, the van sat parked with its back end into the cinder block wall of the neighboring liquor store. Before getting in, Vo walked around and detached the magnetic signs bearing the church's name in English and Vietnamese from the driver's door, the side sliding door, and the rear door. He left the plates on the van. They'd previously decided that driving without plates was too big an invitation for the police to pull them over, especially at night.

The Trans were silent as they entered the van. Through text messages, Vo knew they'd be waiting for him outside the stash house just north of downtown Oakland.

"Let's go!" was all the elder Tran, Aaron, had to say. No air of arrogance or braggadocio. No macho energy or holiness in this hunt. The young men had a sadness hanging around them as if they didn't want to do this. But do it, they would. Vo drove silently to where they needed to go, their harvesting field.

The areas north and east of the Oakland County Coliseum may not have had the worst signs of homelessness, poverty, and crime, but the wide, empty streets and sidewalks gave a blank canvas to display the array of tents, camps, vans, and campers that held all manner of permanent and temporary transient residents. Market prices, land value, and good sense had moved out many of the area's more sizable warehouse and manufacturing businesses. The smart ones moved further inland. Gone were the companies that spent money on their external upkeep, weed management, outside security, or outreach programs. Those who remained did the bare minimum, spending as little as possible to stay afloat, leaving dark corners, torn fences, weeds, and overflowing refuse piles that attracted drifters looking for building supplies.

Where there stood one van or tent, there were two. Where there were two, there were four. Small shanties quickly built up along ragged edges were torn down, either by choice or by a city bulldozer, then rebuilt. Over the last few years, a spiderweb of humans had formed in the dark spaces between the gutters, sidewalks, walls, and fences. They covered the whole of the industrial area. Communities sprang up, relationships were made, and tonight—lives ended.

Vo drove past the east end of Julie Ann Way, where Aaron and Roger had seen their target family the night before. On that scouting mission, the brothers had verified their source's information. The family was there. They did have two girls, twins, in the age range they were looking for. Aaron had watched as the mother emerged outside to grab clothing from the drying line she had strung between the camper and the fence across the sidewalk. She was carrying four garments when she appeared to have forgotten something and called back inside. Moments later, a tall, slim girl stepped outside carrying a laundry basket. The girl, obviously one of the twins, wore shorts that were too tight and small for her and a T-shirt that was too large. She wore her long black hair in a loose and messy ponytail. Her feet were bare, which her mother scolded her for, even as she thanked her for bringing the basket.

That's a BINGO! Aaron thought, a line from one of his favorite movies, *Inglourious Basterds.* He'd yet to knowingly meet a German, but he imagined they all spoke the same way as that character, Hans Landa, did. Their mission was on.

Though none of the men felt chatty, they went over their plan again: drive Coliseum Way twice to look for any activity. If none, they'll head to the camper and take care of it. Vo would pull up ninety seconds later, get out, open the van doors, shut them after everyone gets in, and drive slowly back to the stash house. Simple and clean.

After midnight, Coliseum Way was a ghost town. Best for everyone, usually. For the residents, it meant the police weren't around to cause trouble. The lack of sirens meant a good night of sleep. The nearby train tracks had some traffic now and then, but one could almost get used to that noise, mentally morphing it into the sound of waves crashing.

Vo dropped the Trans off on Joe Morgan Way midway between Kevin Court and Julie Ann Way, then drove south. He pushed his glasses up the bridge of his nose, more out of a habit than for the need. Now, to disappear for a few minutes and wait for a text. After that, his only mission was to avoid attracting attention.

The Trans silently exited the van and walked along the quiet street toward their target, hugging the shadows and dark corners as they moved. The whole time, they were looking and listening for anyone looking and listening for them. They were the invaders here, and there may be eyes and ears alert for danger, but nothing so far. The night was silent, and the bay air brought moisture that maintained a blanket of the industrial area's funk and pollutants. One block north ran another stormwater runoff creek that doubled as a local bathroom and sewer for the locals. A lucky pedestrian could pick out those smells in the air.

They turned the corner to where their target family lay. A tarp leaned off a fence next to the family's camper, but neither Tran spotted nor sensed anyone near it. A tent was pitched on the sidewalk close by, but there appeared to be no activity in or near it. Everything looked clear. Across the street sat the burned-out shell of a minivan, more than likely stolen, used in a crime elsewhere, and dumped here after its useful life had ended. *That's a good sign. If the police didn't care to check out the area, it's safer for us.*

Twenty-five feet from the camper, in the darkness where the streetlights couldn't find them, they reached into their coat pockets to retrieve their tools. Each had headlamps. Aaron had a Taurus .38 tightly wrapped in a towel to muffle some of the noise. Roger had more gear: a pry bar, zip cuffs, two canvas bags with drawstrings, a small assortment of rags, and a roll of duct tape. Each brother had their mission. Aaron looked at Roger and mouthed, "You ready?"

Roger's face and body language said no, his eyes wide, his shoulders tense, and his mouth agape. He nodded his head anyway. This wasn't their first kill, but they weren't yet seasoned enough and inured with death that snuffing out two souls and snatching little girls away would be easy. They were ready. Aaron sent a text to Vo.

90 seconds. Go!

With a nod, they covered the few feet to the trailer door. Using the pry bar, Roger made quick work of the cheap door lock and stood aside for Aaron. They had assumed the parents would sleep in the larger bed at the rear of the trailer, and the girls in the smaller one at the front. They were correct. By the time Aaron entered, Roger was already rushing in behind on his way to the girls. Aaron shot the father as he slept, but the mother woke before the first round was even fired. A quick bullet fired into her mouth snuffed out her scream quickly. The towel worked better than they had hoped.

Only one of the girls was roused by the commotion inside their tiny home. She leaned up, horrified by the strange men with headlamps, and let out the beginning of what would have been a blood-curdling scream of the kind only young girls were capable of. Roger was ready for it and slapped the girl across her face with an open palm, sending her onto her sister. If the twin hadn't been fully awake yet, she was after that. A wrestling match began. Zip cuffs first, rags into their mouths, canvas bags over their heads, all followed by a few laps of duct tape around their necks to keep everything tight.

After killing the parents, Aaron kept an eye on Roger while also watching the street for random passers-by and Vo. He'd arrive any second.

There!

Vo rounded the corner, not too quickly, but still with a purpose, and pulled up beside the crime scene. Roger had both girls subdued, and by the time he and Aaron dragged them outside, Vo had already opened the sliding side door. The Trans tossed the bound little girls inside the van and shut the door behind them. After accounting for all four passengers, Vo returned to his seat and took off too quickly for Aaron's liking.

"Slow the fuck down!" He yelled at his cousin in Vietnamese. "We don't want to get pulled over now."

Except for the crying and mewing of the girls, they were silent the remainder of the way back to their stash house. The girls were on their way to the next level of hell.

* * *

A lone figure stirred under the tarp attached to the fence near the camper. A face blacker than black and eyes yellow from years of drug use and dietary neglect, he said two words to himself. "White van."

He repeated it as if to lock it in his memory, as if the words were part of a secret spell that would bring the dead back to life. "White van."

The man didn't see what happened inside the RV and didn't need or want to check. The sounds of muffled gunshots were obvious enough. The girls had been taken, and he assumed the rest. It had happened before. He'd seen men come and kill people on the streets or at least steal from them. It was dangerous out here. Always has been. Always will be. This was different, though. This was a step above the rest. Or, a step below. He wasn't sure.

When it was safe to do so, with no one around, he relieved himself against the fence near his tarp. Shuffling off, with his rumpled and dirty clothing more piled upon him than worn, he told himself he had to see the mayor.

7

Sergeant Andrea "Andi" Cozens was no longer a true first responder. Despite her experience and seniority with the Alameda County Sheriff's Department, or maybe because of it, she was third in line to be notified of a violent crime, and only if it fit into the purview of her team.

Cozens was the senior detective on the Alameda County Task Force for Major Crimes against the Homeless, ACMC-H. For her to be called into a case at this early hour meant patrol had already been to the scene, brought in Major Crimes from Oakland police, and had determined that, because this incident involved members of the homeless community, her task force should be notified.

She and her small team didn't take the lead on cases like this. Her job, and that of her teammates, was to identify commonalities and patterns among the bulk of crimes committed against the unhoused in Alameda County. This crime clearly fit into her auspices. OPD would take the lead, but her team would have access to all aspects of the investigation.

5:30 in the morning was too early for any type of activity, especially responding to the report of a double homicide and suspected kidnapping. She'd done her time on the streets and had her share of horrors, but this job brought all those joys back again whenever some weak soul preyed upon those who were even weaker.

She brushed her teeth, took a quick washcloth from the shelf, and washed her face in the sink. She made a quick cup of instant coffee and threw on mostly clean clothes before heading out the door—eight minutes from phone call to exit.

The drive from her home in Alameda to the crime scene near the Coliseum took about twenty minutes. Plenty of time to compare the few details she had regarding the event this morning against the others in her memory from the past few years: dead parents, missing girls. There was the Laotian girl in Albany, the Thai boy in Oakland, the two Mexican girls in Fremont, a Venezuelan girl in San Leandro, two Thai girls in Emeryville, and a young Chinese girl in Oakland, only a week before.

There might be more, but that's all Cozens recalled this early in the morning before the caffeine kicked in. From what little she picked up from the phone call, this case sounded like it'd be in the same category: homeless and undocumented family, recent immigrants, questionable paperwork or status. They'd have been living on or near the outskirts of an area lightly populated with fellow homeless wanderers and no security cameras or lights. There'd be no witnesses, or at least none willing to speak with the police, and no significant evidence would be found at the scene.

She and her team had been formed in the chaotic aftermath of the Tennyson Massacre three years prior. Not only were they no closer to solving that case, but they had also uncovered a whole new series of crimes against the homeless: human trafficking, presumably for the sex trade. None of the missing kids on her list had ever been heard from again. Alive, anyway. The responding department had conducted a full investigation into each case, but only so much can be done without witnesses or evidence. The task force kept the cases open, hoping that enough commonalities would emerge and something would break in the trafficking operation's mechanics. Or maybe the team perpetrating these crimes would make a mistake. Maybe a witness would come forward. Maybe this. Maybe that. Too many maybes and not enough evidence.

Cozens exited 880 at 66th. The area, a warehouse and distribution hub, was coming to life, even at this early hour. A few dead, homeless victims weren't going to slow down business. When she arrived at the scene in her work unit, a 2020 Dodge Charger, she looked first for what she always looked for: the investigator in charge and, more importantly, any spectator paying too much attention to what was happening.

Her days of working major crime investigations were behind her, but she still knew what to do and what not to do. Most importantly, stay out of the way when you're not the lead. From the periphery, she tried to form an initial opinion of what happened based on the scene's layout and generally tried to get a feel of the area before getting her briefing. Despite the strong scents of the industrial zone, tar, metal, and unknown chemicals, the spilled blood wafted through the air and mixed easily with the smell of garbage and human funk from the built-up community.

Only one television news team had arrived on the scene, but two press photographers were at work, along with a few print reporters.

Way off in the back of the circle of light stood the mayor. Not the real one. She wouldn't come out here for this. "The Mayor," Marcus Williams, a homeless man and advocate for the unhoused community, had his fingers in everything and knew everyone. Cozens always wondered whether he was into anything illegal, but could never confirm anything. She kept things civil with him because he had more street knowledge, more about the goings on in Oakland's underbelly than anyone else. He stood chatting with the reporter from the weekly, Mike Finney. She'd made a name for herself following the corrupt escapades of city hall and how they'd been negligent in handling the city's burgeoning unhoused population. If these two were sharing notes, she'd want in on the conversation.

Cozens had to admit she got a small thrill when she realized Mike was there. She sometimes wondered if she had a low-key crush on the tall and lean reporter. Finney stood next to the mayor, looking like she had just rolled out of bed and worn the first thing found strewn on the floor, but still looked great: jeans with rolled-up cuffs, a thick, white V-neck t-shirt, and a dark linen sports coat better suited to a man, but which looked natural on her. Her close-cropped blonde hair was messy, but that was part of the charm of the rough-hewn appearance.

"Mike, Your Honor. Good morning," she said, stifling her schoolgirl silliness. "You know anything we don't?"

Mike stayed silent, but Williams spoke up right away. "Probably." His response was curt, leaving silence in the moist, unpleasant air.

Cozens wanted to hear what it might be, but she waited him out. It didn't take long.

He pointed to a tarp across the street. "Charlie over yonder heard the commotion and knew what was what. He got hold of me, then I called 911." He spoke succinctly, clearly, almost angrily.

Cozens looked at Mike. "How'd you find out?"

"A chirping bird," she said.

Fucking Twitter, or whatever it is now. Finney had her shoulder laptop bag with her. *Shit! By now, she'd probably already posted a 1000-word article with photos and videos to her paper's website with links to all the social sites. More than likely added a few extra videos to Instagram for good measure.* It was as admirable as it was frustrating.

Williams continued. "This is them baby fuckers again. They killed the parents and took the kids, the twins. Gonna sell them off for sex or some filthy shit. Y'all need to get your shit together and stop this."

Now that the caffeine had kicked in, making her more alert, Cozens remembered similar cases in the East Bay and beyond. It wasn't just happening here; it was more than one team doing this—maybe one group working on her home turf, but there were more elsewhere. She didn't have a single goddamn clue to go on. No witnesses, no survivors, no evidence left at the scene, and so far, no way to track where these girls had gone. Once they're taken, they simply disappear.

If that were her only problem on the task force, it'd be bad enough, but she also had some type of low-key serial killer out there picking off members of the homeless population. Every few weeks, there'd be an extra death, an unusual death that couldn't be explained away by any other means. People died all the time on the streets, in bad health, accidents, overdoses, and fights. A hundred ways to die out here, but these were premeditated murders: stabbing, strangulation, shooting, and one broken neck. What they all had in common was that they were all done in dark places where only the unhoused roamed, the professionally homeless. Not the casual ones. Her team had another sting operation in the next week to help with that situation, but for this one, the kidnapping of children and the murdering of their parents, she had no solution.

8

Braga didn't have a set pattern for where he hunted. Sometimes, he would choose a spot in the Bay Area directly opposite the site of his most recent attack. If he killed someone in Richmond, the next hunt would be on the southern peninsula, Palo Alto or Daly City. Other times, he would stay close to his latest hunt because, to his mind, no one would suspect another attack so soon or so close to the last. An admittedly imperfect plan, but so far, it had worked well.

Tonight, he hunted two miles north of his last kill in Fruitvale, close to downtown Oakland. While the city had its rough spots, urban blight, and human misery, downtown and the Lake Merritt area were full of enough gems that afforded the city an upscale reputation. Over the years, the old and new money combined to make for a thriving metropolis. The city had earned its nickname, "Hub of the West," because of its central location to commerce, easy access to major highways, bustling ports, and ability to absorb newcomers, immigrants, dreamers, economic invaders, and miscreants.

Have a great business idea and the capital to back it up? Oakland can be your home. Escaping a war in your home country? Oakland and the East Bay already have some of your people, and you can find a community here. Murdered a homeless drifter in the Central Valley and want to start fresh? Oakland has a thriving middle-class service industry. We can find you a job as a bartender, landscaper, or security manager to help you begin anew!

The underpasses in the part of Oakland where Interstates 880, 980, 24, and 580 met were not where many homeless families settled. While several shelters and free kitchens were nearby, the underpasses served as a dark highway for solo late-night wanderers and professional vagabonds. The homeless highways under the freeways were active at all times of the night. It was a dangerous place full of dangerous people. This extra black darkness held a constant, slow trickle of forgotten souls perpetually migrating to their next short-term home. Homeless-on-homeless violence was common, but like wild creatures, the drifters would rather avoid anyone than confront them—but if they were drunk, hungry, horny, or angry, anyone in their path could be another victim.

This is where Braga wanted to be tonight: he wanted more thrill or challenge than his last victim had offered. There were times when a quick but messy kill, the shooting of an easy target, was precisely what he needed to make him feel good. Then again, there were times when he had a greater hunger, and that required a greater thrill, a greater challenge.

Tonight was that kind of night. Despite his side hustles, his workday was so tedious and frustrating that no time at the gym or at the bar could scratch his itch. Tonight, he wanted to increase the difficulty level. Tonight, he wanted to get bloody with someone.

Braga parked his truck on a crowded residential street two blocks off 880, a stone's throw east of Laney College. The area teemed with businesses, and each home and apartment was packed. It being California, everyone had their own car. This made parking a hassle, but it also meant one more vehicle parked in the dark would go unnoticed. He'd be invisible in this urban fog of concrete, traffic noise, and general ambivalence.

He wore one of his generic hunting outfits: a dark blue hoodie, a black T-shirt, black jeans, and black sneakers, the cheapest items he could find at either Walmart or a thrift store. The odds of a crime scene team arriving at the site of one of his kills and taking photos or castings of shoe prints were slim in the case of a dead homeless person. Still, on the rare chance a department would care about the deaths of these pieces of garbage, he took extra precautions. The shoes he wore tonight were one size larger than usual. He usually wore a size 11, but these were 12s. Other times, he would wear a size or two smaller than normal with the front toe cap cut, allowing his toes to hang out enough for comfort.

The night air was crisp and cool, a mild breeze from the west, bringing saltiness and a soft hint of low-tide muck. Those scents combined to nearly cover up the acridness of the asphalt and traffic exhaust. It was an almost pleasant walk through the two blocks to the underside of the freeway. Even before he arrived at his destination, the signs of homelessness were obvious to Braga. A handful were camped out in storefronts or behind dumpsters. He passed more than a dozen cars with makeshift curtains in the windows, a sure sign the occupants were sleeping inside. All worthy targets, but they were all too exposed. He moved toward 880 and richer targets.

On Saturdays, the largest of the student parking lots at Laney College hosted a flea market, and many of the merchants who sold wares there parked and lived in their storage vans along E 7th, E 8th, and the nearby feeder streets. These merchants often cast off items they couldn't sell, but the homeless folks who frequented the area could use or trade them. Old toothpaste, used clothing, broken appliances, and all manner of otherwise useless things a thrifty someone could get one more use from. These items littered the gutters and eaves of the underpasses, waiting to be taken up by a new user or to decompose in place.

5th Avenue was a wide thoroughfare that brought him to Embarcadero and closer to the waterfront. The Nimitz Freeway rose above ground level a block south and stayed hoisted high on concrete pillars throughout downtown except for a short stretch near Laney College. Underneath were secured lots, storage areas for ongoing construction, hard-packed dirt fields, and informal pathways crafted by years of unauthorized use, with strategically snipped fences that allowed passage between properties and railroad tracks, providing safe crossing from cars and eyes. City parks and abandoned lots gave short-term shelter from the world.

Jack London Square had always held promise as a hunting ground. It had its share of residences and businesses, but the living spaces were localized to a few square blocks. The businesses were shuttered in the evenings, or, if open as a bar or restaurant, near the water and away from any potential hunting grounds. After hours, this left a large swath of the neighborhood vacant—a playground for Braga.

There were only a few houses in the area, mostly built in the old Victorian style several blocks north. Many had been converted to other uses. The lofts and condos were all more than a dozen floors tall. Each offered ample parking, so the residents didn't have to contend with the area's visitors or business patrons. More importantly, this meant fewer cars circling for a parking space and fewer observant eyes.

There lay a sweet spot in the middle of the area, between the two main street entrances of Webster and Broadway, and away from the water, businesses, and residents, a section of warehouses that only operated during the daytime or early mornings as the sun came up. Some offices and shops, too, but they operated standard business hours. During Braga's hunting time, they were all asleep for the night. The only people out in these twenty or so square blocks this night were Braga and whoever he might want to add to his list.

His last kill felt great, but it was too easy. It was the right choice at the time, as he only needed a quick one to ease the week's tension, but it failed to help erase any of his self-doubts about his worth, power, or place in the social hierarchy. A simple kill for a simple thrill; the harvest of an undesirable, the ridding of another piece of trash. Tonight needed to be something more. Sure, all those things, but he needed more of a challenge. Like a wild game hunter moving up from a gazelle to a lion. No, not a lion, a hyena, or some other scavenging mongrel.

He walked casually along the streets and past their sleeping, parked cars. To his left, several loft residences shone bright lights, but the businesses and warehouses to his right were dark and quiet. *These people in their comfortable homes have no idea what I'm doing for them.* He made a right turn, leading a block closer back toward the freeway overpass, passing a woman, a gazelle, curled up for the night with her blankets and a few belongings in the doorway of one of the closed warehouses. She'd be rousted out of there before sunrise, but she'd have a cozy sleep until then. She wasn't what Braga wanted tonight. She was also too exposed.

Two vans on the street, running alongside the Nimitz, looked occupied. A black Chevy had makeshift curtains over its many windows. The other, a red Ford, had windows only in the front and back, so the occupant had a rod and curtain behind the front seats to keep stray light from escaping. Both vans were past their prime, and neither had a current registration. One set of plates came from Nevada, and the other had no plates at all. Doubtless, they spent their days shuttling from one dead zone to another, down back streets where nobody cared to observe them. They could hold a single person, a team of laborers, or a whole family, but a glance from the outside revealed nothing. From prior experience, Braga knew that once these folks were in for the night, they were in for the night. He continued north.

Where Webster enters and Harrison exits the tunnels beneath the channel to Alameda, the road nearest the freeway is interrupted by ramps dug into the earth to accommodate the slope of the downgrade. Braga had to divert his path around these, but spied a few other candidates in the dark spaces and shadows. In the corner formed by the freeway support wall and the tunnel ramp railing, a messy pile slouched, revealing two people lying on a cardboard bed, a few blankets draped over them. *Was this a couple or travel partners? That might be an interesting twist—a double.*

From inside the nearest warehouse across the street came the sound of a solid interior door slamming. Was it a worker closing after a late night? Someone starting early? It didn't matter. It was enough to make Braga keep walking.

He stayed away from 880 for a block until he returned to 5th Street, where the other ramp railing met the freeway. Nobody was in this corner. *Shame.* Only an empty, secure parking lot and a darkened, one-story warehouse. The several cars parked in the cul-de-sac were a potential risk, though. Many were empty, but a few looked suspect. *Was anyone sleeping inside? Were their owners coming back from the bars anytime soon?*

Where 5th Street ended at the tunnel downgrade, the freeway's underside was covered by what the state thought was a secure fence. Perhaps it stayed that way for the first few weeks of its existence. Soon after, though, someone had snipped enough of the chain link to create an opening, its mouth jagged with iron teeth. This allowed passage into the secure area, yet it looked dark and scary, threatening anyone with a sense of self-worth or preservation from clambering through. Here, the city and county offices nearby stored their vehicles behind a keypad-controlled gate beside a personnel gate with a similar keypad, both on the 5th Street side. Getting out of the storage area on foot was only a matter of pushing the panic bar on the door. After hours, there were no lights in the area, so by heading to any of the edges, whether it be 5th Street from which Braga came, 6th Street to the east, or Broadway to the north, he got a clear look at the surrounding areas without being seen by anyone.

Moving around the lot, he ensured no one else was in there with him. It seemed a good place to camp, but he'd have to be wary in case of an occasional security sweep. There were no cameras in any of the obvious places.

Looking downtown, light vehicle traffic dashed about, but no one was on foot. Moving west a few yards, he glanced down Broadway, where a young couple walked two blocks toward the water. Looking across Broadway, farther down the freeway's underside, he saw a similar municipal storage space, but better lit. In a clump of overgrown shrubs aside the street, the outline of a tent was visible. It would prove a good hunting option if nothing else emerged.

No clear target appeared available, but since he wasn't in a rush, there was no point in stressing. He sat on the hood of one of the fleet vehicles on the lot, heels on the front bumper, and kept lookout while his mind cast back to the words from years ago that set him on this path.

"Any undesirable person who is eliminated from this country makes the average American just a little better. The more we can get rid of, the better off we'll all be."

Over the years, his techniques had changed, as had his motivations, but that old truism still held. He thought that if every region had a few people like him taking out the garbage like he'd been doing, each community would be a better place. He would probably never fit the role of a happy suburban dad, so he would instead lean into it with gusto for as long as he could and do as much good for the world as possible. Some people create art. Some practice medicine or save puppies. *And some, like me, kill pieces of shit to make the world better.*

Movement to his right caught his eye. Across the street and two blocks down Broadway, a tall man with a backpack strolled, hands in pockets, a rumpled coat and loose pants, his head down, bound for Jack

London Square. Braga thought the man looked neither old nor young; he couldn't tell, but he moved like someone who—he didn't have the words—like someone who could move well. Not necessarily a fighter, but someone with physicality. Certainly not a ballerina. Not a gazelle.

As the stranger came a block closer, Braga saw he was a black man. There was one more intersection before entering the Square. The man turned neither left nor right and walked past 6th Street. Braga's excitement rose as the potential target kept heading straight as he approached the corner, looked both ways, and crossed the red light. There was little time to play with. Braga had to make some decisions quickly. He scoured the streets again for traffic.

Nothing. He looked again at the man, his hands in his pockets, his frame, his headphones, and his overall lack of awareness. This would be tonight's kill. But how? So much depended on where the man turned.

Is he gonna walk straight down Broadway or turn left or right on 5th Street? Attack from the front or behind? He could either walk down Broadway on the side closer to Braga or turn left onto 5th Street and pass by him. *If he turns left, should I leave and face him before he arrives or wait for him to pass and follow?*

Braga felt his excitement growing.

9

The cafes in Jack London Square turned their Wi-Fi off when they closed in the evenings. A few of the bars had Wi-Fi, but they also had patrons going in and out, casting glances, and making judgments, so during the nighttime hours, Xavier Travers would get his internet connection from quiet hotspots he knew about downtown.

Just on the other side of Interstate 880, in downtown Oakland, lay a vast jungle of invisible information bouncing through the sky, waiting to be captured. Xtra's only tool to access all this data was the iPhone 11 he'd acquired in a trade. Didn't matter to him where it came from. It was clean and ready for a new user. That's all that mattered. He never had any data to access the cellular networks, but one can do wonders in the world of wireless fidelity. He had a Google account for email and used Google Voice to make calls when in a hotspot. There were enough news sources that he stayed up to date on what was happening around the world; he maintained his VA records and all manner of digital voodoo not generally practiced by those on the streets. He even played Wordle.

Smiling that they changed the name of the social media platform to match his, Xtra logged onto X to catch up on late-breaking news and check in with his homeless network. He was one of many unhoused people with web access and the savvy to navigate it. In addition to them, several caregivers and shelters were available online. The online unhoused network knew this and shared the information with others. Posts and messages circulated a running list of which churches or shelters had meals available, where beds were free, or what calamity had befallen a comrade. Because of the too-often bad news, a random reporter or cop would regularly pop into a thread, rarely in a bad way. They often tried to be helpful or, at worst, get information, but no one ever talked to the police, as far as Xtra was aware. The reporter, @MiFiReports, was another story. Everyone knew Mike, or at least of her. She'd been around the area long enough and was on top of all the times someone harmed one of his people. Xtra admired and loved her. He didn't know why she did it. He never got around to asking, but it earned her a lot of street cred, and people would talk to her before they'd talk to the police.

After he checked X and confirmed the world was still a flaming dumpster fire, Xtra signed into his YouTube account to watch more videos in the training series he followed, an instructional series for spreadsheets. Back in his Army days, Sergeant First Class Travers had been responsible for all manner of administrative and budgetary tasks in his unit, which required using many early web devices and programs. While primitive, those tasks let Xtra feel he had an aptitude for the world of zeros and ones, for seeing a landscape in digital form. Even though his current physical landscape was all concrete and sadness, he did what he could to keep his mind sharp and modern.

He left the US Army at thirty-seven and never looked back. In the service, he had been a leader of men and a problem-solver. With troops, whether highly trained or not, and equipment, whether adequate for the task or not, SFC Travers would unflinchingly attack any goal set for him by his command. His third rotation to Iraq was the final straw. By then, the war had dragged on long enough, with no end in sight and little to show for it other than a growing pile of Iraqi and American dead. He had seen and done enough. At the end of his last tour, he declined another re-enlistment and left the uniform behind.

He'd never had a moment of regret for leaving a few years short of retirement. So great was his disillusionment with his country for its bombings of foreign brown people, its willingness to send young American people of color to war, and its tendency to reward failure that he had no trouble getting out and staying gone.

Enough for tonight. He had only returned to visit a friend and planned to head back to Fruitvale tonight, but it had gotten late. There were a few safe spots nearby to catch some shuteye, and one of the safest lay around the corner near Warren's place. Young Sergeant would be around to share a meal if he were lucky.

He thought Warren an odd one: a well-off ex-cop who drank like a fish and slept on the streets. *Since he's out here so much, I gotta see if he wants to come hit the trails with me for a while.* Xtra had heard Warren talk in his sleep, mostly mumbles when he'd sat with him in the street. Nothing ever clear enough to understand, but once, he seemed to have had a whole damn conversation with someone. *Crazy shit.* He'd seen that before, but only with people on the street.

Xtra crossed Broadway beneath the freeway, far outside the crosswalk. Jaywalking seemed the least of his concerns, yet it was the worst of his offenses. The streets were safe and clear. A few bars were still open downtown, and far into the square, the open pubs showed some light and excitement. The streets around him looked empty, but he was far from alone. He'd been around the streets long enough to know that perhaps up to a dozen people were sleeping or resting within a 100-foot circle of him. They'd all mind their own business even if Xtra screamed bloody murder. They'd stay where they were.

He turned left onto 5th Street, where the lights created shadows and dark angles. The many streetlamps on Broadway added to the effect. Together, they made an ominous yellow haze, yet each maintained their autonomy, crafting a fuzzy shadow on every graffiti-covered wall, decrepit storefront, and paving slab. With hands in pockets, head down, and headphones covering his ears, Xtra maintained a practiced and relaxed look—but it was just that, a look. His several years of street life had taught him to stay alert for any possible intrusion into one's space. No reason to be jumpy and twitchy all the time, but vigilance was key. Feigning invisibility was the best way to be left alone. Ignore, avoid, and evade. Do what you can to not engage. Xtra never asked passersby for money and did everything possible to avoid contact with strangers, even other homeless people when possible. It was a risky existence, but there were ways to play it safe.

The headphones weren't meant to play music to drown out the world. They weren't ever playing anything, not when he was out walking anyway. They were meant to make people think he was listening to something, giving them one more reason not to interfere. He was still well aware of the music of the world around him. That's what saved his life.

Seventy-five feet along 5th Street, something metallic clanged from behind. He thought he recognized the sound, as if someone had closed the personnel door of the vehicle storage area he'd just passed, but he didn't turn around to confirm it. He'd never heard that door close before, but they must all sound alike, and the distance and direction matched. He continued forward, scanning ahead with his eyes and listening behind with his ears. Nothing new in front, maybe some footsteps behind, but the noise wash from the freeway above, though light, covered any delicate sounds.

Xtra's senses picked up two things together. Multiple shadows converged on him, one for every light source on the street, and already broken glass scraped underfoot as someone, the same someone as the many-shadowed figure, lurched toward him. Those observations gave him enough time to step to his right. A knife blade's downward strike at his right trapezius gave Xtra a long but superficial cut to the area behind his left shoulder, the teres major and minor, and the infraspinatus. It wasn't good, and it hurt like hell, but in the heat of the moment, not a huge problem.

As the attacker prepared for another strike, Xtra lost his footing, his spin having left him leaning toward his attacker and unable to leap or lean away. His only chance, a slim one, was to attack, to close the space between him and the blade. It wasn't much, but it was all he had.

Planting his left foot, he pushed himself right toward his attacker, hoping to grab the man and throw him down. At that exact moment, Xtra felt the searing flame of the blade enter his belly. His hands caught material from the front of the attacker's hoodie, including the hood's drawstring.

The attacker's knife entered deeply. The blade may have gotten a good purchase, but Xtra had two handfuls of the man's hoodie, and he wasn't going to let go despite the instinct to clutch at his wound. He felt the blade withdraw from his guts, and the attacker used both of his hands to shove Xtra forcefully away. Xtra stayed upright but lost hold with his right hand, already weakened by the first attack. Only his left hand remained, clutching the front of where the hood gathered at the drawstrings.

As the attacker struggled further, Xtra lost grip of the remaining fabric. Though he still clenched the drawstrings, his hand slipped toward the knots at the ends. This pressure and distance tightened the hoodie's face hole, obscuring the attacker's vision. It was the one advantage Xtra had, and he used it. Stepping away, he swung his attacker in a slow, wide circle, not so firmly as to pull off the entire garment but enough to control his movements and keep him blind.

After one excruciating effort, the attacker began to flail to keep his balance. He managed to grab hold of the drawstrings, regaining some balance while swinging blindly upwards with his blade. He'd tried to cut the strings but instead slashed at Xtra's hand clutching the cords. It slowed the spin but didn't stop it. Another slash with the knife did the job, cutting the strings three inches from where they threaded through the hoodie. While it stopped the spin, it also transferred all that energy into propelling him ten feet away and down onto the asphalt, knocking his head.

Now, Xtra felt the pain from the three cuts: shoulder, gut, and left hand. They were all losing blood, and regardless of internal injury, he had to stem the bleeding soon. First, though, he had to get away. He was less than 100 feet from a safe space *if that motherfucker was home!* More blood was gushing from his shoulder than from the stomach wound.

Xtra spared a glance toward his attacker, who was rising, and ran as best as a man with three bloody cuts could toward Warren's building, still clutching the two severed drawstrings—seventy-five feet from the door. The attacker rose, adjusted the opening of his hoodie, and moved toward him.

He turned right onto Franklin Street, fifty feet from Warren's warehouse and front door. Everything was quiet. Xtra twisted around. His attacker was fifty feet behind. If Warren's door was locked, Xtra was a dead man.

At the door, after what seemed an eternity to reach, Xtra's blood-soaked hand yanked at the handle without success. He thumped the doorbell on the security pad, hoping beyond reason that something magical would happen. It wasn't magic. It was simple technology with no concern for the situation.

Three lights came on together, casting a flood of brightness over the sidewalk.

Xtra froze. His attacker froze. Time froze.

"Hello?" said a voice over the doorbell device. "Anyone there?" It was Warren.

"Young Sergeant. I need some help, young man. Like now."

From a short distance away, the attacker hesitated, torn, before finally twisting toward the shadows and disappearing into the night.

10

In the evenings, after the sporting events had come and gone on TV, Ma usually flipped the bar screen at the Door to a channel replaying Family Feud episodes for hours on end. The new episodes had all been hosted by Steve Harvey, but in the past, I'd seen episodes with Louie Anderson as host and even a few old ones with Richard Dawson.

With the regular crowd present, Troy, Victor, and Duke, Richard Dawson was hands down the favorite, but *I* liked Steve Harvey better. You could tell he had a colorful sense of humor, but he held it back for the family audience the show was designed for. He also reminded me of an old neighbor from childhood. Carl—something. Carl, with a C, raised fainting goats, among other things, on his acreage outside Columbia, Missouri. He'd always been a kind presence and a helping hand through the many gaps left by my father's absence.

"He doesn't kiss any of them," Victor said. "I always thought it's cute the way Richard Dawson did that to all the women."

"Yeah, well, a man can't go around kissing random strangers anymore. That's called sexual assault nowadays." Troy countered with an officious air. "Or, I suppose he could level the field by kissing the guys, too, but that might get awkward," he said, finishing with a laugh.

"Best keep all that man-kissing to yourselves," Duke said from the far side of the bar, in the tone of a man who wasn't fond of the image of men kissing.

"What do you know, Duke?" I said with the humor and confidence of someone with too many drinks in him. "Maybe you've just never met the right man."

Troy and Victor laughed. Victor harumphed and returned his gaze to his drink. My phone dinged with the particular notification letting me know someone was at my front door. I thumbed in my passcode and opened the notice, which revealed a looming figure in the top-right corner before it scurried away.

"Hello!" I said into my phone. Nothing. "Anyone there?"

The screen showed nothing, but Xtra's tinny, digitized voice said, "Young Sergeant. I need some help, young man. Like now." Xtra was holding a hand up in front of the lens, and despite the scant light, blood was oozing from a cut, more than a casual scrape would produce. I sobered up real quick.

"I'll be right there, Old Sergeant. Three minutes. Hold tight!" I heaved myself up and, as I always paid cash while drinking my way through the night, was all evened up with Ma. I scooped up my remaining money, threw a $20 back down, and looked at Duke. "Xtra needs help. He's outside my place, bleeding."

My panic and concern must have shown. Duke's rusty, crusty, old, out-of-shape frame didn't hesitate despite its condition. He rose to leave, stopped because he hadn't been paying as he went, and gave Ma a blank stare. She understood right away and simply said, "Go!"

The tab for a few drinks could wait. Duke looked at me and told me not to wait for him. I didn't. The Door stood two blocks down and one block over from my building, but that distance seemed to take forever.

When I reached my door, the scene looked worse than I imagined, as the small amount of blood I saw on the camera failed to indicate how much Xtra had already lost. The pool of red I found him sitting in was larger than seemed healthy. By this point, I'd have guessed there was as much outside him as inside, so stemming the blood loss was as important as calling 911. Luckily, Duke was already fumbling with his cell when he arrived sooner than expected, his heavy breathing showing his grand effort. His shock at seeing our friend in such a state froze him, but I brought him back by yelling at him to be quick with calling 911. He knew my address and would know what to say to get an ambulance here soon.

Xtra was leaning against my door, and I didn't want to move him yet, so I used the keypad to open the rolling garage door for my bay instead. I ran inside to the laundry area and grabbed a handful of small towels.

When I returned, my friend didn't look good. Bad, in fact. He was paler than I'd ever seen him: sweating profusely, barely breathing, and non-responsive. A quick survey revealed his wounds, but those on his shoulder and hand had stopped bleeding. Only his stomach wound gave me worry. The hand was easy to wrap, and I held a towel against his shoulder before leaning him back against the wall to keep it in place. As I grabbed his left forearm, two thick strings dropped from his hand onto the concrete beside him, but I didn't have the time or mental bandwidth to deal with them yet. For the stomach wound, I had nothing to bind it with, so instead, I used my hand to hold pressure until the paramedics arrived.

Though a patrol car might show up first, a fire station stood within a few blocks, so unless it were an already busy night, help would be here soon. I hoped my friend held on for a few more minutes for the medics to stabilize him with a few pints of fluid. He'd need lots of blood over the following hours, but first, he needed to hold fast. The ambulance's siren wailed from the direction of downtown. *Yes!* They were coming. I told Duke to stand in the middle of 5th Street to flag them down and guide them to our bleeding friend.

When I looked back at my friend, I again noticed the strings he had dropped. There were two of them, both the same, neither matching anything he wore. I noticed flashing blue lights around the corner, two blocks away, and made a mental note to make sure the responding officer did, too. The police car arrived and blocked the road, followed closely by the ambulance, their lights whirling and flashing. In all my time on this sleepy little street, I had never seen such excitement.

Of course, it had to do with violence, and, of course, it had found its way to me.

11

The shortest path to a goal was often the most dangerous, but it was worth the risk in this case. Braga ran toward 5th Street and turned right toward the same fence line he had ducked through earlier to access the vehicle lot. Instead of following his steps, he crossed the lot to get to the downtown side and 6th Street, where another equally inconspicuous cut in the fence allowed him through to the sidewalk. He decided to conceal his limp during his escape in case anyone saw him flee. Already on fire from the struggle and short run, his lower back and right hip would be sore as hell the next day.

Here, in the brighter light, he finally noticed how much wet blood had sprayed over him. His groin and right hip were awash with it, as was the entirety of the front of his hoodie and right sleeve. His hand was splattered, and he now felt the blood on his face. He reached up under his hood and felt more from when his head hit the pavement after getting wrenched and heaved around like a sock in a washing machine.

Fuck fuck fuck fuck! That motherfucker! That motherfucking doorbell! Braga cursed himself, his target, whoever this "Young Sergeant" was, and technology in general. They all combined to ruin his hunt and put him at risk. Not only did the hunt fail, but his target saw his face. *There'll be no time to be pissed if I don't move now!*

Braga hid in the shadow behind a parked delivery truck, stripped off the hoodie, and turned it inside out. Using the rough texture from the interior, he wiped as much blood off his face as possible and tied the hoodie around his waist to cover the blood drenching his pants. There were a few drops of blood on his shoes, but they were barely visible, and nothing could be done about them now. After the hasty clean-up, Braga moved out.

6th Street was quiet, but with every passing minute, the city would begin to rouse with more delivery trucks and early risers coming to life. He turned off onto a side street lined with Victorian houses, all in good repair. A pleasant neighborhood, but not someplace he wanted to be right now.

Further south, toward his parked truck, were schools and municipal buildings, a community college, and a runoff slough that led to the estuary. Six, maybe eight more blocks to his truck if he diverted around bright areas. From the south side of Lake Merritt, there were only a few ways across the wide slough: Embarcadero and Lake Merritt Boulevards, but both were too far out of the way. 7th and 10th Avenue, though both were too well-lit and traveled. That left the pedestrian bridge in the park near the college campus. Risky, but the path was dark and looked empty. The campus, too.

Checking that nobody was around, Braga entered the property from 8th Street. The college grounds were modestly lit, and as he was unsure if there were cameras, he kept his head down and stayed in the shadows as much as possible. He had to pass four buildings before reaching the park and the footbridge over the slough.

At the bridge, Braga stopped to feel the breeze. As often happened, the cool air of the bay slowly pushed up against the hills on Oakland's eastern side. Because of the tide pattern at this hour, the breeze carried the stench of muck and all manner of decay that comes with the low tide. It wasn't a pleasant aroma, but it was close enough to the scent of the marshlands near his home in the Central Valley that it brought an instant of peace—followed by reminders of pain, failure, and childhood shame. Quick images filled his head: his schoolmates seeing his addict mother, school administrators knowing his father had run away, his own failed attempts at fitting in. He shook his head and crossed the bridge.

When he was ten feet short of the other side, a faint, floating light moved in the middle distance behind him, deep in the campus. He didn't stop, but he did slow his pace. As the light approached and passed a streetlight, Braga recognized what it was and began sprinting to his left, away from campus property.

The school's security control room likely notified the private security officer on a Segway that a pedestrian had entered the campus and asked them to take a look. Braga had trespassed by walking through the campus, but the park and bridge were public property, as was the trail he was currently running away on. This was irrelevant at the moment, and Braga simply wanted to leave the area to avoid any contact. Checking quickly for cross-traffic on 10th, he entered the street and proceeded up 2nd Avenue for two blocks before turning right on E12th Street and finally slowing back down to a walk. Private security wouldn't follow, but there was an ever-so-slight chance they might call for the police to do a drive-by, so he wanted to be out of the area quickly. This would probably be a footnote in the night's security report, though he wanted to keep any more trouble to a minimum.

Two more blocks, and he'd be able to drive away. More of his clothes were stashed in his truck, and Braga needed to change and remove the current bloody set before leaving. On the slim chance he'd be pulled over, it wouldn't serve him well being covered in someone else's blood. He could make up a story for his head scrape, but the other blood was too much. Sirens in the middle distance made him pause until he determined their direction and distance weren't a direct threat. He continued.

He had parked in front of what appeared to be a Korean-owned butcher shop, a two-story building with the business on the bottom floor and offices or residences above. Across the street stood an auto repair garage, its lot enclosed by a tall iron gate. Both properties looked asleep.

Upon reaching his truck, he grabbed the key fob secured in the driver's wheel well. He opened the passenger door and grabbed the change of clothes, then, before changing on the sidewalk, checked around again for stray vehicles or early risers. Nothing. He used baby wipes to clean the blood, his own and his victim's, from his face and hands as best he could. He slathered the knife with hand sanitizer and wiped it down with his hunting shirt to remove his fingerprints. It went into the bag with the clothes. After a quick change, he was ready to go, but first, he had to lose the bloody garments and shoes.

He glanced around and found an overflowing garbage can on the corner. No. He'd make a mess trying to squeeze his bag inside that. Before turning onto this street, he had passed a convenience store with a waste can in front, but that area was well-lit by both the store and the road. He looked the other way down the street, where many residences and businesses had their blue recycling bins out, ready for pickup. It wasn't the best choice, but it was a way to separate himself from the bloody evidence and remove it from the area. He chose the closest bin, the one placed out by the butcher, quietly removed a few of the cans, bottles, and boxes to make room for his plastic bag of crime, placed his items inside, and covered it with what he had removed.

With one last glance around, the escape was secure, and no further damage had been done. *This night was fucked!* Again cursing himself and the world, he eased his truck into the street and disappeared into the dark morning.

* * *

Chung Bak knew every vehicle on his street. Of the ten houses, there were fourteen cars in total, plus two delivery vans, one of which was his. Armando, the garage owner across the street, kept all his customers' vehicles on his lot if they stayed overnight. This didn't mean outsiders never parked there, only that Bak knew when they did.

Sixty-three, happily divorced from his unhappy wife of thirty-two years, proud of his business, and with a bladder the size of a pea, Bak woke up to go to the bathroom a few times every night. On his most recent trip, a disturbance directly under his second-story window caught his attention. Living at work meant he could never escape, but he could always keep an eye on his business. He'd never been robbed, but the neighborhood did have its share of vandals, vagrants, and all-around troublemakers who caused more grief than Bak liked. So, whenever possible, he would pay attention to anything unusual outside and, when necessary, call any affected neighbors.

Tonight, it was his shop's turn to be vandalized. Or was it? The guy was just changing clothes. No harm. Odd, but nothing that would damage the shop. Bak watched the man take the plastic bag of clothing he had removed from his truck to his recycling bin. He'd already received a few notices from the refuse company reminding him about the proper items for the recycle container, and used clothing was certainly not on the approved list.

It was a minor matter, but even that tiny thing would annoy him enough to keep him from sleeping. After the man drove away in his pickup truck, he put on his slippers and robe and went outside to deposit the bag in the proper bin. Recyclables were picked up bright and early Thursday mornings on his street, but garbage wasn't collected until later, so he kept the can, the gray one, locked behind the gated area until then.

The air outside was crisp but refreshing. Cool compared to what midday would be like, yet warmer than a winter afternoon. Pleasant. Opening the blue lid, Bak didn't see the bag right away. He removed a few items before finding what he was looking for. Reaching in again, two fingers slipped inside the bag and into a cool stickiness he was not expecting. Startled, he withdrew his hand. Blood ran down his right pinky and index finger into his palm. Had he cut himself on something? No. There was no pain, and the blood was cold. He'd been a butcher long enough to know all about blood. It wasn't his.

Bak delayed calling 911 long enough to wash his hands thoroughly with a restaurant-grade sanitizing solution formulated for handling raw meat and blood.

* * *

Braga took a long and circuitous route home. He'd gotten rid of enough blood through the clothing swap, baby wipes, and hand sanitizer that he was sure he had no prosecutable evidence on him. If he were ever questioned about why he was out and about so late, his job gave him cover to say he was performing quality checks on his team's patrols, ensuring his clients were getting the security they paid for.

He stuck to the bigger streets as he traversed the city toward Interstate 580, listening to the scanner app on his phone. Among the wonders of modern technology was that you no longer needed a radio scanner to eavesdrop on emergency responders' calls. Because the frequencies were publicly available, various companies created websites that captured transmissions across the frequencies and digitized them for web broadcast. Each site played only one frequency at a time, but for monthly or annual fees, you could subscribe to a service that let you download an app on your smartphone to serve as a scanner. Altru had an Enterprise-level account, and his work gave him ample excuse to listen at all hours of the day.

Selecting Oakland Police, Oakland Fire, BART Police, Alameda County Sheriff, and California Highway Patrol, he set his phone to flip through their channels at ten-second intervals so he could monitor anything concerning him. There was some commotion on OPD regarding the scene he caused in Jack London, but there was no follow-up.

With a few minutes remaining on his drive home, he was unsure if sleep would come. He'd be concerned over any evidence left behind, but more likely, he'd beat himself up about his failure to kill his last target. *That shuffling piece of shit.* His failure now meant the man would incur thousands of dollars in care that would never be repaid, money that could have gone to someone he felt was more deserving.

Braga was angry at the waste of it all, but he was angrier at himself for failing, for being such a failure. He might have to lie low for a while, but he was bound and determined to make up for this night.

12

By the time the ambulance arrived and began tending to Xtra, two more police cars had pulled up and taken up station at various corners near my building. The officers had already mapped out and marked off the scene of the attack on 5th Street by following the blood trails Xtra brought with him to my doorstep. A sergeant coordinated the flurry of activity while two other officers checked the fence line around the vehicle storage area and the County building across the street.

Oakland and Kansas City had roughly the same population and police size. Back in my day, a late-night non-fatal stabbing would not have necessitated sending a detective out for a deeper dive, and I didn't expect one for this.

In the seven minutes they were on scene, the two medics quickly gauged that the cuts to the wrist and shoulder were ugly but non-critical. They correctly focused on the significant stab into X's gut, and they knew better than to try any voodoo in the field other than to stuff it with a clotting pad, apply a pressure dressing, and load him up to go. One of the silver linings of all the unnecessary deaths and injuries in Iraq and Afghanistan was the great leap forward in emergency medicine and prosthetic technology. It was a shitty way to learn, but

EMTs and medics can now easily access and use tools like hemostatic gauze to save lives that formerly would have bled out.

"Where you guys taking him?" I asked the medics as they lifted my friend into the back of the ambulance.

"MCH," said the guy closer to me. "We can be there in six minutes."

Merritt Community Hospital. Ten minutes away unless you're running code in an ambulance. Then, six. I was covered in blood and half-drunk, so there was no way they'd let me go with him. I wasn't family anyway. The police wanted me first. The interview might not take long, but they'd clog up my doorway for a while. A glance at my phone told me it wasn't 2 am yet, so I walked over to Duke, who'd been standing around looking like a lost dog.

"How you feeling?" I asked him.

His eyes were wider than usual, and I'd never seen him this alert and concerned. "I'm good. I'm worried about X. He looked like shit."

"Yeah. Those dudes got him steady real quick," I said, trying to comfort him. "They stopped the bleeding and got fluids into him. He'll either make it or he won't, but we've done everything we can. He's a tough old fucker. If it's just intestines and muscle, he'll be fine." I sounded confident and almost believed it.

Handing him $60 from my wallet, I said, "Look, I think I'm gonna be stuck here for a while longer, and you're more than welcome to keep me company. Wanna run to the market down the way to get us something to drink? Some beer and a bottle of something."

Duke was a good guy, a concerned citizen when he had to be, and one to look out for a buddy, but it was clear he'd had his fill of excitement for the night and needed an excuse to get out of there.

"Run? Hell, no. Had enough of that shit tonight," he said with wide eyes, still breathing heavy. But he composed himself. "I'll get something for Pearly, too. The good girl can drink with us." He gave me a wink and headed off. I stood, not knowing whether to smile or cry at the thought.

The police didn't think he was anything but a passerby, so they didn't stop him as he left the scene to head downtown. It was a spot that I usually hit before 2 am, and I wondered if they'd miss me tonight. The old vet wasn't a speedster, but he'd make it there on time. Depending on how long the questioning from the police officer took, Duke should be getting back around the time my night's buzz and adrenaline from the excitement wore off.

13

The Altru Security office was in Walnut Creek, where Braga had a nice, comfortable space all his own, but he spent most of his time working from home or on the road. As the Regional Manager, he was the point man for securing new contracts, overseeing existing ones, and managing operations across their current arrangements in various hospitals, municipal buildings, and private businesses. He also had his own endeavors to tend to. Despite the pain in his hip and back after the early-morning adventure, he had to keep up the appearance of a normal day.

Most of his work could be done from his phone or laptop, but he also needed to be on the road, checking in with his teams, meeting with clients, and searching for more business and hunting opportunities. Braga, at an even six feet, was already taller than the average guy and was stout, carrying himself like he was still in the Corps. He had a few extra pounds but was still a startling sight in his tight polo shirt, buzz-cut hair, and goatee. In conversations, he came on strong, with a firm handshake, a steady voice, and an air of confidence that came from being in charge. The Marine Corps globe and anchor tattoo on his right forearm showed proudly every time he shook someone's hand. He was always pleased when someone noticed or mentioned it.

Today, he was at Hillside Medical Center, a small private hospital in the San Leandro hills, ostensibly making the rounds among the staff and checking in with the administrator for some face time. He had another reason, too.

Leaning on the hood of his black Ford F-250, Braga asked Lloyd Sgamba, "What's new?"

Braga had not yet made his official hospital rounds with Sgamba, the unit leader, or chatted with the hospital administrator to see if she was happy with everything. First, he needed to talk about actual business.

"My guy in the pharmacy is back from his training or whatever the fuck it was, so we can get back to making money there. While he was gone, I didn't have anyone else with access, ya' know, so to get around inventory checks, I had to use up the last marker I had. We wouldn't want the counts to be correct during the time my guy was gone, so I traded the pharmacy supervisor the footage of him sucking off that dude in the storage room."

"Do you still have a copy?"

"Naturally. Anyways, the count looked normal while my guy was gone, and we're back in business now." Braga nodded but didn't interrupt. Sgamba continued. "There's a new RN up in Palliative Care that I'm pretty sure is a user. I'll chat her up to see what her poison is, and maybe I can use some stash to make her happy for a while. We'll have someone on that floor with a hook-up to the good shit, you know."

"That hospice stuff is the best! Well done." Braga said. "How's the new kid working out?"

"Keen?" Sgamba said. "Good kid. Make a good cop someday." Sgamba's tone implied it wasn't a compliment.

"Well, fuck!" Braga said. "That won't do. Keep him on a short leash and keep an eye on him."

Braga looked away and sighed as if these decisions weighed on him. They didn't. They were the tiresome details of running his operation within an operation. Compared to the fuck up of last night, these minor concerns were no more bothersome than fleas to a rhino. He put his hand out. Sgamba handed over the zippered pleather pouch he'd been holding. Braga looked inside and made a quick visual inventory: a bundle of cash and two clear bags of pills.

"What's the count?" he asked.

"Should be seventy-five Valium and a hundred Percocet," Sgamba said. "Less than usual, but my dude is back, so we'll be on track now. Cash is $3300. About average, but we just got a new girl in the vegetable patch. She's done for, but her parents are keeping her around for some reason. I'll start working her in ASAP. Cute kid. Guys will pay good cash to fuck her." He said it with a wide grin, as if he were planning to enjoy sampling the product himself.

"You keep your cut?" Braga asked.

"Yeah. I wrote a short note showing the math. It's in the bag." Sgamba said. "I know you don't like records for this stuff, but I figure if they find the note in the bag with the cash and drugs, we're fucked already."

"I hear ya," Braga said, placing the pouch into a small duffel he used for his collection rounds. "I appreciate it. One Dave is enough for all of us, eh?"

The unit leader shook his head. "Fuckin' Dave!"

Dave Limon was another Altru unit leader, but for a different hospital, a larger one in Berkeley. The side businesses were going great there; plenty of drugs were slipping out the backdoor to Braga's team, and men were lined up and ready to pay for the privilege of having sex with the long-term coma patients. They had several staff members on the hook with enough information and evidence to get them decertified from their respective medical boards and charged by law enforcement. Cash was rolling in, and only stupidity could stop it.

Dave Limon, a truly unsavory man with no business being in a security position, had a good thing going and was earning his cut, but he wanted more. He didn't appreciate the effort it took to start the operation and thought his work was enough to earn him a bigger slice of the pie. Dave got greedy, and when he didn't get what he wanted, he made some noise about blowing the whole operation open. Dave genuinely thought he had a shot at getting more of the action. He didn't know his boss well enough.

One of Braga's unsavory street connections was more than happy to kill the ambitious man for the grand total of 100 Percocet tablets. Unfortunately, he'd confronted Dave while Dave was escorting one of the female medical staff to her car one dark night. The street junkie ended up killing both Dave and the nurse. It was a sad end to the affair, but the positive spin was that the hospital took it as a sign to increase security, and Altru was able to add a few more officers to the contract.

"Yeah," Braga said. "Fuckin' Dave."

Sometimes, fuckers deserve to die. He'd made it happen before, and he'd do it again if needed.

Braga's next stop, a private care facility in Castro Valley, proved just as unexciting and administrative, yet still useful. This was where he sourced his Adderall, invaluable for his personal use and his trade arrangement. He took the payout of drugs and cash from the team leader, then went inside to check on his duties as a regional manager, reviewing staffing levels and meeting with the main administrator. Neither role excited him, and he lamented that in both his positions, that of regional manager and low-key crime lord, he was merely a manager now. Not a doer, a manager.

Where's the thrill in that?

14

With the sunset, I had successfully passed the bulk of the day doing as little as possible while avoiding unwanted human contact. My circuit of the area's coffee shops reminded me that my head and body were still heavy from the weight of the previous two nights' events. I hadn't drunk enough alcohol the previous night to cause that, nor did I have nearly enough to take away the pain from the ass-kicking of the other night, the stress and angst from Xtra's attack, and most importantly, my regret for not going with him on his walks or patrols. It was an uncomfortable middle ground of discomfort. Not enough to complain about, yet enough not to ignore. The obvious remedy to this malaise was more alcohol.

I would like to have visited Xtra at the hospital, but he'd need at least another day to stabilize, or so I was told when I called earlier to check on his status. I was now left on my own to ruminate. This rarely worked out well. I had the healthy remnants of a bottle of Blanton's in the cupboard. A few fingers' worth and a single ice cube in a Mason jar made for a fine nightcap. Though tired enough for sleep, I wasn't quite ready for bed as my mind was still restless, so I figured I'd do some stretching while letting the bourbon do its voodoo.

From the basket in the corner, I grabbed my yoga mat and a couple of blocks. Most of the time, I either took in-person yoga sessions at the nearby studio or did them online from the comfort of my own space. I rolled out the mat in my usual spot in the living room, but I wasn't going to use an online helper this time. Right then, I didn't need any extra electric stimulation, only quietude while I worked my body. Turns out I didn't make it even that far.

My beverage was only two sips down, and the ice cube was strong and healthy when I lay on the mat to begin. I placed my hands on my belly to feel my breathing and made minor adjustments by wiggling my feet, hips, and shoulders as needed. It only took a few moments to find a place of ease.

Not "ease" so much. More of a controlled madness. A variety of unhealthy and unhappy images flashed momentarily through my mind as I passed through to what I hoped would have been a peaceful space: the specter of a hand under the stones, the way Mallard's backside fell straight down when Williamson placed some lead into his brain, and the drops of Husted's blood on the chilly Westwood morning.

It would have been easy to stay in these thoughts, and oftentimes I have stayed there, stuck, unable to move forward in my practice, instead reaching for a bottle to drink. This time, though, I breathed my way through them and found a little bit of nothingness where only a few thoughts intruded, but only for a moment.

Then the ghosts came on stronger.

Visions of dead cops came, yet I was able to put them aside and regain track of my breath.

Memories of Laura came, and all that I'd done to ruin that relationship, but I shook those thoughts away and regained my breath.

Cassandra visited for a moment, hanging naked in her closet, but I blinked her away and began a new cycle of breathing.

What I couldn't shake was the mental video of how Xtra's blood had swirled and played in the water as I hosed down my property after the police were done with it.

As I sprayed the pools of blood off the door and front wall, they divided and came back together again. The water ran crimson, whirling and gathering as it headed toward the gutter in the street. As I added a natural soap to the concrete and scrubbed it with a brush, I created dark purple bubbles as the chemicals did their trick, removing the simple proteins in blood from my home. Xtra's essence was washed away into the gutter, down a storm drain, and into the bay.

The image of purple bubbles heading down the drain was one vision too many to banish from my head during my session. Drinking seemed like a better option. Instead, I resisted that urge, got up, put my yoga gear away, and got dressed and ready for a walk.

I walked a different path than I usually did. Instead of sticking to the environs around the Square, I passed under 880 and into Oakland proper, with the idea of heading to Lake Merritt and maybe circling the whole thing. Naturally, I took a path that brought me through quieter streets and darker areas, away from traffic and any businesses that might be open. One of the liquor stores I occasionally visited was on my path, and for once, I didn't stop there.

It was a cool night, in the fifties, and the air was different here than a half mile west. Closer to the water, in the Square, you could more easily smell the salt in the air and the muck in the tide lines. Here, in the city, the scents of asphalt, exhaust, and garbage almost overpowered the metallic tinge blowing in from San Francisco Bay. There were no seagulls here. In the Square, even at night, you'd usually find gulls soaring above, sitting on a light post, or scrambling for anything edible that had been cast off. None of that here. I walked alone until I arrived at a little pocket park.

Wilma Chan Park had an assortment of tents and campsites set up, enough to make the entire perimeter and small grass fields seem covered. I made a mental note to pass by during the day to see how many would still be there. There seemed to be plenty of activity in the camps, and I wondered how the community dynamic had been affected by the string of killings of homeless people. Had they formed bonds to watch out for each other? Were they distrustful of anyone around them? If I were looking for a target, this wouldn't be the place.

My walk brought me to a trail along a lightly wooded area near the lake. Here and there, tucked away in brushy pockets, were more campsites. Some were tents, but others were people sprawled on the ground, inside sleeping bags or piles of blankets. These sites looked more established, as they didn't have to be out of the way for anyone the next morning. Still too many eyes around.

At this time of night, the walk around Lake Merritt lacked the usual walkers, joggers, and cyclists I would see during the day. One must be either brave or stupid to run around this area unnecessarily at this hour. I understood the area had been cleaned up since its darkest days, but it still emanated dangerous vibes. I expected to find more people camping around the lake, but instead, I saw few, and of a different sort: overnighters with no visible possessions.

A single person would be under a tree or on a bench, stretched out all on their lonesome, seemingly without a care in the world, oblivious to any danger. If I had come to create havoc or end someone's life, this would make a much better targeting area than anywhere I'd yet seen tonight. If the damage were done quickly and quietly, there'd be no witnesses if the mark was chosen wisely, and you'd have ample avenues of escape. With the residential neighborhoods nearby, it'd be easy to disappear quickly.

What am I doing? I had just been practicing yoga, and now I realized I was mapping out a killing. This seemed unhealthy. Then again, it seemed like a good exercise to learn more about what may have motivated Xtra's attacker and how they carried out the attack. If it was the same person who killed all the others…

I was hooked on the idea—no, not of killing someone, but finding what kind of target would make a good one. It would be nice to know more about all the past killings, but I didn't have that. Neither did the killer when he started. He had to figure it out as he went along, and he's had success. This wasn't the place. I needed somewhere darker and more out of the way.

It took twenty minutes to walk to where I wanted to go. I crossed under 880 again but made it to a part of Oakland that shuts down after 6 pm, an area of old garages and small warehouses near the Home Depot on 37th Avenue. A few gentrified lofts and condos were thrown in, and perhaps the whole area would look different in a few years, but for now, at this late hour, it was a dead zone.

Here, I found what I was looking for: potential targets. They were tucked away in the eaves of the overpass, leaning up against pillars or backed against wire fences. There was almost no light in some of the places. How many more people would I find if I used my flashlight? Walking further into the neighborhood, I found people in doorways and several cars with overnighters. At the ends of the streets, I saw RVs and campervans looking like they'd been there a while. Some of them were standing off alone, asking to be violated, and their occupants attacked.

In the doorway of a cinderblock garage, a man was bundled in a sleeping bag, surrounded by a protective wall of his belongings. His snoring was loud enough to rise above the wash of traffic on the nearby freeway, signaling his status and letting me know I could approach. We were on a side street with no traffic. The garage was between the streetlights, all its lights were off, and there seemed to be no one else in sight. If I wanted to make a kill, this would be the target. This was— thrilling.

I moved closer, within ten feet, while his snoring persisted. My rubber-soled shoes made no sound against the sidewalk. Closer. Five feet. I moved until I was beside him, and he was less than two feet away. What would the killer do? Again, I wished I knew more about his past kills, as it would tell me how to do it, but the killer's not here now. I am. How would *I* do it?

Would I give a hard heel to the head to stun him before stabbing him in the throat? No. Why give a warning? A quick stab through the heart, or an eye. Slashing the throat might work, but even if I wanted to experience the struggle, to grip him hard enough to perform the act, there'd be a risk of having blood splash over me. I'd bet that had happened at least once with all these killings. How did the killer prepare for that? I should have read Mike's reports better.

The novelty and thrill of my stunt wore away quickly, and I soon found myself backing away from the sleeping man, turning, and heading home. The killer must have had an exit planned for each kill, or at least a contingency for if things went wrong—and a lot could go wrong: witnesses or getting his clothes soiled with his victim's blood. From what little I'd heard about the guy, he always succeeded in his attempts until he met Xtra. Then what did he do? I reasoned the best way to answer such a question was to become a killer like him.

Going on a faux hunt probably wasn't what X had in mind when he asked me to walk with him. I had turned his idea for a neighborly safety patrol into a plan for murder. Not an ideal mindset perhaps, but it did strike a match of sorts. It got me thinking about the world marginally outside of my own. I may have a nice home and a few bucks in the bank, but this was my neighborhood, and these people had been my peaceable neighbors throughout my time here.

My walk home was more direct. Plenty of people were sleeping or camping for the night in safe spots. Many of the benches along the waterside were taken up by sleeping forms. Two men were sharing a palm tree near the marina as a backrest. One industrious person had rigged a series of tarps and bungee cords to form a makeshift tent where two fences met. I'd never looked at them as targets or prey before, but my experience just now opened my eyes to how vulnerable these people were, living the way they did. It was clear how easily the homeless community could be preyed upon, and with the greater world's uncaring attitude toward them, catching their killers would not be a top priority.

When I arrived home and showered, I washed off more than simply the night's sweat and grime. It was a layer of ignorance and ambivalence that I wasn't aware existed.

15

Braga sat in a Danville bar that was much too good for him, and he was well aware of it. Tonight, he needed to visit the opposite end of the spectrum, a place with no human filth. The other patrons might have been comfortable paying $20 or more for a glass of wine, but he wasn't. More than once in his drinking history, he'd stood at the supermarket deciding which three-liter box of wine to buy, but here he was sipping a Napa County Cabernet blend that cost more for a single glass than any of those boxes. The bartender said it would be earthy, with a hint of blackberry and minimal tannins, yet with a full reminder of the grape's richness—some white pepper on the backside. To Braga, it tasted like wet dirt, but he wasn't here for the quality or bargain prices of the wine.

Coming from Central California, joining the Marine Corps, and traveling around with the working stiffs in the Central Valley, Braga had been in more than his fair share of dive bars, beer pubs, and shitholes than he would care to admit. He'd had enough Pabst Blue Ribbon in cans or shots of cheap whiskey to affirm himself in the club of reckless drinkers. Now and then, he liked to step outside his history, his past, and try to acclimate to another world. Sometimes, he experimented with an upscale bistro in Walnut Creek or a refined cocktail lounge in San Francisco. These social experiments ended with the night, highlighting his awkwardness, his outsider-ness. Often, though, he would make it through most of the night before all the second-guessing and negative self-talk came on, but tonight, those feelings started early, and he was already feeling his loathing for people creep up around his defensive edges.

The concrete countertop was a modern touch, quite unlike any place he'd seen in Lodi or Redding—nothing like this outside of Camp Pendleton. There was probably plenty in Palm Springs near the Marine Base at Twentynine Palms, but he'd never been allowed to go there. This bar didn't have a single neon beer sign. Nor, he noticed, did they have any decent beer—lots of IPAs, Hazy IPAs, and dark ales. PBR wasn't his beer of choice anymore, but he'd choose one over what they served here. Instead, he chose the red blend.

This place, Il Vino, was in the heart of Danville's well-to-do downtown district. It had long been a part of the upper-middle-class lifestyle, but in the past few years, the city had made an extra effort to create an urban space catering to the upper crust of Contra Costa County. Gelato shops, Yoga studios, fine dining establishments, and in-house breweries dotted the local landscape. This wine bar made Oscar feel, for a short while at least, like he was worth more than what his upbringing entitled him to.

Keeping an eye on everyone who came in through the front doors, he would quickly judge their personality and character: that guy was gay, that one was a loser pretending to be cool, that married woman was on the prowl, those are fake tits. Often, he'd joke with the bartenders about the other patrons. It's a trick of the weak-minded and middle-school mean girls to make themselves feel better by teaming up with one another to laugh at the flaws of others. Sadly, Braga never realized the bartenders always knew more about those patrons and played along with him, hoping for a sizable tip. Bartenders may not always be the brightest in any room, but they're never the dumbest. If there's a buck to be made, they'll find a way to make it. If they have to tolerate a blowhard for a while, they will.

Oscar took a nose of his wine. He wasn't overly knowledgeable about wines and their qualities, but he had the basics. Smelled like dirt to him. He could fake the talk, though. In his various visits to more upscale places, he'd learned the different attributes of the reds. He had the language and lexicon to give a base explanation of the whites, especially the central California varietals, but he wasn't nearly as cultured as he wanted to be. So, in exchange for actual wine wisdom, he'd bullshit his way around the different grapes with whoever happened to sit in his orbit at the heavy concrete bar in Il Vino.

Tonight, next to him was a Spanish-sounding man in his forties or fifties with what may have been a younger female co-worker or employee. Braga sensed the older man had designs on his younger friend. *Too bad he's so fucking ugly. He doesn't stand a chance unless he's rich.*

He rarely initiated conversation. Braga had nothing in common with these people. They weren't Marines. They hadn't seen what he'd seen or done what he'd done, but he prided himself on the fact that they slept at night under the blanket of safety he provided. He wasn't in the mood to chat, anyway.

His day driving from station to station had taken him through the worst parts of the East Bay, through the most exquisite collections of human trash and filth in Hayward, Oakland, Berkeley, and Richmond. His job was mostly done by phone and laptop, but he had to make a presence now and then. He had to keep his team on their toes. He had to meet with his clients' contract coordinators and check in to see if everything was in order on their end.

The contract didn't require these visits, but the previous company wasn't renewed because they had grown too comfortable in the position. They failed to keep an ear to the ground and a management presence at the sites. Being tired from the day was one reason Braga didn't chat with any other patrons that night, but mostly, he was disgusted with all the filth and tired of how little was being done about it.

Since his kill spree three years ago, he'd added twenty-four more victims to the tally, each one satisfying on its own, and more so as the number grew, but ultimately, he still felt like he was battling the tides. As he was told so many years ago at a dive bar in Red Bluff, "If you squish one roach, there'll be ten more to replace it." Not every kill was a challenge. Some were just a release of tension. Not a sexual one. It was never that. *I'm an exterminator, not a sex offender*. He'd read about guys who got off by killing. Not him. He considered it more of a public service, even if the public wasn't aware they wanted it. *They did, though. Who could possibly want so much filth near their homes and businesses? Who wants to pay for all their sicknesses and injuries and addictions and filthy babies and immigrant kids?*

Brage felt that most people secretly wished that someone, somehow, would sweep through these camps and get rid of everything and everyone so the streets could be clean again. *There are so many places where it's not safe to walk down the sidewalk because it's covered with the disgusting belongings of the filth. It would be doing humanity a favor to rid the community of those people and the trash they carry.*

He thought back to perhaps his greatest kill, a double that resulted in such a great act of community service. The two men had set up camp in a small park in a residential neighborhood in North Richmond. It was an area the city had set aside to keep green, landscaped, and safe from development, perfect for a duo of trash looking for a camp space. Braga had noticed them a few nights earlier and seen how quickly they set up tarps, cardboard, and support ropes to make a cozy little home for themselves, depriving the community of its peaceful oasis in the city. After their dead bodies were hauled away, a city work crew cleared out all their belongings and trash, giving the public back their green space. Public service through murder and physical labor.

"What are you thinking that brought such a smile?" the bartender asked him.

Braga hadn't even known he was smiling.

The bartender gestured to Braga's empty glass. "Can I get you another, or would you like to try something else?"

"You caught me daydreaming," Braga smirked and shook his head. "Just thinking about good times. I'll try that Pinot you mentioned earlier."

"On the way," she said.

Braga liked her. Big, toothy smile. Big chest. He liked that a lot. It reminded him of another bar, another big chest, and another Pinot Noir years before.

It might have been Redding, Stockton, Merced, or any of the small cities in the California interior along the Interstate 5 corridor that countless contractors and salesmen called their home away from home. But that night, it was Red Bluff. It might have been any of the seedy bars that serviced the merchants and truckers near the interstate, but that night, it was Connie's. There was no longer a Connie, and nobody knew if there had ever been one, but the cinder block building adjacent to the Super I-5 Motel had been in its place long enough to become a staple for those who worked the central corridor.

Braga was one of those souls. He worked in sales and delivery for a flooring wholesaler, and Red Bluff was part of his route. He was there to make an early delivery, check on other client needs, and head south along I-5 for additional deliveries and stops in similar towns. It had all been mapped out for him. His company would arrange overnights at cheap motels, and he would head where they told him— a cog in a machine.

Tonight, at Connie's, his fourth night on the road, he sat silently nursing his third bourbon and cola, stirring his drink absent-mindedly, waiting for his life to change magically, knowing it wouldn't. Yet it did. Charlie walked in and, because some people are just weird, sat two stools down from Braga even though the place was nearly empty and there were plenty of seats elsewhere. He smelled of cologne, breath mints, old sweat, and whiskey. His short, gray hair was messy from the day. He wore tan slacks and a blue polo shirt emblazoned with the logo

111

of a company Braga had never heard of. If he weren't loud, robust, and sitting within arm's reach, he'd be utterly forgettable and indistinguishable from any other traveling salesman in their mid-sixties. Connie's was not his first bar of the night.

The bartender said a warm hello and had a glass of Pinot Noir poured and ready before he was fully seated.

"Hello, darlin'," he said to the bartender. "How's my girl been?"

"Oh, fuck you, Charlie!" she said in the sweetest way possible. "How many 'My Girls' do you have up and down the state?"

"Oh, maybe a few, but you know you're my favorite. You're one to talk." Charlie pointed at Braga. "I leave town for a few weeks, and you take up with another man."

The bartender laughed, and Braga, just getting into the conversation, put his hands up in mock defense as if to say he was not involved in this mess.

"I'm bullshittin' ya, friend. Let me buy you a drink. I had a great day. Erika, would you get this man a beverage for me, please?"

Erika complied, and pleasantries were exchanged. If his ebullient manner didn't give it away, Braga learned that Charlie was in sales—specifically, construction software sales. Business had been good lately, and they shared common ground in the construction field. However, they differed significantly in that Charlie had more control over his fate than Braga.

"Sure, I've got my higher-ups I need to please and quotas I need to make," Charlie continued, "but I've been doing this for a while. I make my sales by a wide margin because I know the ins and outs of this stuff. I get to pick my clients and routes, and let the kids and new guys pick through the scraps. It may not be fair, but it works out for me. Not like back in the day when I was young, fit, and had to swing a hammer with the rest of the guys. In this Central Valley heat, that was just plain horrible. Thank God for Mexicans."

Charlie swirled his third glass of wine and reminisced. "Those fuckers will work through any condition for a buck. Back in the eighties, when I was starting out, you hired them by the truckload for cheap and got your project done under budget. Nowadays, you gotta check their papers and pay them well, but the work quality is the same. Hell, most of them are Americans now. Good for them."

Braga was only half listening. The problems he faced with his own staff were different, and it was proving damn near impossible to keep a flooring team together for more than three months before one of them got busted for some drug offense or pulled a no-show because they'd rather stay home and get high. The drug of choice was usually oxy, but there were others to choose from. Fentanyl was becoming popular. Far too often, a crew member would show up stoned or get high on the job, and someone would have to roust him off the site before the client saw him.

"Heroin was popular back in the day," the old salesman then leaned in closer. His breath was sweet from all the wine and sour from the long day. The wine made his tongue loose, too, "and it was more than once that we would disappear a guy into the foundation if he was a fuckwit. If he was an immigrant, then we would consider it a public service. No one would miss a hammer-swingin', loner junkie."

Why the fuck would you tell a stranger something like that? Braga thought, stunned.

Charlie leaned up straight again and continued as if he were asking for lawn care tips. "You ever kill anyone?"

Braga was shocked by the course change and boldness of the question; one you're not supposed to ask. "I was in the Marine Corps for a while. Saw some action over in Iraq."

"But did you kill anyone?"

"Had some incoming." He obfuscated, stunned by the whole conversation. "Had some outgoing," he lied, knowing he'd never fired his rifle at a human target. "Never had a confirmed kill."

"Oh." Charlie sounded disappointed. He returned to his wine for a moment, and the conversation hit a lull for a few moments before he piped up again. "You should try it sometime. You'd like it. Especially if you liked what you tasted over there."

Braga said nothing, but his mind was on fire. He wondered how this man knew he'd been longing to know what it was like to take a life, to see the energy drain from a person's eyes, to watch their color fade as their blood drains. How did this stranger know that for years he'd hated anyone who allowed themselves to be caught in traps, to be dumb enough to be victims like he was? He'd seen people die. His mates. His Marines. Good people, not piece-of-shit junkies, drifters, or bums. He'd seen enough people in his post-military days who only deserved to be scraped off his Marine Corps boots. Nothing else. People who needed to be wiped off the earth so that the rest of the decent people had a better chance at living a good life. The more of the filth gone, the better.

After a pause, Braga looked down at his drink and answered. "That's a horrible thing to say!"

After an equal pause, Charlie said, "Maybe, but it took you a minute to answer, so you thought about it." The old salesman/murderer had a good, deep laugh. "You can't fix all the problems in the world by killing, and you can't kill all the cockroaches in it—but you can kill a few, ya know? At least then you'll have the satisfaction of having killed a roach or two."

* * *

He wasn't smiling now, but he did catch himself frowning before the bartender said anything. He had remembered his first kill: a Mexican drifter with no business being where he was. It was a sloppy, messy attack, but it was necessary to get the ball rolling. A cockroach was dead, and many lessons were learned. That's what mattered.

After what the media called the Tennyson Massacre, he lived in fear enough that he stayed out of action for five months, but soon hunted every four to eight weeks again. It had all felt good, but he needed more. He needed a score. Perhaps it's like a bank robber who wants to make one more big heist before retiring. Except he didn't want to retire. His failure from the previous night didn't just throw him off his pattern. It reminded him of all his failures and shortcomings.

Braga drained his glass and paid his bill. He'd been normal enough today. He was tired of pretending.

16

Braga had been with Altru Security for seven years, starting as a patrolman and quickly rising to supervisor. That was more due to the difficulty of retaining talent than to any great skill of his own, but Braga made the best of the role and learned as much as possible about the operation. Three years into his tenure at Altru, the company received a major break: a series of contracts with Alameda County for security patrols at its remote parks and buildings in the coastal hills east of Hayward, Oakland, and Berkeley. Shortly after, Altru won an even bigger contract with a major healthcare provider for patrols and static security at twelve of their clinics and hospitals in Alameda and Contra Costa Counties.

The potential income from these two contracts alone would increase the company's revenue by 420% annually, and the ownership team was hell-bent on ensuring nothing stood in the way of making it happen. They had only sixty days before the changeover of responsibility for the County contract and ninety days before the healthcare security contract went live. Time was critical, and a lot needed to be done.

Braga was given the opportunity to relocate to the area to oversee the vetting of new employees and determine the staffing needs for the healthcare contract. The staffing needs wouldn't be too troublesome. Braga used the previous security contractors' work as a template. He factored in a few requirements and details from the new contract and developed a staffing and rotation schedule within a week. There was some give-and-take in the schedules and some fudging of numbers, but the client didn't need to know the ugly details. They were happy as long as the prescribed coverage was in place and backed by verifiable reports. Sometimes that meant a roving supervisor would stand watch while a resource was shuffled from one site to another, but it got done. In the first year, Altru Security was unconcerned with overtime. The directive from the highest echelon of the administration was to get everything covered and to worry about the rest later.

The first part of his task, getting and vetting new employees, was much more difficult. Braga knew the realities of hiring in Alameda and Contra Costa Counties, where almost every aspect of life was more expensive. What they paid out in Merced or Turlock was decent, but it wouldn't be nearly enough in El Cerrito or Walnut Creek to make someone jump from another ship to Altru Security. The area's unemployment rates were low enough that people weren't desperate. They had a ceiling on how much they could offer per hour, but they could mention the overtime potential for the first year.

When you can't pay for top-tier talent, there's a shortage of workers, and if you need to fill spaces quickly, what do you do? You lower your expectations to fill those slots and hope to fix mistakes as you go forward. This was how Braga began building his empire of information and favors.

Four years into these contracts, Oscar Braga was responsible for almost every hire in Alameda and Contra Costa Counties. Initially, he did his best to find reliable employees, but quickly realized that his high standards would leave the contracts unfilled if he stuck to them. If you had a felony conviction, were on a sex offender registry, or were on a no-fly list, he couldn't help you. Short of that, you were a candidate. If your paperwork, to be legal and work in the US, was verifiable, regardless of whether it was actually valid, he could work you in. Accused of a few nefarious things but not convicted yet? He put you in service and worked around your court appearances until a guilty verdict was rendered. The state laws on who could carry a firearm were clear and solid enough that he had clear limitations there, but since most of the postings were unarmed, that was not an issue.

Being part of the company's administration gave him access to a wide range of background search tools, many used by police. Because they weren't actual law enforcement, he wasn't beholden to the same internal limits and rules about boundaries. Most employers wouldn't dig overly deep, but Braga quickly learned the more information he possessed about the past of a potential hire, the more power he'd hold over that person's career path.

Braga could name every patrolman in his two counties, even though he rarely worked with them. It was the supervisors he was most familiar with, as he had hired or promoted each of them, and they all knew it. A few got their jobs on merit, but for many, loyalty to Braga was merit enough. As long as they pulled their weight on the collective side hustles and did an occasional extra task for Braga, they were all cool in his book.

During his killing missions, he knew not only where Altru patrolled but also where the other security companies were. His constant research of the opposition and their routines revealed their many routes and contracts. Between that and the scanner app, his knowledge of where and when the various security and law enforcement patrols occurred was complete.

Braga's work the other night hadn't received coverage by any TV news stations, and only one of the news sources he found on his phone posted a tiny blurb about a random stabbing as a footnote of the week's police activity. It wasn't until he searched the website of the area's weekly alternative paper, *The East Bay Hub*, that he found an article with usable information. The report was short on details, but it did list the victim's name and that he had been taken to Merritt Community Hospital. *That's good. That's one of our places.*

The remaining details were scant, so he clicked on the writer's name, Mike Finney, and read his other articles. A few concerned local politics, but most detailed a broad range of homeless concerns, including the crimes committed against them. Over the past few years, it looked like Finney had written at least twenty articles covering suspicious deaths of homeless persons Braga had been involved with. How had he not known about this before?

He took the time to read every article. The attacker was never described, always disappearing without witnesses. Finney outright said the unhoused population had told him things they'd never tell the police, yet there were no identifying details about a suspect. Finding the previously unknown articles surprised and frightened him, but learning they contained nothing threatening put him at ease.

Braga wanted to hunt some more, but he had to clean up the current mess before continuing. The wounded hyena would have to be eliminated to make him pay for his failure. It started with a phone call to a service desk.

"Yeah?" The sleepy voice on the other end said.

Sitting in his truck smoking a cigarette, Braga disliked the lazy tone and had to fight against the urge to snap back. The painkillers hadn't taken hold yet, so the fire in his back made him irritable. He let it go.

"It's Braga," he said to Carlos Guerrero, the daytime shift supervisor for Altru's team at MCH.

"Yessir," Guerrero now spoke with more energy. "What's up? What do you need?" Guerrero was one of those Altru employees with a colorful history that would preclude employment with most other companies, let alone a security company. All the supervisors knew Braga wanted to know everything happening inside every Altru-contracted location. If a hospital employee was dealing, Braga wanted to know so he could either take his cut or get the person fired, whichever was most advantageous. If a doctor or nurse showed up drunk or high, he wanted to know so he could either protect that person's career for a price or derail it.

"What's up with that Edgar guy? He still dealing?" Braga asked.

Edgar was a new man on the janitorial staff who sold weed on the side. Guerrero found out and told Braga. Instead of firing him, Guerrero kept Edgar on to see if he could be useful in other ways, perhaps moving other items.

"Far as I can tell," Guerrero started, "he doesn't bring product inside the hospital, only the parking lot. That's both smart and stupid."

Braga understood what Guerrero meant. Edgar was smart to keep his sales in the parking lot, where there were fewer witnesses and security outside the hospital. It was stupid because the number of cameras had doubled since the Limon incident, and no one could move anywhere in the lot without being seen by the electric eyes.

Already bored with the conversation, Braga told his lead to put Edgar on probation, have him move a few other products, and make sure they received their cut; otherwise, Edgar would end up in a dumpster. Right now, there were more important things to do, like finding out about a recent stabbing victim, whether the police had spoken to him, and learning the details on any of his visitors.

"I can get you a few details now if you want," the shift supervisor said, "but I'll have to track down a couple guys and ask about cops on the floor. I can call you back as soon as I know."

"Save it all for later, except for his name and DOB if you have it," Braga said.

"Stand by," Guerrero said, and Braga heard the keyboard's clicks. "Xavier Randolph Travers." He told Braga the date of birth and that no permanent address was listed, just a PO Box in Oakland. He said he'd get back to him as soon as he knew more.

A name and date of birth were more than enough information for Braga to begin. Even if Travers was homeless, he had to have some pattern. If he had a PO Box, he would have to check it now and then. If he took any benefits from the state or federal government, there would be a trail. If he'd been in the news in the past twenty years, he'd be in an archive somewhere. It was simply a matter of knowing where to look and how to access the information. Braga decided this Travers guy would be easy enough to find and eliminate, and Guerrero would be smart enough to keep his mouth shut.

Exhaling and sitting in a cloud of smoke, Braga cursed brown people in Iraq, black people here, filthy people of all colors on the streets, poor people, the unemployed, junkies, and he'd think of more later. Taking another drag, he cursed himself the most.

"Fuck!" he said quietly to no one.

17

October 2004 - Al-Sejar Neighborhood, Falluja, Iraq

The Marines were tired from the long hours on the road, but they were so close to returning to base that they'd be back within two hours if they kept going without incident.

Their mission had been simple: to circulate through all the Coalition outposts in the area to service the water purification systems, refill water and supplies, and replace any worn filters or valves. The heat and sand were hell on the machines. Still, with these monthly trips, the troops and civilians in the area had a steady supply of potable water to augment what they got from the local wells.

With seven filter camps on this circuit, it took a whole day for the convoy of two trucks and two support Humvees to reach them all and ensure they were good to go for another month. In addition, this day's mission only serviced a quarter of the total units in the area, so after a day of resupply and loading, the same team would head out for a different circuit in two days.

Today's mission was almost done, and the team knew it. They had finished servicing the filter at a small outpost east of Al-Sejar, near the shopping district, and were returning to Camp Fallujah to wrap up their day. They chose a different route each time they left base. Even when they planned their route, the convoy leader, usually an MP sergeant in one of the two support Humvees, had the authority to change it at their discretion.

The unit had been at this for almost seven months without incident, until today. This day, even with precautions, they had been watched and tracked since arriving in Al-Sejar. Unseen watchers had planned almost any route the team might make on their return to base.

USMC Private First Class Oscar Braga rode shotgun in the M-35, a two-and-a-half-ton truck. He and his team had been together on these service trips since April, sharing thousands of miles and tons of dirt and sand, but so far, every trip had been uneventful. Their convoys had often been halted by slow-moving carts, kids playing in the road, herds of goats, and even a flock of ducks being shepherded by a small boy with a stick. None caused any great concern.

The closest they'd ever come to a problem was a soccer ball being kicked at the lead Humvee. The team inside hadn't known it was a soccer ball, and the driver had panicked, accelerating through the 'danger zone.' Braga saw it happen. He and his team leader, Sergeant Ojeda, thought it was funny as hell that these combat MPs got spooked by a kid's ball. After a good laugh, Ojeda told the MPs over the radio what it was, and they resumed normal speed.

The insurgent who had called in to report that the service team was arriving at the camp in Al-Sejar also called in when they left. Unknown to him, his mates had been planning for this day. They didn't know which road the team would take back to base and had made contingencies for several possibilities.

At a strategic point along the potential paths, preparations had been made. Where the attack would occur was dependent on where the convoy went. Two main roads would lead them back. One was a mostly straight shot from the center of Al-Sejar, leading them directly to the main highway. From there, the convoy would have to head east for several more miles before reaching safety. Alternatively, they could take the smaller roads east of town. These would take them through several small neighborhoods and villages, but the streets were wide and had been safe on previous visits.

Sergeant Randall Yee made the last-minute decision to take the longer route. The team wouldn't want to add an hour to their day, but it was the right choice. They had taken the shorter, more direct route on their last two trips, so repeating this for a third time was risky.

It didn't matter which path he chose. Consequences were waiting anywhere. Had he taken the more direct route, they would have taken fire from two men waiting with RPGs and AK-47s—a quick attack followed by an even quicker vanishing into the evening desert.

Yee's choice made more work for the insurgents in planning and communication, but not enough to deter them. It meant a few more options had to be ready. In two areas, other men were waiting with RPGs, and in five different spots, IEDs had been placed. The insurgents had to keep an eye on the convoy and keep in contact via cell phone to let the others know.

The timing would be tight, but enough eyes were watching the Marines that any turn would be relayed to the team. If the convoy stayed on its current path, it would be met with force. If it took the left turn near the mosque, it would go around the busiest part of town, but there were two other paths. Both were prepped for violence.

The last time Yee had led a convoy through here, he made a left turn by the mosque and headed away from the center of town. This time, he decided to remain on the main road and continue. Home was waiting.

An unseen insurgent called, and a man and his cart went into action. One kilometer after the mosque, the road narrowed before a slight bend. A modest-sized home obscured the view around the turn, and the Marines could not see what awaited them. Unfortunately, the man waiting for them had pulled his donkey onto the roadway, blocking most of it. Then, with all the force his older body could muster, he kicked at the spokes of the left wheel, breaking two of them.

Sergeant Yee didn't see the cart at first. The first sign that something was wrong was the brake lights of the old Toyota truck in front, which had been moving slower than he would have liked, though it hadn't seemed like a threat for the 300 meters he had been behind it. Then, the truck braked, and a moment later, his driver did the same. It was a sudden stop, and the two trucks and the Humvee behind them had to brake hard, bunching them together on the road.

It didn't take long to see the problem. A broken donkey cart blocked the roadway, and the small man who owned it was trying to drag it away. Unfortunately, his progress was far too slow for Yee's liking.

"Goyle," Yee said to his turret gunner. "Stay alert. You, be ready to move," he said to his driver. He exited his Humvee, gave a quick radio update, and moved forward for a better read on the problem.

Stepping back to the passenger side door of the M35, he turned, looked directly at Braga, and hollered, "You! Come here!"

Oscar Braga froze.

He wanted to stay in the truck. The truck was safe. It had always been safe, and there was no good reason to leave. His driver made him move.

"Braga! Get the fuck out there!" David Hansen wanted to waste no more time on this trip and return home.

That snapped Braga out of his blankness and brought him back to earth. He stepped out of the truck, rifle in hand, and swiftly approached Yee.

"Okay, Marine," the sergeant explained as they walked toward the cart. "We're gonna lift the side of the cart and let the donkey drag it out. Got it?"

"Aye, Sar'nt!" was all Braga could come up with.

He was scared as hell, but managed it well. Walking toward the cart, he slung his rifle across his back like he'd done a thousand times before. He and Yee had barely put their hands on the side of the cart when the explosions began.

Unknown to the Marines, the man with the cart wasn't alone. Another man was on the roof of a nearby building, where he had a clear, unobstructed view of the convoy as it stopped.

Buried at the base of the wall at the corner of the house were two IEDs shaped to spray a deadly shower of metal across the roadway. With two phone calls placed from separate phones, the IEDs exploded, belching a storm of stone and metal and fire across the vehicle beds.

The civilian vehicle, the Toyota, remained untouched. Because the cart was placed farther along than ideal, there was room for the small truck to stay safe. The lead Humvee and the first of the two trucks both received the full and complete power of the bombs. Yee's driver and the gunner, Goyle, disappeared in dust and smoke. The blast rocked the vehicle hard, shrapnel obliterating the nearest flank and setting it on fire, though it remained mostly intact.

Goyle was still in the turret, flopped over to the left at an appalling angle. The driver, Lance Corporal James Earnhardt, was also motionless, his face an unrecognizable mask of red.

Braga unslung his weapon as he ran back to his truck. He didn't need to open his door to see what had happened to Hansen. The door had been blown off, and Hansen had been eviscerated by shrapnel. The only part of him that now moved was the blood leaving his body. Blood and dust were everywhere, the blood, Jackson Pollock-style, on the cab's ceiling, and the dust, a gentle mist, wafted around inside. A metallic tinge clung to the air, and Braga couldn't tell if it came from hot shrapnel or Hansen's blood.

What little remained of the truck's canvas canopy was in flames. Braga raced to the back opening to see if his two other teammates had fared any better. They hadn't. Will Salazar appeared to have been killed instantly as he sat with his back to the main force of the blast. He had been blown into the steel support bars opposite, then bounced back against the truck bed onto his back, his blood pooling ever larger as Braga watched.

Nina Guarino was alive, for now. Her face was mostly untouched, but shrapnel had ripped through her neck and throat, removing flesh and sinew. She sat upright, barely moving from her position before the blast, holding her throat, willing the blood to stop pouring from her. It didn't.

Just as they made eye contact and Braga watched her life disappear, a third explosion designed to kill or wound anyone who came to assist those injured in the initial blast rocked the truck. The force of the IED's blast picked him up and sent him flying. Shrapnel pierced his backside, and his right hip was shattered as he was folded sideways over a half-wall opposite the explosion. He found himself in a small courtyard where frightened chickens cawed and scattered about him. He tuned out everything after that, not knowing whether or who on his team was still alive.

During the confusion, the man who'd placed the cart on the road walked away, removing his outer wrap and head covering. Underneath, he wore a darker shalwar and vest and covered his head with a Western-style baseball cap. Hopefully, the donkey would forgive him for being left behind.

18

Merritt Community Hospital was a newly built medical center located where several freeways meet, making it convenient for paramedics and ambulances to enter with their charges. The hospital was owned and operated by a corporation that owned several similar hospitals up and down the West Coast. It had contracts with most local municipalities and governments to treat anyone involved in incidents requiring medical care.

If you arrived injured and with insurance, they'd treat you well if you were in their network. If you had insurance with another provider, they'd do the bare minimum to keep you alive before shipping you somewhere in your network. If you arrived without insurance, for instance, you're an unhoused drifter recently gut-stabbed, a variety of government programs, charitable organizations, or grants might help cover the cost. The hospital would take care of you when you arrived, but they'd surely do their best to get paid for it.

Xtra had arrived in the early hours, transported by an Oakland Fire Department ambulance. Due to his blood loss, the emergency room team had given Xtra top priority. As they opened him up, they soon realized the wounds were messy but not fatal; a few slices here and there, with only one severe cut in the abdomen. This one required the bisection of a few inches of his small intestine but was otherwise harmless. X would have bled out before the organ damage killed him, but the medics on the scene had mitigated that before he even arrived at MCH.

The ER Doc, AnnaLisa Fiero, was an Army veteran who, back in her old life, had sewn up wounds more catastrophic than this a dozen times every day. Three deployments to the Middle East as a surgeon with the 28th Combat Support Hospital would do that, so she wasn't too impressed with an old man who'd been stabbed once in the gut.

I arrived at the hospital a few minutes after 3 pm. The front information desk held a lovely older lady and a security guard who looked like he should have been supervised at a remote maximum-security joint. After sharing my ID, they gave me X's room number and a visitor pass. Fourth floor. No elevator music, simply the whir and dings of the lift.

Exiting the elevator alcove, I noticed a woman leaving Xtra's room: tall, lean, with close-cropped blonde hair. She wore little makeup but had a naturally colorful face, pale skin, and bright freckles on her nose and the tops of her cheeks. Her black low-top Chuck Taylor sneakers completed a simple outfit of sleek maroon corduroy pants and a snug blue Oxford shirt, its sleeves rolled up. She walked as if she had somewhere to go, radiating confident energy, grace, and comfort. She also smelled nice.

We nodded politely as we passed, making the briefest of eye contact. I paused a few steps later and watched her enter the elevator car. As the doors shut, I felt a gentle pang of loss, but a loss of what?

I'd lost Laura years earlier to my anxiety, stress, and drinking. Since then, I'd resigned myself to a solo life, one without love. Sure, I missed sex, intimacy, and a sense of belonging, but at this point in my life, the effort required to be present and aware for a partner of any kind was too great. So I created a safe space for myself in the world.

Once in a while, like now, a woman crossed my path with the right mix of electrochemical transmissions to be greeted warmly by my electrochemical sensors. I could never explain how or why it happened. The woman had a level of non-traditional beauty, but there were beautiful women all around. What made this one different? I didn't have time to solve the mystery tonight, so I shoved the thought aside. When I entered his room, Xtra was awake but weak and groggy. It was a three-person room, and both other beds were empty.

"You just missed my buddy, Mike," he said.

"Mike? Like, Michael Mike? Yeah. I think I saw her." I said, intentionally skipping any further chat of her. "Scale of one to ten, how shitty you feeling?"

"About an eleven," Xtra croaked. "I just need some sleep, and I'll be alright."

"I'm sorry I wasn't there for you, Old Sergeant." I had to say it. "I'm sorry I wasn't at home to help you."

"You helped plenty. Your lights and camera thing scared him off. He didn't want to get recorded," he said wearily.

"Well, then, I'm sorry I wasn't out walking with you. Had I been, dude wouldn't have got you."

"Then he would have killed someone else. Look here, young man. It happened, and it happened the way it happened. It's all over with, and I made it. You and me, we're all cool, man."

I let the words hang in the air, along with the sounds of his heavy breathing and the heart rate monitor. There wasn't anything more to say—except I still talked out of my nervousness and guilt.

"When you get better, I'll go on those walks with you."

He needed more rest, not me poking around. His eyelids were heavy, and he played with the idea of shutting them solidly.

"I'll let you get more sleep, Old Sergeant," I said. "I wanted to come say hey. You can stay at my place for a while when you get out. You know I have the spare room for you. You can store your stuff and relax for a bit."

"Cool," he said weakly, then added, "You meet the mayor yet? I told him to check you out."

"No, X. Who's that?" I asked, but he had closed his eye and drifted off.

He must have been pretty well doped up. I wanted to tell him about my walk the previous night. I'd probably leave out the part about planning the murder of the homeless guy, but I at least wanted him to know I'd gone beyond my comfort zone to check on his people. I wanted to tell him I was sorry I hadn't done it sooner. I wanted to tell him a few things about my guilt, about being a selfish drunk, wasting my life sipping poison, and walking the dark streets alone, looking for trouble. Instead, I stood silently as my friend slipped into sleep.

I stayed for a few minutes to ensure he was breathing well enough and that no monitor alarms were triggered. His phone, already plugged into a wall outlet, was in his hand. His friend Mike must have gotten that for him, as I didn't see any of his other belongings.

If a nurse saw me in his room while he was sleeping, they'd probably shoo me away, so I left of my own accord.

19

Frederick Cooper again found himself to be a cog in machinery he had little control over. Not too long ago, he was an enlisted soldier in the US Army, a Private First Class, doing almost precisely what he was doing now: patrolling the back roads of a big city.

Then, it was in and around Kabul, Afghanistan, as part of the last regiments involved with securing the country's capital before all US troops were sent home. Throughout his seven months there, his mission had been to patrol his assigned area and report any abnormal activity or players on the street who appeared suspicious. The problem for him, a twenty-year-old cherry away from California for the first time on his first deployment, was that everything looked abnormal, and everyone acted suspiciously.

The woman and her child buying fruit from a merchant; suspicious. The kid playing with a ball by himself on the side street; abnormal. The old man sitting in the doorway, talking on his phone while staring at Cooper's patrol; suspicious and abnormal.

Everything and everyone there was suspicious and abnormal. The streets smelled like shit, the people all talked and acted funny, and everywhere he went, they looked at him like he had personally destroyed their homes and families.

During those months in-country, Cooper was afraid on every patrol, with no control over anything outside his vehicle. Violence could come from any direction. The Taliban held control of some neighborhoods, private contractors held others, and Afghan government-approved warlords held the rest. His mission was a joke. He was only out there to keep the bad guys distracted while forces more powerful than him did the important stuff, whether actual security needs or more profitable ventures. There was a lot of heroin to move out of the country. Everyone knew it.

Cooper had nothing to do with that. He just bided his time until the withdrawal. When that came sooner than expected, and he was discharged, he found himself a civilian back in Oakland without any resources or family support. He was an easy mark for targeted Google ads that highlighted the awesomeness of Altru Security, the fun and flexibility they offered, as well as the excellent overtime pay and opportunities for promotion. It all sounded great, but after he was hired, trained, and sent out on his own, he discovered that he was right back where he was in Kabul, patrolling ugly streets full of abnormal situations and suspicious people.

On these streets, here, today, was a slightly different story. Here, in his backyard, despite the weirdos, night owls, ne-er-do-wells, homeless drifters, and derelicts, he was more comfortable than he had been in all his time overseas. Here, despite all the dark corners, filth, and human sadness he witnessed while on his patrols, he had more autonomy to chart his course. Here, he made deals with the low-level drug dealers who worked the corners and alleys. Here, he took a cut from whatever was stolen from a neighboring property as long as he was prepared to look the other way. Here, he provided an extra set of eyes and a deterrent, in case someone like the Trans needed a few uninterrupted minutes to do whatever it is they do.

Just an hour earlier, he'd received a call from his big boss, Braga, asking him to do some extra work. It wasn't anything complicated. He simply had to pay extra attention to a building near his patrol area for anyone coming or going through the door at the far end. "Get pictures of him and follow his movements as best you can," Braga had said, and Cooper had to keep the extra patrol out of his logbook. His vehicle's GPS would track the activity, but it could always be explained away. However, the only person likely to ask about it was the one who had asked him for the extra work. So, no problem.

Cooper would get to it after his other side hustle of the night. His instructions from those guys, the Trans, were to park at the corner of the northbound lane of 12th Street and 17th Avenue, near where 16th Avenue crossed the train tracks and 880. There was a small homeless camp there, and even late at night, some foot traffic or cars might pass by. His job was to be a visual deterrent to anyone who wanted to get closer, and, if they did, to turn on his flashing yellow lights to warn them away and alert the Trans.

He had a good idea of what they were doing, but never asked questions. They paid well enough for such an easy chore that he never bothered to inquire. They didn't need him necessarily. They needed a security vehicle to scare people away. Cooper had done this a few times already, and the longest he'd ever had to sit on station in his patrol vehicle was twelve minutes. He had to flash his yellows once, and there had been no more excitement than that. Easy money.

20

Upon my return home, a man standing near my garage door highlighted my building's most significant security flaw. I couldn't safely drive into my parking space while keeping someone from entering on foot at the same time. This forced me to keep my vehicle on the outside, parked across the street.

He was short and stout, with a boxer's stance, his low center of gravity giving him a look of strength. When I pulled up, he turned his complete attention in my direction, shoulders and body facing me. For an instant, I thought he wanted a confrontation, but then his body loosened and relaxed, not how one might stand before a fight. He seemed peaceable—for now and wasn't loitering; he had a purpose here.

He was a black man, maybe in his fifties, with a short beard, dark cargo pants, a black zippered hoodie, and black boots that had seen better days. A man of the streets, but with an air of some dignity. Military maybe.

"Hey, Young Sergeant," he said as I exited my Honda. The man was partially hidden in the shadows, but as I neared my door, he stepped into the remaining rays of the sun to show himself. "We have a friend in common," he said.

"So it would seem," I said back.

"Xtra says you used to be a cop."

I hated it when this topic came up in conversation. I'd begun to believe being a cop was something I did and no longer a part of my personality, but everyone else who had ever met me disagreed.

"Used to be," I said, not knowing where this was headed.

"He also said you've got some free time on your hands."

Well, that might have had some basis in fact. I may use some of my free time to drink and walk, but my social calendar isn't exactly packed.

"Not really," I lied, "but go on."

"Xtra said you're a good guy," he said.

"Yeah? He's a liar."

"He said you'd say that. He said I should talk to you."

"Who are you?" I asked, hopefully not impolitely.

"I'm the mayor!" like that answered it. "Marcus Williams. How ya' do? Listen up," he said in a tone I'd heard before, the kind of tone spoken by a sergeant to his troops before an op order was given. Something important was about to be relayed. "I've been watching you. I seen you on your walks at night. I seen how you walk. Figure you just might be the man X says you are." Williams paused, looked me up and down, and gave me a chance to say something. I chose not to.

"We've been having trouble on the streets. Lots of trouble, and not just Xtra, what with him getting his ass whooped. Homeless folk have always been preyed upon, sometimes even by one another, but the past few years have been especially bad. Sometimes folk wind up bein' dead for no reason. Other times, folks end up dead with their little girls kidnapped for who knows what. Well, we know what, but—ya know.

139

Two nights back, we had a couple killed and their two young 'uns taken away. That's happened way too much lately." His pace never quickened, nor did his voice rise. He spoke clearly, with weight in all of his words.

"What are the police doing about it?" I asked, even though I already knew the answer.

"Not a damn thing, far as I can tell," he said. "Nobody cares if some bums get bumped off or raped. There's thousands of us around here. Who's gonna miss a few?"

I let that sad truth sit for a while in the late afternoon air as I digested what he said. I could have added to his argument by saying that I, too, didn't give enough of a shit to go out walking with Xtra. I hadn't wanted to be bothered or burdened by yet another mess of death and violence. It wasn't too long ago that I'd stumbled into a multi-body graveyard and drug-dealing kill spree simply by turning over a few stones in the dirt of my farm. The thought crossed my mind that perhaps I should have let those fucking stones sit where they were. I wasn't growing any crops. I wasn't planting any seeds for veggies. I wanted happy soil for grasses and wildflowers. Instead, I got dried-up dead girls, a murdered cop, and drug-running Canadians. All after a move away from exactly those things.

Yet here I was, about to turn over another stone to see what lay beneath.

"You want some coffee or something?" I broke the tension after the lengthy silence.

"Yeah," he said. "Coffee'd be good."

We went inside and up the stairs to my living area. I told him to make himself comfortable while the coffee brewed, then opened the curtains to let the last of the day's light in through the windows. Marcus sat on one of the stools around the kitchen island, and I did the same. He dumped his modest pack on the floor between his feet.

"Why are you coming to me with this? Why not a reporter, another cop, or...," I began, but his heavy, even tone cut me off.

"Cuz no one seems to give a shit. I thought you bein' an ex-cop and seeing what some fucker did to our boy. You might want to do something about all this. There's a reporter who's tracking all this stuff. I think maybe you could get with her and see what's what? She's been tracking killings and disappearances for years now, and I think she knows more than the police." He tilted his head. "You on Twitter or X or whatever?"

I told him I had an account but didn't use it much. Then he had me open the app and search for her username, @MiFiReports. It was easy enough to find her profile tucked away amongst the celebrities, bots, and regular Joes.

> Mike Finney
> Reporter/Streets Editor for The East Bay
> Hub. Author, Survivor, Freelancer.

I enlarged the picture and was astonished to see it was the same woman who'd visited Xtra earlier that day. She visited him before the police did—if they ever did. How did she know he'd been hurt? Did he text her, or was there an update on their magical network?

I clicked to follow her and promised I'd look into it further, though I wasn't convinced I actually should. Marcus told me more of his story, and I wasn't too far off in my earlier guess. Like Xtra, he had been in the military, though his time hadn't been as fond a memory for him as it was for Williams. Marcus had been in the Air Force during the '70s and '80s, a time, he said, when it was still perfectly safe to be openly racist toward colored airmen at Air Force bases in the South.

"The Brothers," he said in a lighter tone than before, "loved being stationed in Japan or Italy or Germany. Sure, you had racist crackers in the service, but you get off base, and the civilians were much cooler. Hell, being black was a novelty to some of them foreigners, and we enjoyed the hell outta that. Know wha'Im sayin'!"

I did know what he was sayin', and I smiled, hoping he enjoyed his time overseas in the service of our great country. Our chat wound down after that, and we said our so longs with a promise to stay in touch. I almost meant it.

Later at the Door, while sipping my Jack and Coke, I followed through on my promise to look into Finney and her work by scrolling through a number of her articles. Most of her earlier pieces concerned city planning, budgets, and local elections, but almost everything in the past three years was about the crimes committed against the homeless. Unhoused, she called them, and had covered a lot. Dozens of murders, kidnappings, and disappearances had occurred since the Tennyson Massacre three years ago. There were several articles about that event alone, each with more details as they were revealed, but none identified a suspect.

The most recent article was about the attack on Xtra and concluded with a call for any public information to be sent to Finney via her X account or email. She was a busy one, that's for sure, a wealth of information, too, and scouring her articles brought me up to speed on what Williams had asked me to look into.

There was a story I read as a child that stuck with me: about a woman, Lorelei, a siren who sat high on a cliff above the Rhein River in Germany, drawing sailors to their deaths on the rocks below. She was so lovely, the poems and tales said, and her song was so hypnotic that men helplessly followed the sound of her voice. They threw themselves in her direction, heedless of the cost. They had to have her, to be with her. My Lorelei, my siren song, wasn't a beautiful woman high on a cliff, with golden hair or a sweet voice. It was the suffering of humans, found in the form of dead and missing bodies.

It was earlier than I usually came home from a night of drinking, but still late enough that the sun had long since slipped away, and the artificial pink, orange, and yellow lights had taken over the night. The light was cast in all directions, but because there were so many structures, vehicles, and posts, so were the shadows. In the darkness, I heard Lorelei's faint call.

21

I used Facebook to keep in touch with family and friends around the world. Unlike some others, I kept a tight circle on that network, only about 110 friends. It used to be much larger, but over the past few years, I realized I just didn't like many people. I certainly didn't like many people knowing what I was up to, so I kept the circle to family, long-time friends, and a few cool weirdos I'd met along the way. Still, it was a platform I didn't use much.

I went through an Instagram phase years ago, when Laura and I were a hot couple, living large in Kansas City and the envy of everyone else. That was before the world took a dump on me, and I allowed the ghosts to take over. Since then, I've deleted most of my old pictures and haven't posted to that app since moving to California.

Twitter, or X, was a creature I hadn't played with much. I knew it had the new name now and occasionally slipped and called it the old one. I'd had an account for a few years and would open the app occasionally to try it again, but every time I did, the platform seemed full of angry people yelling about sports and politics. I could get that anywhere in real life. I'd only been sniffing around it since hearing more about the network that Xtra, Marcus, and this reporter were a part of.

My profile and banner pictures were still blank. I was okay with that for now, but I supposed it would look suspicious if I reached out to someone with an empty profile. A red flag, I suppose. I'd have to work on that—later. For now, I checked out Finney's profile to see what her deal was. Most of her posts were articles or reposts of similar reports about homelessness in the Bay Area. A few were about local government problems, and federal budgeting issues for State and County-level programs were sprinkled in.

One article in particular caught my attention. It concerned the recent slaying of a homeless person in the nearby Fruitvale neighborhood.

Oakland's latest homicide victim was a man in his 30s who was living under a pedestrian bridge where his body was discovered by a jogger on Monday morning.

The body was that of Peter Blum, investigators said in a news release issued on Tuesday morning. In recent months, Blum had been living in and around a homeless encampment on 37th Avenue.

Emergency crews attended the area and attempted to revive Blum, but were unsuccessful.

"He was clearly suffering from physical trauma," police said via a statement.

His cause of death has not been released, and no suspect information has been provided by officials at this time. Investigators have released a photograph of Blum and a map showing his location.

"It is important to the investigative team to determine if anyone saw Mr. Blum alive in the early morning hours and at what specific time," police said in the news release.

"In addition, officers are appealing to the public, if they saw or heard anything out of the ordinary in that area between midnight and 5 am on Monday, to contact the homicide squad immediately."

Oakland Police will set up a command post in the area on Tuesday morning "in an effort to stimulate witness participation," officers said.

The article provided the official phone numbers and email addresses for OPD and the Alameda County task force. Finney concluded by stating that she could be contacted anonymously by email, phone, or X if anyone had something to share and wanted to avoid talking to the police.

I clicked the three dots on her profile page and looked at the lists she was a part of or had created. There were several, but two immediately caught my eye: Street - Indv and Street - Orgs. It looks like she was the creator of both. Opening each, I got an idea of what the lists held. 'Orgs' was a roster of accounts for non-profits, businesses, and Government agencies that dealt with street-level demographics. 'Indv,' just as obviously, was comprised of people; many seemed involved with the groups in the other list, but some had little to no information in their profiles. Were these folks actually living on the streets?

Another list caught my eye: 'the tempest-tost.' Initially, I noticed the oddness of the wording and the apparent misspelling, but after a moment of reflection, the phrase 'tempest-tost' hovered in my brain, but I still couldn't place it. Upon opening it, many people were either proudly or professionally homeless, advocates for the homeless, or at least tangentially in the community. Many used the phrase unhoused or houseless. I didn't see the difference. There were 1,134 names on the list, and scrolling through them took a while, but I finally found Xtra's account and followed him. I saw Marcus's as well and did the same. Maybe I'd hear about something terrible in the neighborhood from this list before I read it in the news.

I'd never sent a message through Twitter, but the process was the same as any other platform. Clicking the little envelope on Finney's profile page opened a dialogue window. The rest was easy.

> Ms Finney,
> A mutual friend suggested I reach out to exchange information about recent crimes against the homeless community. Can we chat sometime soon?
> Karl Warren

Though I knew how to send a message, I wasn't aware of the proper etiquette or even whether such a thing existed. There probably wasn't a point to a greeting or closing, since she knew who she was and from whom the message was sent, but I did it anyway, out of my tech awkwardness. X didn't have a feature to show whether the recipient's account was online, and I couldn't see whether she'd received the message. I assumed, like me, she'd check her phone at intervals throughout the day. As I put my phone away, it vibrated with a notification. It was from X, a message from Finney. She must have been online already, or, like a good reporter, she was quick to respond to messages about information for her stories.

> Who is our mutual friend?

> Marcus Williams.
> We have two, actually.
> We also have Xtra. In fact, you and

I passed each other while visiting
him at the hospital yesterday without
knowing it.

Ah! Young Sergeant. The former police
officer turned mysterious recluse. Yes, we
should chat. Send me your number, and I'll
text or call when free. Should be later today
or tomorrow.

Xtra must get chatty around women. Or, it's the painkillers that
made him share too much. I did as she asked, thanked her for her time,
and put my phone away, but there it was again—that feeling from the
hospital—that feeling that made me wonder what she might be wearing
to our meeting.

22

Donald Vo sat parked in one of the diagonal spaces on the northbound side of 12th Street. He was alone in the white van because his cousins had already left to walk the site and ensure their girl was still where they expected her to be. They hoped she would be with her mother, either in their car, parked in the same row as the van, or inside a tent beside the parked cars, against the fence that kept pedestrians out of the triangle median. They didn't see anyone sleeping in their '92 Ford Taurus Wagon, so they must have been in the tent twenty feet away.

Plenty of lived-in cars lined the street, and nearly as many adjacent tents. Vo suspected the homeless people had to keep their options open. Though small, this tent city had enough full-time residents to form a type of neighborhood watch so they could drive to work without having their tent homes molested. One of the many ways the downtrodden stuck together.

One way they did not stick together was that one of the tent city's members was always on the lookout for someone the Trans might want for their operation. The *someone* was always young, almost always a girl, an orphan, or soon to be one. Sometimes, the orphan status was induced, like tonight. Two days prior, a text from one of the Trans' street sources had alerted the brothers to someone matching their description.

With a nod from Roger to Aaron, the Trans first approached the Taurus to double-check that no one was inside. They then turned toward the gray tent that housed a Salvadoran woman and her eleven-year-old daughter. Pausing briefly to look around again for stray eyes, he caught sight of the Altru SUV he was paying for. After they switched on their small headlamps, Aaron cut through the flap while Roger pulled out his towel-wrapped .38.

Within a second, the two were inside the tent and quickly spotted the woman and girl. The dim light from outside cast silhouettes of their faces even before the beam from the headlamps found them. Before the mother was fully up and alert, Roger shot her twice in the chest. Even with the towel, the report from the barrel was louder inside the tent than they had hoped. The little girl roused immediately, but Aaron was waiting to take care of her. He pushed her small frame down firmly against the pile of blankets and quickly tightened zip cuffs around her slender wrists. He stuffed a rag in her mouth and a small bag over her head, then grabbed the girl by the shoulders, made her stand, and dragged her forcefully outside into the early morning air.

* * *

The old veteran didn't sleep much anymore, not at night anyway. It had been more than fifty years since his time in Vietnam came to an end, but his continued service in the US Army kept him sharp, and the many subsequent years of homelessness kept him vigilant in the dark.

Besides, considering all the nighttime demons that visited him over the decades, sleeping deeply rarely appealed to him.

He was awake but in a mental trance when the unmistakable sounds of the two muffled gunshots erupted so close by. He wasn't sure of the caliber, but he recognized small arms fire when he heard it, muted or not. Even over the low-level din of all the other city sounds, the two pops had brought him out of his trance.

Removing one of his cardboard curtains, he looked out the window of his old van toward the direction of the sound in the tent city across the street.

* * *

When the Trans left the tent, Donald got out of the van. Walking around to the front and passenger side, he opened the door, letting the Trans bring the girl inside. Aaron half-carried and half-dragged the girl along the sidewalk. He moved around the front while Roger peeled off two parking spaces before the van, stepping between the two parked cars for a better lookout position closer to the street, finally reaching the side door as his cousin did. Aaron entered the van with the girl to keep her under control, but Roger noticed something in the back that set him off. Moving to the van's back doors, he felt his heart stop.

In Vietnamese, he yelled at his cousin Donald, "What is that?" He pointed to the magnetic sign on the van's right-rear door, advertising the First Vietnamese Baptist Church, listing its name in both English and Vietnamese, along with its phone number. "How could you forget to take that off, you dumb ass?" he continued, too loudly for the occasion.

Donald dragged a hand through his hair and spoke with a soothing tone. "It's no big deal," he returned in Vietnamese. "I'll take it off now. No one saw anything."

"How could you be so stupid?" Roger said, stripping the magnetic sign off and throwing it at his cousin. "That's the stupidest thing you've ever done!"

Donald was younger than Roger, but he was also bigger, and he wasn't going to take any shit from him. He shoved Roger forcefully. "Watch yourself, cousin, not to make your own fuck up here."

They eyed each other warily. "We're so close to the transfer," Roger said in a softened tone. "We can't make stupid mistakes like this."

Donald, abashed and knowing he was wrong, said nothing. Instead, he picked up the sign from the asphalt. In the damp Oakland air, alongside the northbound lane of 12th Street, they stared at each other until Aaron, inside the van, knocked on the glass and gave the international "What the fuck?" sign by raising his hands, shrugging, and shaking his head. He thumbed for Donald to get in the driver's seat and glared at his brother. Both men went to their seats. Donald started the engine, backed up enough to clear the curb, and left the scene.

* * *

Inside the old van, the vet had been transported back in time. The language he heard and the letters on the van's sign brought him back to Vietnam and the little people who had tried so hard to kill him and his buddies all those years before.

23

Billy Burke was an old man, a rusted shell of his former self. Deep into his seventies, he had no family he claimed or that claimed him. He was a willing feather in the wind. Since 1986, after his last divorce, he'd been a Ramblin' Man, as The Allman Brothers might say. He'd done his best to navigate the civilian world after his time in the Army and the Vietnam Conflict, but often wondered whether dying over there might have been the better option.

With few jobs, two divorces, a kid he didn't want, and more unfulfilled promises than anyone should bear, he'd traveled the back roads of America for the last forty-odd years trying to find salvation and hide from it at the same time. His memories of Vietnam were filled with images of burning villages, dead buddies, dead civilians, heroin from Burma, and multiple layers of American greed and incompetence. The few happy memories he retained from his childhood in Montana stood no chance against all the horrors he carried with him.

In one of his few clear-headed moments, he visited the co-op clinic, a multipurpose office outside the heart of downtown Oakland that served all the wretched refuse in need of assistance. The place was run by a contracted nonprofit agency with connections to the administrations of all levels of municipal, county, state, and federal programs. You're an undocumented person who needs legal help?

They could help you. A battered spouse who needs to escape a bad husband? They would find a shelter. You're an old vet needing assistance getting VA medications refilled? This place had resources to help you wind through the system.

It was a modest building outside Oakland's downtown that had yet to be gentrified—though that was coming soon. Until then, Oakland's ignored and invisible residents got the help they needed. Because it was near railroad tracks, abandoned buildings, and city parks, the area's homeless made it a casual hangout, whether they had business there or not.

Burke sat in an uncomfortable chair in the sterile lobby of the utilitarian building, waiting for his number to be called. The humming fluorescent lights lit his paper tag, which read *54*. He'd already presented himself to the central admin clerk to state his business. Now, he was waiting for his number to be summoned to see a counselor. A clerk called number thirty-two.

He sat, leaning forward with his elbows on his knees, trying to create a mental world where the waiting didn't matter. He thought of home in Florida. He thought of Lily, the girl he loved when he was twelve. He thought of the new soldier from his hometown who entered his unit in 1973. Simpson, Sampson, Thompson? He never remembered his exact name, but he still saw the boy's face, partially removed by the Vietcong's sniper round less than a week from the kid's entry into the bush.

Billy Burke wasn't the same after that. The kid from Bozeman was the last straw who sent the older soldier, Burke, into his mental cave. After that death, no one could get close. No one. No buddies in the field, no lover back home, no wife, no child of his pierced his heart and made him feel love for anyone ever again.

"They didn't have to kill her," he said to no one. "They could have just pushed her down and taken the kid. No one was gonna stop them." He spoke to no one, but someone was listening.

"Hey," the younger man sitting two seats down began. "You talkin' about that lady got killed?"

Burke said nothing and made no movements that gave away the fact that he'd heard the man.

"Hey," the younger man said again. "Are you talkin' about Flora and her little girl?"

With the mention of the name, Burke's eyes opened, and he lifted his head as if he'd reacted to a train horn. "Flora," he said. "That was her name. Nice lady. Spoke shit for English, but she was nice. Cute kid, too."

The younger man leaned forward and put a hand on Burke's shoulder, shocking the older man enough that he recoiled and pulled away. "Did you see what happened to Flora?" the younger man asked.

"Yeah! I saw it!" Burke was alert and present now. He looked directly into the younger man's eyes and said, "I saw the whole thing. I saw them come into the village, and they separated her from the rest. Her and the girl. They grabbed them out of their hootch and took the girl to their van. As soon as Mama-san made a sound, they shot her. The girl they dragged to their van. Fuckin' Charlie was quick and silent. They wanted the girl, so they took her."

"What?" The younger man said. "What are you sayin'? Who is Charlie? What village? I'm talkin' about the stuff over by the park a few blocks away." To connect with the old man and help him make sense, the younger man placed a hand too firmly on Burke's knee. "What did you see?"

Burke clamped his hand around the kid's wrist with unexpected strength and speed, quickly stood, and rotated his arm. As physics dictated, the younger man was forced to his feet and was thrown onto his back when Burke made a quarter turn.

The younger man went from a mildly confrontational questioner to a submissive subject in a second. He'd had his ass kicked on the streets before, but not like this, and not by such an old man. As Burke straddled his chest, ready to commence a beatdown, the younger man did the right thing. He capitulated.

"I'm sorry, I'm sorry, sir," he whimpered. "I just wanted to know more about Flora and what happened."

"What happened!" Burke said firmly to the young man. "What happened is that three guys came for the girl. The Vietnamese, man. They didn't give a shit about the mom. They just wanted the girl. They just fucking took her. They took her and killed Mama-san."

The younger man was waiting to be punched in the face, even as the conversation was still going on. "What the fuck?" he said. "Flora wasn't Vietnamese. She was Guatemalan or some shit. The fuck are you talkin' about?"

"Not her, you fucking punk," Burke snarled into the younger man's face. "THEY were Vietnamese! I know that fucking talk when I hear it! They came into the vil' and took what they wanted and killed who they wanted. This time, it was the girl. Next time, it'll be more."

The younger man, supine on his back, his left wrist and shoulder searing with pain, listened to Burke scream from a foot away, his eyes and mind wide open.

"They took the girl and put her in their fucking church van and drove back to wherever the fuck they came from and wherever they go to fuck little girls."

"Wha..?" The younger man was shocked and unable to make sense of Burke's ranting.

"The fuckin' Vietnamese Baptists, man!" Burke half-screamed at his victim. "Don't you fucking get it? They're still fighting this war. They're taking us one by one. Kid by kid. Village by village. They're doing to us what we did to them. They're not gonna stop 'til all of us are gone, man! Don't you get it?" Burke was beyond sense and reason now, deep into his demons and ghosts. "The fucking Vietnamese Baptists, man! They're killing most, but they're grabbing a few in their fucking vans, man."

Burke glared deep into the younger man's eyes as he lay still on the floor beneath him. In that instant, he knew beyond a doubt the boy didn't understand him. He loosened the grip of his wrist and, with both hands, grabbed the lapels of the boy's coat, pulled him close to his old face, and screamed.

The scream was several years coming. A scream built on the back streets and underpasses of California. A scream that came from all the lonely miles of wandering the southwest and seeing other vets drift into the wind. A scream that came from years and years of social impotence and worthlessness. It came from dozens of deaths seen and memories of buddies unalived by the enemy.

Burke finished screaming, paused to catch his breath, and then dropped the younger man back onto the over-waxed linoleum. Then, heaving himself to his feet and without saying another word, Billy Burke turned and walked out of the sterile waiting room and into the bright, cleansing California sun. The number counter inside the waiting room showed *33*.

* * *

The younger man, Willie Caudill, no stranger to violence, picked himself up from the floor quickly to have as few witnesses to his embarrassment as possible. He was concerned with only one thing, and it wasn't his pride. Flora was dead, and Ligia, the daughter, was gone. He knew them from the streets and shelters. He'd seen the girl play in the park, watched by other homeless mothers while Flora was off making money with her job at the college or any other way she could. Willie's mother had been killed on the streets years before, the killer never found. The news of another dead homeless person would ripple through the community and add fear and shame to an already overly preyed-upon demographic.

With the tiny bit of power Caudill possessed, he did what little he could by posting something on X. His username was @starlight9450, and he had a small following. As of this moment, there were ninety-seven, but his name was on a list of homeless people and voices followed by Mike Finney, the Hub reporter. As long as he used the hashtag *#tempesttost*, it would be noticed.

24

Mike texted to say she would be a few minutes late for our coffee meeting, so I ordered for myself. I asked her if I could get her something, but didn't hear back. She was the one with a job and deadlines, so I didn't mind.

The sun's heat hadn't gathered yet. It was out, but the gentle bay breeze kept it in check for now. The gulls weren't yet squeaking or swooping. They were resting in clumps of a dozen or so around the harbor and pier close to the café where I was waiting. It was after the morning rush, and two other customers were inside: one typing on their laptop and the other appearing oblivious to the world, lost in their latte. Neither paid me any attention, and I appreciated being ignored.

I also appreciated that Mike was tardy. It gave me a few extra minutes to figure myself out. The feelings I experienced when she passed me in the hospital yesterday were unwelcome because I knew what it signaled. I didn't like it, and I wasn't ready for it. Back up in North Idaho, I'd tried dating Hannah, the police clerk, for a short time, but that didn't feel right, so I cut it off in what I thought was a polite way. She didn't. It got weird.

Mike's Twitter bio said she was a survivor. A survivor of what? How rude would it be to ask? Fart in a quiet church-level rude? Probably. I'd better skip it unless she brings it up. What's Mike short for? That was fair game, though. I'd never been fond of short hair on women. Longer hair always seemed more feminine and appealing, more alluring. The first twenty years of my Midwestern life ingrained me with many anachronistic gender expectations, but the more recent twenty or so have done a helluva job tearing all those notions apart. Her short hair wasn't unappealing.

Just as in meditation, you're supposed to catch your focus when it's drifting away from your breath. I caught myself drifting away from the matter at hand and instead thinking about Mike's hairstyle. I never thought about Xtra's hair or any of the guys at the bar. Why should I care about Mike's? And why should I care about the sharp-looking maroon slacks and sleek Oxford shirt she wore yesterday? I shouldn't care—but I did notice how she looked.

If she were a ninja assassin, I'd be dead. She came to my table from behind, and though she politely announced herself from a few feet away, it still startled me.

"Karl Warren?"

Standing far too quickly to look cool, I reached for her already extended hand. "You must be Mike. Good morning. Can I grab you a coffee or anything?"

She set her bag on a spare chair and sat opposite me at the salvaged-wood table. "No, thank you. I'm over-caffeinated as it is. I've been up early and busy working. This chat is a needed break. In fact, I visited with the mayor this morning. He told me a little about you already."

"Oh, really!" I said, feigning a little shyness. "I feel exposed. And I know so little about you." I assumed she, being a good journalist, had done a deep dive on me before coming here. Playing mysterious was probably out of the question.

She smiled politely, a smile that held its ground, and jumped into the meat of the meeting. "Williams said you wanted to help with trying to sort out some of these murders and kidnappings in the East Bay and Oakland. The police are already on it, the county has a task force, and I do what I can to accurately account for all that happens accurately. How can you help?" Her emphasis on "can" was spoken in a way as if to test whether I was worth her time or not.

"Well," I said slowly and leaned forward, "since moving here, I've done what I can to stay quiet and mind my own business. I have a nice place, and I've made a few nice but low-class friends. I drink too much, and my late-night walks are dangerous, but all in all, I like it here, and I like all the people that surround me. Xtra is my favorite person in this small world I've crafted here, and if he were to be taken away, I'd be rather upset. So the idea of someone trying to kill my friend has pissed me off. The odds of finding that guy are slim to none, but if I can stop someone else's murder, I want to help."

I didn't like having to sell myself and didn't want to lean on my bona fides as an ex-cop. Neither of us was clear on what I might do to help, so I wasn't sure what part of myself or my skill set to offer. I've stolen money from the Kansas City mob and North Idaho drug runners. I've killed a dirty cop. I've thrown a handcuffed child molester down some stairs. I don't think any of those things would have impressed her. She sat unmoved and unmoving in her chair, waiting for me to continue.

163

"Not knowing much about what's going on, I don't know how I can help, but I suspect that X and the mayor have told you a little about my past. I'll add that I'm a late-night wanderer with a knack for spotting trouble before it happens." I paused again to gauge whether she was impressed, bored, or wanted to laugh. So far, none of the three. "I'd be a good set of eyes in all the dark corners you and the police can't go."

Mike leaned forward, resting on her crossed forearms. "Huh!" is all she said. She got up quickly and headed for the door. "I do want some coffee. You need anything?"

I shook my head, and she went inside. She either took offense or thought I was a loon. I couldn't tell, but she looked great in that mid-length black pea coat and untucked button-down men's dress shirt. Instead of thinking about fighting crime or what I said, I thought of Mike's fashion choices again. Her time inside was either quick, or I had been lost in thought longer than what was good for me.

"Let me show you something on my laptop." She pulled out her MacBook and avoided any conversation about what I had said about myself. The screen opened to a custom Google map she had made. It had several layers, but she cleared them all, revealing only a limited area. "This is Alameda County."

She clicked a box on the left column that said 'Homicide,' and dozens of pinpoints appeared on the map. She unclicked the two boxes labeled 'Tennyson' and 'Traffick,' and most of the pins disappeared.

"The remaining pins you see are the unsolved homicides of unhoused persons just in Alameda County in the last five years that do NOT fall into the two categories I'm about to talk about. These murders on the screen are explainable as drunken squabbles, territorial disputes, or other such things common in the underground world." She removed all the homicides from the screen and added the pinpoints for the 'Tennyson' tab. Thirty-one popped up. "I believe most of these murders are committed by one person!"

"You think there's a serial killer hunting homeless people?" I asked, stating the obvious.

"They're not homeless. They're houseless or unhoused." She leaned her head down, made direct eye contact, and spoke with a particular emphasis as if trying to get me to catch her point. "But yes. Same killer."

I knew the terminology better after seeing those descriptions on X and in her articles. I got the distinction and was embarrassed by the correction.

She continued. "Three years ago, he started with what we all call The Tennyson Massacre that killed ten, and he's been adding victims every two months or so. As far as the police are concerned, he's doing everybody a favor. The public doesn't seem to notice, and the media won't sell any ad space for the deaths of poor people, so there's no benefit. It's a quiet and slow genocide. Look here." Mike added more Bay Area counties to the map, and the body count increased, but it was easy to see that Oakland was the main target area. Truly the Hub of the West.

"What's the other category? Traffick?"

She removed 'Tennyson' and the other counties and showed the 'Traffick' pinpoints. Again, they were dispersed throughout the county, but Oakland was the hub. There looked to be at least twenty pins.

"These are both murders of parents and kidnappings of children."

My stomach dropped. I'd heard of one happening a few nights ago. A mother and father were killed, and their twin girls stolen.

"That's why I was a little late. There was another one this morning. I went to the scene and got a story out already."

"Another one!" I said softly, gripping the table in front of me.

"Yeah. Marcus and I were at that one, too. It's fucked up. In neither case do the police have any solid leads despite the pile of dead bodies left behind."

I leaned back in my chair. I wanted to tell her I have some experience with sifting through piles of dead bodies, but getting points for a cheap joke didn't seem worthwhile.

She checked her phone. "Holy shit! I think we can call this a clue!" She held the screen toward me so I could read the post from @Starlight9450 that had been reposted at her.

"I'm a few years off the force, but I think you're correct. What now?"

"I'm gonna message him, talk to him, and I'm gonna find the witness to confirm." She paused as if weighing the gravity of her next words. "This is a big fucking deal."

A moment passed, during which we both thought—she about the story and me about her. I wondered what kind of flowers she liked and if she liked sports.

"Karl," she stood abruptly, "we never actually got around to talking about how you could help, but maybe just being around you is good luck enough. I've been waiting for a break like this for a while now. If I figure out what you can do to assist, I'll reach out, but I gotta go find this kid."

Just like before, she reached out her hand, and after a brief shake with a firm grip of her soft hand, she was on her way. I didn't get to ask what Mike was short for.

The bay breeze had subsided, and the sun's warmth decided to join us. The gulls remained where they were, waiting for whatever made them happy and gave them a reason to fly. My walk home was direct because I wanted to be home and safe, not exposed to the elements with emotions in my head. Perhaps emotion wasn't the right word; it was sensations. I needed to be safe to let all the sensations pass me by, to get them out of my system like a flu bug.

I knew what was happening to me. I knew I was developing an attraction to Mike. I couldn't put my finger on why just yet, but it was happening. I had learned so little about her, yet my receptors were picking up whatever electrochemical signals she was sending through my circuits, firing up long-dormant machinery. The reaction was unwelcome.

A block from my house, on the other side of the street, a security patrol SUV sat, blue with gold lettering. Altru Security. I was sure the produce business was cutthroat, but it didn't need security. Altru had some contracts in the area, but nothing in this part of the square. So, why were they here?

As I walked past, a man in the SUV, a redhead with a mustache, made it a point not to make eye contact.

25

Willie Caudill wasn't anyone unique or influential. A part-time homeless person himself, drifting from borrowed couch to borrowed couch, he was a student at nearby Laney College and came to the co-op clinic for help with his Pell Grant. His grades were good enough to keep the funds flowing, but not enough to qualify for any of the scholarships he had applied for. The old vet's mumbling had caught his attention. With the broad spectrum of oddballs in the waiting room, it was usually easy to drown out other people and their ranting, but this one was noticeable.

The victim of this morning's murder, Flora Oliva, had worked at the college as a custodian. Her death happened a few blocks away from the campus, and news of the event spread quickly through the school's staff and students. Apparently, few people at Laney were aware she was homeless or that she had a daughter. She was a perfect example of the adage, "Everyone you know is battling demons you don't see." Now, after her death, everyone was going to know about her demons.

The younger man didn't have much, but he did have an online hive of local folks who kept their eyes and ears open for such events. He was an active X user, and whenever he posted using the hashtag

#tempesttost, others in his online orbit who cared about issues affecting the area's unhoused community would notice.

> Hey #tempesttost. Talking rn to a dude who witnessed the killing and kidnapping this morning. Don't know how long he'll be here.

The post was made at 11:12 am.

* * *

At 11:22, Mike sent a direct message to @starlight9450:

> This is Mike Finney of The East Bay Hub. Is the man you spoke with still there?

Within thirty seconds, an answer came back.

> Yes. He's outside the building now

> Thanks. Be there in a few.
> Can we chat? Are you still there?

He said he was, and they arranged a meeting place. The co-op clinic was a few blocks east of the Square, adjacent to Laney College.

Because her home was near downtown, she had ridden her bike to the meeting with Warren, but she could still make it to the clinic in less than ten minutes. She knew the building and had been there many times to meet interview subjects or to help some of them access services.

After securing her bike to the crowded racks out front, she sent another DM to @starlight9450 asking where he was. Again, the response came quickly.

* * *

"I wouldn't really call it a conversation. He was mostly just mumbling to himself," Willie said. "I asked him a few things, but he kinda went off on his own about the Vietnamese and a church van, some guy named Charlie coming and killing women. He kinda snapped and sorta assaulted me, but he was out of it. Didn't hurt, but it scared the shit outta me."

Mike saw that the young man was embarrassed at not handling himself better. "It's okay," she said. "His mind doesn't sound right. You did the right thing by letting him vent like that. I'm glad you weren't hurt, and I'm glad you didn't hurt him. He saw something bad, and it might help."

As they rounded the corner of the building and the wide lawn spread out, Willie pointed to the old man, who was sitting on the grass. "That's him right there."

"Billy Burke!" Mike said in a surprised and pleasant way.

"I don't know," Willie said. "I didn't catch his name."

"It's cool. I know him from the streets. His name is Billy." She turned back to the younger man. "Thank you, Willie. I appreciate all this. Can I reach out to you if I need something more about this?" She noted his slight reservation and gave him a reminder. "I'm not a cop. Just a reporter."

That did it. "Yeah," Willie said. "Whatever you need. I don't think I ever really talked to Flora, but I'd seen her around campus. She seemed nice. I hope you find that Charlie guy," he said as Mike walked away and headed toward Burke.

Mike approached the vet from the front and stood in the full sun, several feet away, so that the old man could get a good look at her. "Billy Burke. Do you remember me? I helped you get those parking tickets reversed."

Burke was slow to look up for fear of being blinded by the sun. Once he did, he was equally slow to recognize the person before him, but without changing expression, said, "Yeah. You're that reporter— with the boy's name."

"That's right," she said, "Mike. Mike Finney."

"What can I do for you, Miss Finney?"

"I understand you might have seen some of what happened earlier this morning. With Flora and her girl."

Burke looked back at the ground as if remembering hurt, as if he wanted to avoid the conversation. "Not really," he said meekly. "I just heard them jabbering to each other in Vietnamese a little before they took off."

"Did you hear what they said?" Mike asked hopefully.

171

"Nah, but I could tell they were pissed at each other for something. My Vietnamese is shit nowadays."

"I'm sure it's better than mine. What's this about a white church van? Is that what they were driving? What makes you think it was a church van?"

"The sign on the back kinda gave it away," he laughed and snorted. "It said something about a Vietnam church and had some Vietnamese writing on it. English, too. Had a phone number, too, but I didn't get that. The driver guy had glasses. Saw that. I went to check on that woman after the white van pulled away. I saw that her tent had been cut open. I saw the mess. I saw the mess, and I was back in-country again." Burke's breathing picked up pace. He paused and looked away. Mike knew better than to interrupt.

Still looking away, he continued. "That's why I came down here this morning. I wanted to get in to see a counselor and get some more meds. I kinda messed that up for today by screamin' at the kid. I'll try tomorrow." He looked back up at Mike. "Tomorrow seems like a long time from now, now that I saw what I saw this morning. I haven't seen that kinda thing since I got back from the jungle in '74, and I was hoping I wouldn't see it anymore. I just wanted to talk to someone." He looked down, silent again.

After a moment, Mike had an idea. "You know the mayor, Marcus Williams? He's a brother vet. He won't tell them to me, but he's got some stories, too. Maybe I can have him find you to chat."

Burke answered quickly. "Oh, I don't want to be a pain in anyone's ass."

Mike was equally quick. "You wouldn't be. You're one of his people. Plus, you may have told me something that could help us find who's been doing this. This isn't their first time stealing kids and killing parents."

"No shit?"

"No shit!" Mike replied. "You're the first one to give a piece of information about a church van. I don't know what it means, but it means something. What I'm saying, Billy, is that you saw a horrible thing, but you did a great thing."

There was no way Burke would talk to the police about this. He'd had a colorful history and trusted them as much as they trusted him. Mike could tell them about it a little later, but only after she added all this info to her research.

Before leaving, she messaged the mayor about reaching out to Burke. She didn't say much about why, other than that he was a brother vet and needed to talk. She thought that would be enough.

26

To say that Mike Finney had an affection for spreadsheets would be an understatement. Perhaps it was more of an affection for data and its storage, and for placing it into useful tables, fields, and maps. More accurately, it was an affection for gathering as many facts as possible, so that her stories and reports carried the weight needed to make the change she hoped to bring about in the world.

Journalists can manage their data in several ways. In the days of paper and pen, they'd keep stacks of notes or journals handy and then retype the information into something sensible or valuable. As computers became more common, the same could be done electronically. Soon, though, spreadsheets went digital and linkable, opening a whole new world to journalists.

By the time Mike entered the journalism scene, the hard work of developing these skills had already been done, and she dove headfirst into using everything that had been discovered before her. She learned every trick possible in her journalism studies at Cal State East Bay. Her early years in the business, bouncing from freelance gig to soon-to-fold periodical and back again, taught her even more about information management and many valuable tricks never taught in school. Once she landed at the Hub, she put all she had gathered into practice. She even expanded it in her own way, a way that gave her instant access to any data she had encountered over the past few years on the streets. Easily manageable and accessible folders of all stripes and sorts populated her cloud account.

Her most valuable tool, her event intake sheet, began with a Google Form. The form was simple enough, with blocks to enter information about parties involved, locations, and notes. There were checkboxes to select the types of offenses committed and the layer of the master Google map where the newly added data should be placed, if any. Additionally, there were upload frames for images or recordings, with links stored in designated cells in a spreadsheet for easy access.

The various form fields were linked to corresponding cells in a master spreadsheet, keeping all this data in one searchable space. Finney set up various formulas and sub-sheets so that follow-up information from subsequent interviews or police reports could be added to the original entry without causing conflicts.

Similar to what she had done earlier in the day with the initial report on the murder and kidnapping, Mike entered her interview data with Billy Burke, starting with the anchor point, the subject's name, Flora Oliva. That gave her a reference for all the other data stored around her location, crime scene info, witness statements, links to published reports, maps, photos, web links, and anything else she'd accumulated for each of the houseless persons in Alameda County since 2019 who'd been a victim of a major crime against their person. 214 in total, including homicides, attempted homicides, assaults, sexual assaults, and kidnappings. Other offenses might have been included there, but only if they were part of a larger event.

When she entered "Oliva" into the form, her formulas handled the rest. She'd enter what Burke shared, along with known information from the police report, and that would autofill into a Google Sheet whose fields were preset to send the new info into other sheets, tabs, or maps. In cases with multiple intakes or interviews per person, which there always were, Finney might have to sort and merge occasionally, but like everything else, she had functions and shortcut keys set up for that. Using Burke's info, she entered details that automatically created three new entries in her master Google Map: where the incident occurred, where the interview took place, and where they were when the crime occurred. Each entry had its own "type" on the map and was assigned a layer; thus, it could be searched for individually and removed if one needed less information on the screen. If Finney wanted a map of every instance in which Burke and a woman in her system had shared time and space, a few checkboxes would find it. That wasn't the case here, but it meant Finney had the makings of a fantastic search tool.

In addition to the bare facts and figures of an interview, she included a link to a digital audio recording and a typed transcript, along with a dedicated field for tags, keywords, or phrases unique to the situation that could help highlight the case. For this interview, it was easy. She tabbed her cursor into the 'Tags' field and entered *veteran, van, Vietnam, white van, Vietnamese, male, young, Oakland, three males, Latina, young girl, church,* and several more that came to mind as relevant to the interview and the incident.

Afterward, Finney ran a duplicate check and, as she had already entered a new form for each of the two news articles she'd read about

176

the latest murder and kidnapping, as well as for the young man who led her to Billy Burke, she would already have several FLORA entries to dedupe. A similar process told her which other cases had identical tags. Many were obvious, such as girl, Oakland, or kidnap, but there was one Finney looked for, as it was only a couple of days old in her mind. White van.

Now, she had something about a Vietnamese church to add to the overall picture. She had some access to public vehicle records, but she couldn't run a broad search to determine whether a particular church owned a van. Fortunately, she knew of another, slightly more tedious way of discovering whether a particular church owned a white van. Once again, Google was her friend.

The search began with Google Maps to find all the Vietnamese churches in the area, which appeared to number seven within a thirty-five-mile radius. A thorough review of all the images on their websites turned up no white van, but the Facebook pages were another story. The churches had plenty of pictures to sift through, images revealing their community outreach and good deeds. Two of these churches used white vans for their missions, though Finney could not read the signs well enough to know what they said.

Two churches. Two vans. Both in Oakland. Finney considered visiting the churches to see for herself, but it was getting late, and she had other work to do.

She texted Warren, wondering if he'd be game to stir up some trouble.

> Would you still like to help? Have
> some legwork for you.

27

Oscar Braga considered Carlos Guerrero "Employee of the Month" material. Braga liked him because he was loyal, greedy but not too greedy, smart but not too smart, ruthless, and it was in his best interest to keep his mouth shut. Since he was working with an entirely fabricated identity created by Braga, Guerrero owed his entire existence to his boss. His sole purpose at this point was to be the head of Braga's operation at Merritt Community Hospital. That meant he oversaw running the prostitutes who serviced the medical staff, funneling the prescription drugs and the money that came with them to Braga, and pimping out select staff members in exchange for their drugs of choice.

The most lucrative hustle was the payoffs from those with essential licenses and certifications caught in compromising positions. Braga estimated that at one point or another, 4% of the staff had been trapped in their web for stealing pharmaceuticals, inappropriate behavior with patients, drug abuse, or any manner of offenses that would get one fired or de-certified by their governing board. Paying the security staff a few grand to keep it all quiet was much easier than losing your license forever. Braga had entrusted all this to Guerrero, so learning more about a gut-stabbed bum was nothing in comparison.

"I don't know," Guerrero said. "I don't see any history of the two before the attack on the old guy."

That was odd. It wasn't the first time a homeless person turning up at a hospital had tried passing off some fake address as their own, nor was it the first time they'd listed their buddy as next of kin. This was different. Guerrero had discovered the Travers guy listed this Karl Warren as his residence and next of kin—and Warren had signed off on it at the hospital. He wasn't living there before the attack, but he'll be there now.

"What more do you have on Travers?" Braga asked.

"Just what I gave you. The basics that he gave when he came to after surgery. He's on the city's dime, so he didn't have to give all his personal info—no social security number. As for Warren, I got nothing but a name and an address. You're on your own there, Boss."

"Cool, thanks." Braga hung up without another word from Guerrero. *Who is Karl Warren, and why did this bum run to him? Was Warren "Young Sergeant"? Why is he staying with him after he gets out?*

Finding out more should be a matter for the internet. The first search, 'Karl Warren Oakland,' returned everything except what he wanted and everyone else he wanted to see except *his* Karl Warren. A broader search returned Karl Warrens from all over the country, Karls of every shape and color. It reminded him he needed to figure out what he looked like. He'd have to check with Cooper to see if he had any pictures yet. Braga had only a small amount of information from Warren, along with the guard's basic description from when he checked in to see Travers at the hospital: name and rough age, around

6'2", well-built but still lean, no facial hair, short hairstyle. That's it. Pretty slim, but it might do.

Braga typed in what he thought was an easy one, 'Karl Warren' and 'police,' just in case he'd had any newsworthy arrests. It was a small gold mine. Karl Warren, this. Karl Warren, that. One Kansas City newspaper article highlighting a 'responding officer, Karl Warren,' caught his attention.

A Kansas City, Missouri, girl, 11, was found dead in the bedroom of her home in the Ward Estates neighborhood of Kansas City, Missouri, on the morning of Jun 25 after police responded to an emergency call from a housekeeper.

The Kansas City Police Department has since said that a note left inside the house indicates that the girl recently decided to end her life. Police believe the girl died by suicide. Police said there were no signs of forced entry or struggle and no evidence that anyone else had been present.

There were other police-related articles regarding Warren. More assaults, domestic violence, and sex crimes, all with Officer Warren either responding or testifying about something, according to the reports. One of the articles even included a photograph of Warren that matched Braga's rough description of his appearance.

So, our boy used to wear the blue. The last date on the mass of articles was roughly four years prior. He clicked forward to another page of results and found another article on Karl Warren, but this was in Idaho.

> Kootenai County homicide detectives responded to the area and spoke to witnesses as they processed the crime scene. The owner of the property, Karl Warren, lived on the land for less than two years and is not considered a suspect, as all the bodies are in states of decomposition that required far longer than that, sources say.
>
> Police did not reveal what caused the deaths of the individuals but said the Idaho State Police Medical Examiner's Office would determine the causes of death.
>
> Residents in the local area admitted they were concerned about the discovery of the bodies, with several suspected of belonging to those on the state's list of missing persons.

The article was only about two years old, which vexed Braga, but he stayed in his chair and let his wheels turn. He was entering a different phase of his hunting, of his game. Only one person alive knew he was a hunter and had seen his face. Now, that person would be living with a cop. *Probably armed and has some security*, he thought.

He grabbed his phone, hit three buttons, and listened to it ring. Cooper was off duty, but the redhead knew better than not to answer. Braga was aware of his extra gig with the Vietnamese.

"Yeah, Boss?" came Cooper's eager voice.

"The gig I have you on, I need you to add two things to it. First, get the guy's license plate number. Make it a priority. Look through the windows of his garage door if he has one."

"He has a motion video camera on his front door, so I can't approach too close without him knowing, but it doesn't matter. There's no windows on the front of the first floor. I can take a picture if he drives in or out," Cooper said.

"Okay," Braga said without much confidence, trusting somehow that Cooper would fuck this up. "The second thing. While you're there, take a picture of the security device he has on his door, okay?"

There was a pause on Cooper's end of the phone. "How do I do that without setting off the motion sensor?"

"Take a picture from about twenty-five feet out and at an angle, not straight on. Use your zoom the best you can. That'll get me a clear enough picture to work with. I need to know what kind of device he has."

Another pause. Braga knew Cooper wanted to ask why. It would be a natural question. Why would a security company manager want to know about the security situation of a private residence? The pause continued, but Braga waited Cooper out. The delay was only a few seconds, but during that time, Braga made tentative plans to have Cooper "Limoned" by one of his street stooges for a handful of drugs. Instead, Cooper saved his own life by ending the pause.

"Okay. I'll get it all to you ASAP."

Braga ended the call a little disappointed he'd miss out on the cheap thrill of a proxy kill. He headed out the door of his townhouse for his "bunker" to drop off some supplies. It was a storage unit, built inside an old brick building in Oakland, but it looked and felt like a bunker. He didn't pay anything for it. He and the owner had an ongoing arrangement: safe, secure storage for a steady supply of Adderall. Braga gave a modest supply to the owner, and the owner kept the paperwork on the sizable space clean and away from Braga's name. He also made sure the cameras around his unit never worked.

The building had only twenty long-term storage units, so in-and-out traffic was minimal. Braga heaved up the roll-up hatch, stepped inside, and secured it behind him before turning on the lights and reaching into the dark to the spot where the switch would be. A 20'-by-20' space, lined with metal shelves along the walls, blinked awake under the fluorescent lights. In the middle of the unit were two motorcycles, both with clean titles, awaiting new owners. Lastly, in the right corner stood a large, stand-up safe that could have been pulled from a turn-of-the-19th-century bank. It held his cash and fake documents, all valid and issued by the proper agencies: Social Security, DMV, and the Department of State for passports. The identities were real, matching his age and description, but the photos were of Braga.

It was easier than he would have thought to get fake documents. All he needed to do was find enough homeless people his age and race who were willing to give up their information for a few bucks. He'd need their names, social security numbers, dates of birth, and a few other facts about them to begin. With that, he could get a copy of their birth certificate and a state ID. A passport was easy after that. Braga had the resources to check if the person was clean of warrants or felonies before applying for anything. In total, he had four whole new identities to choose from.

The shelves on the left wall held stolen medical equipment, monitors, infusion pumps, mobile devices, and all manner of apparatus that garnered demand on the black market. On the far wall was the pharmacy. Everything was separated and stored by type: OxyContin, Xanax, Adderall, Ritalin, Vicodin, Percocet, Valium, and almost anything else that would get someone high or save their life. There were also several small refrigerators filled with insulin, alongside blood sugar monitors.

The right wall had half a shelf full of tactical gear and ammunition. The other half was covered with handguns and long guns, all illegal and unregistered. Altru Security had an official armory, and this wasn't it. Possession of each of these was a felony, and there were nearly fifty felonies on the wall.

Braga was fastidious about the next step, not wanting to mix the salt with the pepper. Unslinging his duffel, he unloaded his collections for the day. He'd made three stops, and three different security supervisors made their payout to him, one larger than expected to make up for a past shortage. Good. All even now. Each hospital was its own operation, and each small trickle helped create a larger stream from which they all drank. With each container safely tucked away, Braga made a call.

"I may need you and your guys to do some work for me soon."

28

Mike's mission sounded easy enough: check out two Vietnamese churches and see if their vans might fit Billy Burke's descriptions. She filled me in on a few other details, mainly by phone, but we chatted by text enough for me to see she texted like a real, live human adult. I couldn't help but add this to the imaginary plus column, even though I wasn't even thinking such things, even though I was thinking such things.

I prepared for the night more than usual. In addition to my typical keys, phone, wallet, small folding knife, and flashlight, I also brought a phone charger and a few pairs of zip cuffs and wore my thin tactical gloves. It's hard to tell what may happen, but I liked being prepared.

Mike had sent me a useful digital tool: a Google Maps overlay for my phone app that showed locations of accessible electrical outlets, free Wi-Fi hotspots, pay phones, homeless shelters, and food kitchens. I was sure she sent it for electricity and Wi-Fi information, but I also assumed she had given it to any of her tech-savvy street friends or used it in her reporting. I didn't plan to be out there long enough for my phone to die, but it was handy information.

I wasn't sure how much I could help her or whether either of the vans was the one in question. Short of finding blood splatters or hogtied

186

girls inside, I wasn't sure what grand clues might present themselves. As I was without a single thing to do in the world except drink coffee or booze, I supposed I could help out. These weren't the people who hurt my friend Xtra, but they were the same type of people who preyed on the weaker, unseen folks who lived around me. If I could help a little, I would. It might do me good to come out of my shell a little. Steve Harvey and the kids at the Door would have to do without me for the night.

A Lyft took me to the first church, Vietnamese Presbyterian Ministries. It was nestled between a donut shop and a bingo hall in a strip mall on the outskirts of a less-than-lively shopping center on Dutton Avenue, where Oakland kisses a corner of San Leandro. I had the driver drop me off a block away, but upon seeing the van, I could tell immediately it did not match Burke's description. The church owned two vans, both parked in spots in front of the bingo hall. Small as bingo halls went, it was a lively place.

The vans were white. Anyone looking at them would have easily seen the name, printed in bold English on the sides and back in large red letters, with no Vietnamese writing. They were not a match, though I took pictures of both vans and their license plates to be sure.

It took twenty minutes for another rideshare car to arrive. During that time, I called Mike and left her a voicemail saying I was heading to the other church further south.

The First Vietnamese Baptist Church made its home in a one-story stucco building and, according to their website, had been there for over thirteen years. It wasn't much, but it provided them with private parking along the side, next to a tire store. Here, they kept their used but rugged van, currently parked tail-in against the tire shop's wall.

After having my driver drop me a block from the church, I walked to the other side of the street for a broader view of the place. No lights inside. No activity, but a white van was parked in the lot. A lone light perched on the church's outer wall, and some wash from the streetlamps shone into the parking spaces. I walked a few more doors down and crossed the street again at the crosswalk. Heading back to the church, I checked for anyone camping in doorways on either side of the road. There was someone with an overflowing shopping cart in the doorway of a hair salon across from the church, but other than that, the late Sunday street was quiet.

The van appeared to match what we were looking for: white, with magnetic signs mostly in Vietnamese. In English, it read *First Vietnamese Baptist Church*. That and the phone number were the only things I understood. I walked around the van and found signs on both front doors, the slider, and another on the back doors. That's the one Burke described. Stifling my excitement, I took pictures with my phone, stepped away, and called Mike as I crossed the street and a couple of buildings down to a used-car lot on gravel that made too much noise under my boots.

She answered on the first ring, and I told her, "I think it's our van. I'll text you some pictures."

"Holy shit, dude! That's hella cool," she said, highlighting her California upbringing. "Is there anyone at the church right now?"

"I don't think so. Looks pretty dark here."

"Well, let me tell you what I found out. When you told me the first church looked like a dud, I looked around the VBC Facebook page, hoping to find pictures of the van and who drives it. Most of the posts are in Vietnamese, but some are in English. Some photos were taken inside a van. I couldn't tell if it was our van, but I saw a few pictures of a driver. Kid named Donald Vo. The name Vo pops up on their website a few times. I think his grandparents help run the church. I found he has a few minor arrests for petty stuff, but I don't have access to deeper info like known associates or other contacts the police have had with him. He wears glasses like one of the guys that Burke saw. It may be time to call the cops and loop them in. I know the head of the county task force for this, Sergeant Cozens."

A Hyundai pulled into the lot near the van.

"Hey!" I moved further back into the shadow. "What kind of car does this kid have? Did you find that out?"

"Yes," she said, "hold on."

The rhythmic sounds of keystrokes and mouse clicks from her laptop came through the phone. A young man in glasses stepped out of the small car and headed toward the church's side door.

"Yeah, he drives a 2018 Hyundai Elantra. Why do you ask?"

"Because he just showed up."

Mike gasped. "Karl, get the hell out of there, please."

"I will. Soon. But I want to sniff around a bit more. I'll call or text if there's anything. If there's nothing, I'll reach out and update you tomorrow."

Off in the distance, on the cliffside, I heard Lorelei singing her rich and intoxicating tune.

29

There wasn't much around me in the gravel lot I'd been using as my observation point: some discarded clothing, a dozen feet of nylon twine attached to an old sign, rocks, and broken glass, all swept over to the side or blown there by winds. I didn't see any sticks or pipes I could use as a blunt instrument, but there was enough to make a simple weapon.

Vo would likely be armed, probably a gun, so I needed something more than the small folding knife I carried. I hadn't planned on going on the offensive while on my expedition, but I didn't expect to run into one of the suspects. With my knife, I cut an 18" x 18" section of fabric from a discarded denim shirt I'd found. Placing a couple of handfuls of sand and pebbles in the center of the square of fabric, I grabbed the wad from the other side of the denim and gave it a firm twist and tug before tying the bundle closed with a length of the nylon twine. It wasn't perfect, but I had a disguised, easily concealed, readily deployable blackjack. All I needed to do was get close enough to use it before he used whatever he had.

How did I know that he had something? Well, I'd have a weapon if I were him. If I were setting up for a night of scouring the streets for more victims, I'd be packing something. I'd already concluded that this was one of the people responsible for the kidnapping and murders of the girls and their families. Between the tangible elements, such as the witness statements about the van and ethnicity, as well as the intangibles, like a guy taking a van from work at an hour when there's apparently no work to be had, I had enough of an idea that this was one of my guys. I also wanted it to be him and had prepared accordingly. I wanted the action, and I was sure enough about the whole thing that I was willing to risk assaulting a church worker to get some.

On my earlier trip to the lot, I checked for cameras around the church. I didn't see any, but I got a pretty good view of the area, and I figured my best friend was the dumpster in the church's lot.

The sun had long since dipped, and the traffic had diminished. I noticed a handful of other folks walking about the streets. None did so with a particular place to go. They were wandering for the sake of wandering, passing the time until salvation or death came knocking—just another day. For me, they provided both a distraction and camouflage. One more lost soul like me shuffling around would be invisible and easily ignored.

I got up slowly and made a lazy, irregular path down the sidewalk away from the church, then walked a block up and crossed the middle of the street, where there were no cars—one of many legal infractions of the evening. I turned back toward the church on the other side of the quiet street—no new activity. The van was still there, and no new drifters had slipped in, so I kept my slow pace in that direction. At the tire shop, I stopped to adjust the slouch of my watch cap, taking a moment to scope the church's side lot for any movement before walking closer. Nothing. I slipped around the corner of the tire shop's wall, behind the church's dumpster, and into the dark corner of the lot to wait. A light was attached to the church wall, casting its mung yellow glow over the lot. While I'd have to hide from the glare when Vo came out, at least the shadows would fall in my direction.

Having parked tail-end in, he'd have to step into the space between the dumpster and van to enter. I'd only have a quick moment to cover the fifteen feet between us without being noticed. I wasn't the fighter I was a few years back, but my confidence was high. There was some rust, some wear and tear, and some self-esteem issues that kept my mind in check, but when it came to doling out unrestricted violence, I was still good at that.

Hearing Vo leave the building, I headed closer to the van. For a moment, the racist, Midwest portion of my brain pushed through with a nugget of information: all Asian people are good at martial arts. My time in the military and police force disabused me of that notion and taught me there are no absolutes when it comes to ethnicity and fighting skills. The only exception I made was for Tongans and Samoans. To this day, I will not fuck with either without a good reason—and even then, it had better be a really good reason.

Vo emerged and unlocked the van door. His waistband showed a telltale bulge. My boots scuffed against the asphalt, the noise making him freeze long enough to allow a solid strike with my makeshift blackjack against his skull. I didn't hit hard enough to kill him, but I did need him stunned. He didn't pass out, but he did go limp, and before he fell, I had the blackjack back in my coat pocket and was hauling him up by the back of the neck. He was dense with muscle, but the simple physics of his body weighing eighty pounds less than mine was against him. With a firm hold, I pinned him solidly against the wall, his feet resting on the ground, but with so little purchase, he could not get any leverage to spin away or struggle.

Keeping Vo's head pinned to the wall, I grabbed his phone, wallet, and weapon from the rear left of his waistband. The pistol looked like an old 9mm Beretta knockoff, a Taurus, or a Girsan. Nothing fancy, but it would give anyone within fifteen feet a reason to have a bad day. I relieved him of the potential guilt of hurting me with it and, making sure its safety was on, slipped it into my coat pocket. I had also relieved myself of the potential guilt of harming an innocent person. There had been a chance I was wrong about this guy—until I found the weapon. His having a gun made me feel better.

The alley was dark, and the dumpster concealed us from passersby, giving me a few minutes to play.

"What...," he sputtered, "what the fuck?"

"Hands behind you," I said softly.

"Who the fuck are you?" he groaned.

"Hands behind you, please," I repeated, still calmly.

"What the...," he started, but didn't finish.

I punched him in the back, below the left side of the rib cage, with my left hand. It's not my strong side, but placement was more critical than pure power. Young Vo must also have understood physics, because after a few light gasps and flails, he complied when I gave the command a third time. Within thirty seconds, I had him secured in a pair of zip cuffs and moved him away from the wall and into a cross-legged seated position on the gravel between the dumpster and van. His glasses flew off as I moved him from the wall to the ground. He was in more fear than pain, but struggled to contain both.

"What do you want? Money? I don't have any, dumbass!" he said with an air of defiance his body language failed to project.

"I want information," I said. "I want to know things only you and a few people know. I need to know these things, and I need you to tell me now, or I'm going to cause you large amounts of pain. You are a bad person, and you've done bad things. I'll have no problems hearing you scream and beg. I'll have no problems watching you bleed and squirm, so I recommend that you be as honest with me as soon as you possibly can at all times, okay? I already need to go to therapy for a bunch of stuff like this, so adding a little more to the pile isn't going to set back my development much. Do you understand me? I don't want to kill you, but I will hurt you a whole lot if I need to. I won't enjoy it, but it won't bother me, either."

Vo nodded.

"Good," I said. "Tell me about the girls."

His eyes widened, and he looked down. "What girls?" he hissed.

"So, we're gonna go that way, huh? Okay, son. Here we go," I said as I removed the blackjack and knelt at his side. The ball of sand and rocks was too big to fit in his mouth, but the tail of denim fabric wasn't. All wadded together, it fit nicely in his mouth. It was snug enough to trap all his whimpering and prevent the weight of the stones from pulling it out.

The kid didn't weigh much, and he didn't struggle when I lifted him to his feet and shoved him toward the van. I reached into my coat pocket and pulled out the 9mm. With the safety on, I tapped him on the right temple with the barrel to remind him I had it, pushed him toward the passenger-side door, and bundled him inside before buckling him in. Instead of going all the way around the van and giving him a chance to escape, I entered through the sliding door on the right and slid into the driver's seat, shifting the pistol and laying it on my lap, pointing at Vo.

"Where are we going?" Vo whimpered through the wadded material in his mouth.

"You had your chance for me to play nice," I said. "I even said *please*. I'd like to do this as smoothly as possible, but how smoothly it goes is up to you."

Within minutes of driving, I found what I was looking for. The industrial area near the Oakland Coliseum has no homes, many warehouses, and empty corners. I needed somewhere out of the way, with enough disquiet to mask a few minutes of light screaming. This street had scant light, no traffic, and plenty of noise wash from the interstate.

I parked the van between two trailers without attached trucks and looked only partially out of place. It was worth the slight risk, as the kid grew more scared with every passing minute. I didn't know if his eyes could get any wider, but I was about to find out.

I exited the van the same way I came in, through the sliding panel door. Once outside, I opened the passenger door and gave the kid a once-over. He was zip-cuffed and seat-belted in, but it was more than that keeping him in the seat. It was fear. He was used to being the one to dish out the violence, not being a victim of it. His fear did most of my work for me, so there was a chance I wouldn't have to perpetrate any more unfortunate violence on the young man, but I was more than prepared if I needed to.

"Tell me about the girls," I said as I grabbed the bulk of the blackjack and roughly pulled the rag handle from his mouth.

He didn't look confused by the question, but didn't answer immediately. He seemed to be formulating an answer that might save his life, or at least spare him further discomfort.

"What girls?" he finally answered.

I responded with a strong, gloved right fist to the side of his head. Again, not enough to incapacitate, just enough to serve as an unpleasant reminder of the rewards of truthfulness.

"Upon all that reflection," I said, "that's the best you can come up with? C'mon, young man. You can do better. Let me remind you, I am not a part of any law enforcement agency, and I'm not beholden to any laws of decency here other than my word. In this case, my word is that I will punch you hard every time I don't like your answer. We'll do that until I get bored or my hand gets sore. Then, I'll move on to something new and exciting. If I get the information I need, the punching stops. At this point, I can't promise that I won't kill you because I don't see it as a need just yet. Ya got me? So, tell me about the girls, please." I added some emphasis and a pleasant tone to the last word.

"They'll kill our family back home if we don't do this," he pleaded.

"Back home? As in Vietnam?" I said. "Shit! I'll kill your family right here if you don't help me. We'll start with your family at the church. It's only a matter of looking through your phone and Facebook page to find them. How do you think we found you?" I made sure to emphasize the "we," hoping he'd pick up that I wasn't alone out here, even though I was totally alone out here.

I'd never murder anyone. Well, no one else after the last time. At least not if I didn't have to or the person didn't deserve it. But that's not really murder, is it? Anyway, I'd never harm his family, assuming they didn't have anything to do with the kidnappings and killings. Vo didn't need to know that part, but the theatrics were helpful. I had an idea and sent Mike a text.

> Send me a picture of Vo's
> grandparents. I'll tell you why
> later.

"Hold on a sec, kid."

Thirty seconds later, a photo of a smiling elderly couple came up on my phone. I showed it to Vo.

"Your grandparents, right?"

With wide eyes, he did some mental calculations and decided to write off the family back home in the old country. He hung his head. "They're in our stash house near the port."

Truth be told, that was easier than I expected. I had prepared to do more to learn more, but I'm glad I didn't have to. I've got enough demons as it is. Right hand to God, in all my years in the Army or KCPD, I never once intentionally harmed someone in my care, well, mostly. There was that one time when I didn't make a 100% effort to help that one handcuffed, accused child sexual assault suspect back in Kansas City. Perhaps I could have made a better effort to stop him from falling a few flights of stairs in his apartment building as we were removing him from the home where he was molesting his wife's daughter. Officer Sheila Black and I received written reprimands, and we promised our Precinct Captain that we felt bad about the guy's broken wrist and rotator cuff injury.

"So, kid, where we headed now?"

30

It looked sleepy enough from my spot in the van a block away, some sort of garage in an old Quonset hut. The kid was more cooperative during the drive than I would have thought. He said I could expect two of his cousins inside, no cameras, and five girls. I'd have guessed three girls, so I didn't know where the other two might have come from. He also said they were awaiting a phone call from their buyer, who would tell them where to take the girls and when to meet them. Vo wasn't what I'd call chatty, but he was more helpful than I had hoped.

"What do you do with the girls?" I asked on the drive here.

"Nothing," he said, looking down. "We bring them where we're told to, and we get paid. Supposed to be tonight."

"Where's that?"

"There's a warehouse close by we've used a few times. We'd probably use that tonight, but we wouldn't be sure until they called."

He told me where the warehouse was, and I filed the information away, but right now, I had this current mess to deal with.

Without leaving the van, I searched the far back for anything useful and found a roll of duct tape and two ratchet tie-down straps. I used them to secure Vo to his seat, ensuring his legs were immobile. I probably needed the blackjack, so I stuffed it in my pocket before applying a length of tape to his mouth. There was little else of use inside the van. Since I never took off my gloves inside, there was no need to wipe away any prints. I grabbed my gear and stepped outside into the now-chilly air.

I stayed across from the garage but headed toward it slowly, taking a visual and aural audit of the area. We were at the confluence of three freeways and two busy thoroughfares. It was late, but there was enough traffic to make far more noise than I usually heard at home next to a freeway. If I were to step on a twig or piece of glass out here, someone a few feet away would be hard-pressed to hear it, let alone determine a direction. Some of the street's buildings looked like they were still active homes, but mostly, the neighborhood was made up of businesses. A few were inside buildings that were newer than the rest, but many were newly refurbished houses turned into either offices or who knows what. What mattered to me was that few lights were on, and no human movement was apparent.

I continued walking, passing the garage on the opposite side of the street. On the north side of the hut, I noticed a small parking lot, but it was empty. Was I here too early? No. Seventy-five feet from the garage, a too-shiny Honda Civic was parked in front of an abandoned steel building across from the empty lot. There was no other place in this neighborhood at this hour where the owner of such a car could be except at the garage.

There was no apparent motion inside the Quonset hut, but I'd check more closely once I got to that side of the street. I stayed on the opposite side and watched for a while longer. No movement on the road or in any of the buildings along it. A quiet and peaceful night in

Oakland. No violence or murder. No kidnapped girls or drug-based misery. Just another fine American city, all settled in for the evening.

If I had walked away, I'd have been home in thirty minutes. Only one bad guy had seen my face, and he'd never say anything because he'd get worse from his family than anything I did to him. I had invested nothing in this yet, and nothing to lose. I'd be home way before the bars closed, and I'd be back on track with my drinking in no time.

Five Cassandras. Five little girls who would have their youth and innocence stripped away. Five little sirens, singing their song, calling me closer to the rocks.

Cassandra. In my mind, she looked at me again and said, "Do something."

I called Mike, and she answered on the second ring. "Can I be a protected source of yours?" I asked.

"For what?" she replied, mildly confused. She must have been wondering what type of trouble I'd been involved with that I needed anonymity. Mike hadn't known me long enough to know my way of thinking and how I could be once my siren's song was sung. Hell, sometimes I didn't even know what I was thinking or feeling about the world from one day to the next, but here I was: lurking in the dark outside a criminal hideaway with a zip-cuffed and duct-taped kidnapper in the passenger seat of a van I had stolen.

"I have located information and individuals that may eliminate as many as twenty names from your boards," I said flatly, hoping to strike a serious tone and let her understand the weight of the topic.

Her scales worked. "Yes. Provided whatever you tell me leads toward an actual story or assists with an investigation, you shall remain protected," she said with equal weight and seriousness.

"Good," I said, relieved but not surprised. "I'm going to text you an address in Oakland. Don't come here yet. Park two blocks away and wait for me to text or call. This is happening now, so I'm sorry if I'm interrupting anything. I can't tell you anything more right now, but please trust me that you should stay away until I say otherwise. When can you be here?"

"About twenty minutes, but...," she started, but I cut her off, which I hated doing because I'm sure she had a thousand questions.

"Bring a camera or at least be able to take good pics and video with your phone." I ended the call with a reminder to stay away until I reached out again.

Twenty minutes was plenty of time. My hasty plan was to go in, incapacitate the two brothers Vo had mentioned, and free the girls. Simply calling the police was an option, but this way, I solved the problem immediately.

I slowly crossed the street two buildings from the garage and headed back toward it. I passed a darkened, abandoned-looking duplex, a house-turned-accounting office, also abandoned, then an empty lot before arriving at the garage. Streetlights cast their glow over the front of the building, but the middle and rear sections remained dark, save for the small light shining through the windows. I continued past the garage for a good look beyond it. Glancing down the block toward the van, Vo's silhouette stood out starkly against the backlight of the freeway lights.

Passing the adjacent parking lot with its cracked asphalt and the open field full of weeds on the other side, I stopped in front of the house on the far side. It appeared occupied, with a single light in the front room, but I couldn't sense any activity within, though there was an old GMC truck in the driveway behind a heavy iron gate. The arborvitae may have looked quaint fifty years ago, but they had now grown to the point where they dwarfed anything else in the front yard and covered most of the front façade. You couldn't see much of it from the street or the street from the front porch, and while this was horrible for their home security, right now, it suited my needs.

After a brief pause to survey the neighborhood again, I turned and headed back to the garage, stepped into the abandoned property, and made a wide circle toward the darkened area behind the structure. The Quonset hut stretched the length of the property, so the far end of the abandoned field met the back end of the building. Sticking to the shadows whenever possible, I kept looking through the hut's windows for movement. So far, nothing, but I did see some flurries of light. Slight signs, but I couldn't tell what it was. A TV, maybe.

There was no way to be sure if there were external security cameras. Vo said there weren't any, and I didn't see any, but there were so many dark corners in the lot and the eaves of the front and back of the hut that I couldn't be sure. My best guess was no, so I cautiously went with that assumption. Staying close to the fence, I approached the hut. A door on the far back side of the building was blocked by an old, rusted truck bed sitting all by itself, an oversized doorstop. I guessed there hadn't been a fire marshal inspection here for a few years. Aside from the front rolling door, the only usable entrance was a personnel door on the north side, adjacent to the small parking lot.

Vo's phone vibrated in my pocket. Still in the shadows, I took it out and checked the screen: a short text message.

Where are you?

They're waiting for their cousin and the van. *Is something happening that they need it now, or are they just getting nervous?* I wasn't sure. I wasn't even sure if they were here. I had to get closer. I had to see them for myself. Moving through the grass and weeds was soundless, drowned out by traffic.

I saw the flickering of the TV screen before I actually heard it. Whatever was on the screen also reflected on the windows facing me. The room was dimly lit, with most of the glass covered by taped newspapers, so I didn't notice any movement. Since there was only one layer of paper, light from inside seeped through, and small gaps occasionally offered a glimpse inside. Gathering confidence, I looked through one of these gaps. On the TV, I saw something I didn't recognize—perhaps an interview or a reality show. Two people sat on a couch facing the TV, seen from behind: one with short, dark hair and the other, smaller, with long, dark hair. My limited view didn't show much else—just a similar window on the opposite side.

Retracing my steps, I returned to the shadows along the back fence line and made my way to the south side of the garage. Here was another weed field, but the hut had no doors on this side. The street lighted the front half of the building, but the back half, where I wanted to go, was still mostly in shadow. Again, the freeway drowned out any noise I might have made, but because I was closer to the TV, its sound reached me as I made my careful approach. I found an opening in the newspaper, far from the person on the couch's line of sight, and looked in. There, on the couch, was what I hoped to find—and what I hoped never to encounter again.

The person with the short hair was a young Asian man in his early twenties, no more than twenty-five. He had a pistol tucked in his front waistband, his right arm casually draped over the back of the old couch, and his left hand resting on the thigh of a girl beside him. She looked no more than ten years old, Hispanic, wearing a nightgown whose material was bunched up so he could touch her skin. The look on her face was beyond catatonic. She had been scared and traumatized too much and for too long that she was spent of emotion and energy. Her dark eyes were open and stared lifelessly at the screen, focusing on nothing, waiting for some kind of stimulus to tell her how to behave.

My impulse was to start shooting at the man through the glass. At this distance, there'd be no risk of hitting the girl, but there was another kidnapper and four more girls to worry about—so, horrible idea. *Where were they?*

I didn't have a good enough idea of the layout of the place to make a sensible attack plan like my instincts wanted of me. A part of me wanted a daring rescue with bloody consequences for the kidnappers. However, that was problematic now that I'd better seen the reality of the multiple felonies I'd committed tonight. More likely, I recognized how pissed off I was and how I wouldn't be able to dispassionately solve this without getting one or more of the girls hurt.

It had been thirty-eight minutes since I called Mike. I slid back from the window, retreated further into the shadows, and texted her.

You close?

Yes. What's the word?

I gave her the address of the empty building near where I parked the church van and told her to meet me there as soon as possible.

Don't pass by the first address I
gave you.

Mike rounded the corner. I hadn't known her long, but her image struck such an impression that it stunned me momentarily. Tall and lean with long strides that carried her purposefully, without hesitation. It was a chilly night, but she didn't overdress: dark blue flannel shirt, green khakis, and boots that looked more like hi-top sneakers. Streamlined and ready to go.

She crossed the street and headed toward the light of my cell phone, which I held out for her to see, surveying the street as she approached. I'm sure by now she'd already pulled up plenty of information about the place, but her first question wasn't about that.

"Why is there a man tied up in the passenger seat of that van?" she asked. She must have seen him as she scanned the street while crossing. I liked her more and more.

"That is an excellent question," I began. "May I suggest that I tell you a few of the high points, then you call the police? While we wait, I'll give you even more details. If we have time before they arrive, you can ask me as many questions as we have time for, but when they show up, I have to go. That's the anonymous part. Are you okay with all that?"

I watched the quick calculations behind her eyes. At a bare minimum, she had someone tied up in a van who'd been spotted at the scenes of at least two kidnappings. She squinted. There must be a quirk in her math. "Is the guy in the van dead?" she finally asked.

"No," I said.

"Have you killed anyone?" she asked.

"Tonight?"

"Uh, regarding whatever is happening here," she said.

"No," I said concretely.

"Okay," she said just as firmly. "You're a confidential source. What's happening?"

I took a deep breath. I needed to get the key points out quickly and clearly so we could involve the police.

"When you call the police in a minute, tell them that in that building is definitely one, but perhaps two, armed men involved in the kidnapping and murders of the homeless. Also, inside is definitely one and upwards of five young girls who are missing. They are waiting to be sold and transferred by the guy in the van and the two inside. I don't know when that's happening, but it's supposed to be soon. Most of the details we knew already, but the guy in the van, Donald Vo, told me more about who and when. The two guys inside are his cousins. With my own eyes, I saw one guy, armed, and one young girl, Hispanic. That's more than enough to get a welfare check, but if you call Detective Cozens, I'd guess she'll make sure even more happens."

Her calculations only took an instant, and she decided to call Cozens. Mike relayed what I'd told her and answered any follow-up questions the best she could. All of this needed to be acted upon immediately.

Mike hung up. "She said she'll call back in a minute. She needs to make a few calls, so I should keep an eye on the place and wait."

While we waited, I shared a few more details with Mike about what I had learned and how: the church, my first meeting with Vo, the information I got from him, and his willingness to talk on the drive here. It helped fill in some blanks and let Mike know why some information came to light under less-than-legal circumstances. If the police had been involved, most of this evidence, well, all of it, would have been useless, but if a tip from a reporter came in who heard from a neighborhood source, that's a different animal. In that case, the police are compelled to go to the location and at least conduct a welfare check for a suspected missing person.

Mike's phone rang. "Where exactly are you?" It was Cozens. She must have had Mike on speakerphone because I also heard her read the address over the radio.

"Okay. Another detective, Kwami Scheffield, will meet you by the van. He's already downtown and should be there soon. He knows what I know. We also have a couple cars on the way, but they won't approach until Schef says so. Give him any updates you can, and I'll be along as soon as possible. I'm coming, but it'll be a few."

We continued to wait in the dark, saying nothing until she broke the silence. "You sticking around?"

"No," I said. "As soon as I sense they're near, I'll head out. It'll be all yours after that. I'm anonymous, remember?"

She looked at me as if to ask why I was doing this, but I suspected she knew why. She also knew I had some experience with the names of girls on a board and that they needed attention, no matter how long they'd been there. She knew that if I did something before the girls became a piece of history, so much the better.

Charles Baker was long dead, but the world remained populated with souls like his, souls who needed the misery of others to feed and grow. Someone else's suffering is energy for another. One person's pain is another's pleasure. I could probably continue with this case and derive some enjoyment from causing pain to those who built this network, but that would be selfish of me. At this point, the police would do a much better job of handling this scene and finding out where the other tentacles of this ugly monster reach. I assumed child traffickers didn't have the most accurate administrative systems, but there would be enough data to find out more about the next level. I'd have to be content with that. My work there was done.

I noticed a man headed toward us in the same way that Mike had approached me earlier. He moved quickly, so I assumed it was Sheffield, and I took that as my cue to leave. After disassembling the pistol, I left it on one of the van's rear seats and departed. While still in the shadows, I headed west between the adjacent house and its neighbor. There was no fence between them and no house behind. Others had clearly used this path over the years. I headed west for a few more blocks before turning south onto Union Street. This path took me deep into a blended zone of parks, industry, gas stations, gray fields, abandoned cars, and middle-class houses. A true melting pot with plenty of dark spaces. Easy to disappear if anyone drove by. Few did.

It was late, and I was tired, but I had another thing to check out.

31

I walked to the warehouse Vo had told me about. It was a mile and a half, and I was already beat from the long day, but I didn't want any records of me taking rideshares around the area in case anything went sideways. As I approached the warehouse, I stayed on the opposite side of the street and ambled as casually as possible toward it, staying in the dark. Passing by, everything looked normal: a chain-link fence and gate in front, a loading dock on both sides, and an imposing sliding door facing the street.

Inside the lot, behind the closed gate, a white cargo van with no windows sat alongside a dark SUV. I couldn't make out the model from this distance. Maybe on my next lap, from the other side, I could see, but not from here. I walked slowly for another hundred feet and froze at what I saw: a blue Altru Security vehicle. *What the hell were they doing? Do they have contracts here? What was one of their vehicles doing near a trafficking transfer?* I wasn't sure about the license plate, but it looked like the same type of vehicle that had been hanging around my place, another location Altru shouldn't be. I had to check who was behind the wheel.

Assuming he had seen me on my first pass, I casually walked another block further to avoid the driver's view before crossing again. When I doubled back to the warehouse and patrol car, I stayed in the middle of the sidewalk, indifferent to being seen. I didn't want to startle the man. In fact, I wanted him to see me and to discount me as just another street person. I walked as if I had nowhere to go and no deadline to get there. A lazy amble with no worries in the world; slow, stooped like a drunkard, hands in pockets, and head down. When I pulled up to the tail end of the patrol SUV, he was already looking my way. He must have seen me on the sidewalk or across the street. Good. As I passed his window, I only caught him in profile as he had already lost interest in me, or perhaps he didn't want to make his staring too obvious. Hoping it was the former, I took one glance to fill out the quick mental picture I had taken moments before. Same hair. Same mustache. Same face. It was the redhead with the mustache who had been watching my place. His presence was not a coincidence.

What does this mean? How is Altru wrapped up in this? He had to be part of the transfer.

I wish I had cigarettes, not that I smoke, but they'd make a great excuse to plop down anywhere I wanted to light up and enjoy a quick drag, somewhere like in front of a warehouse. I'd have to risk it, and now knowing this guy was trouble, I felt less bad about what I had to do.

Short of the cyclone fence encircling the warehouse lot, the neighboring property's building abutted right up to the sidewalk, its cinderblock walls shielding me from view of the target warehouse. I made a show of sitting on the sidewalk and leaning against the wall. I'd give him five minutes, and if it didn't work, then I might be wrong about their involvement, and I could find a better place to watch the warehouse.

It took one minute. The guard slid out of his patrol car, and he was already making a rookie mistake. He was a righty, as his weapon was holstered on that side, but he also carried his flashlight in his right hand. He had the mindset that he wouldn't need to draw his weapon. He's not ready to fire. The battle was already mine.

"You can't sleep here!" He hadn't turned his flashlight on and held it like a decoration.

"I'm just resting for a while," I said.

"Well, you can't rest here, either. Find someplace else."

The longer this persisted, the better the chance he would finally recognize me. I kept my face down and moved to get up.

"Fuckin' cops," I muttered.

He made it easy. His holster was a type that required the user to unsnap a flap, then push and twist the weapon to pull it out when drawing. It's tricky at first, but simple enough when you go through the academy and the training team has you send several thousand rounds down range while practicing your draw all day. This guy had never undergone adequate training. The flashlight told me that.

I got up slowly and finally showed my face. When he recognized me, I used that shock and added a slight slap to the side of his head with my right hand to draw up both of his hands. I grabbed the handle of his pistol, gave it the required flip, push, and twist, and moved back two steps into a left-handed firing position.

"Listen quickly and answer quickly, or you're dead," I said earnestly. I had him step into the darkness, put him facing the wall, and moved the pistol to my right hand. For the second time tonight, I applied zip cuffs. With the pistol pressed firmly at the base of his skull while I applied the cuffs, I asked, "What are you doing here?"

His breathing had calmed down in the thirty seconds I had taken to secure him. He sounded scared, but he was a little more under control now. "Just pulling security. That's all. I swear."

I rapped him lightly on his head with the butt of the pistol. "Somehow, I don't think that's entirely true. This isn't one of your contracts, is it?"

"No. It's a side thing."

"What are they doing inside?"

His voice got a little higher now. "I don't know. Shady shit, but I don't know. They just pay me to keep people away."

"Why are you outside of my place?"

Almost embarrassed now, exasperated, he said, "That's a separate thing. I don't know why, but my boss wants me to keep an eye on you. That's sorta my patrol area, and he says to do it, so I do it.

"Well, stop it!"

"Hell, no. I don't wanna piss him off. If he says to keep an eye out, I'm gonna keep an eye out. I'll tell him I didn't see you if you want, but I'm gonna do what he says."

"Why? What's his deal?"

"I don't know. I just know he's the boss, and I want to keep my job and not get Limoned."

"The fuck does that mean?" I grabbed the cell phone from his pocket and held it to his face to activate the facial ID. "What's his name?"

"Look, man. You're gonna get me in trouble," he said.

"You don't feel like you're in trouble right now?" I asked, pressing the gun into his head again and, thus, his face into the cinder block wall.

"Yeah, a little, but you seem kinda nice," he said without irony.

"Then what's his name, please?"

"Oscar Braga."

"What's your name?"

Of all he had already given up, he acted as if saying his name gave him the most pain. He said it slowly while looking down. "Cooper."

I looked through the contacts for Braga's information, found it, and took a picture of it with my phone—low-tech and high-tech at the same time. "Coop, to the best of your knowledge, are the people who paid you for your services inside the warehouse right now?"

We both knew he was going to answer. The only question was whether he was debating or making a show of it. He was sure I wasn't going to kill him. He hoped his boss wouldn't find out, and that the people inside the warehouse wouldn't either, or that they wouldn't be in jail soon.

"Yes. Two vehicles. Five guys in the Escalade and a bunch of girls in the van. I didn't see it, but I heard some commotion back there when they parked."

"I thought you didn't know what was going on inside?" I said and gave him another light tap on his head with his gun.

"Ow! Fuck! I didn't *know*, but I kinda knew they were moving some girls around."

Keeping the gun pointed at his midsection, I told him to turn around. I grabbed the spare magazines for his service weapon from his belt and was about to drop the one in the pistol when two gunshots blared out. Cooper's head rocked from the impact of at least one of them. My stomach turned at the fear and the gruesomeness, but instinct drove me to move.

Cooper's killer had apparently noticed us talking about the operation and decided to end the discussion his way. I don't know where he came from, but I was lucky he chose Cooper first, not me. As I sprinted for the cover of the patrol SUV, I heard two more rounds call out, but thankfully, I didn't feel them. Racking a bullet as I ran, I checked behind for the shooter, and he, too, was making a big mistake. If he were smart, he would have pursued me and kept the distance close as he continued to shoot. Instead, he stood near where the fence met the edge of the gate, silhouetted against the lights of the warehouse yard while also being bathed in the yellow gloom of the streetlights. He was a well-lit target and chose to stay that way.

The SUV would provide all the cover I needed for the next few seconds. The shooter was probably waiting for backup before approaching, but if I waited for them, my chances of survival would plummet. I had to act now, so I popped my head around the left side of the car. A shot howled past me. I ducked back but quickly jumped up again around the right, this time coming up firing, aiming for the center mass of the silhouette. If I got him, great, but the goal was to get him to stop shooting and to either turn and run or to backtrack and retreat. Turned out to be a little of everything.

My second shot winged him in his left hip, causing him to spin in that direction. He continued the twist until he was facing away and made a quick bolt for the gate opening. Sadly for him, doing so provided me with a nice, wide target, and I had no problems shooting an armed man, a killer, in the back. The quick fight was over, but I had to move in a hurry. At the moment, the fact that I had again witnessed death, then doled out some myself, didn't seem to bother me.

I ran to Cooper, opening my knife as I went, cutting off the zip-cuffs from his lifeless wrists, and stuffed them in my pocket. Finally, I slipped his pistol into his hand, closing his stiff fingers around the grip. With growing commotion in the yard, I made a risky choice. Peeking around the corner of the neighboring warehouse, I looked into the yard at the trafficker's vehicles. I saw only the van's license plate, but that would do. I repeated it aloud three times and committed it to memory, then turned and sprinted from the scene as footsteps approached from inside the warehouse. Two blocks away, I stopped my flight, confident I wasn't being followed, and called Mike from a payphone I found on the map she sent me. Rare that these dinosaurs still existed. I had no change, so I had to trade a twenty-dollar bill to a guy on the street for what little he had.

"Hey! Speaking to you as your confidential informant again, I have just left the scene where the Trans were to have transferred the girls to their buyers. The buyers are still there, or they were as of a minute ago. I need you to call the police, relay the location, and report the vehicles, and I need you to do it right now."

"Holy shit, Karl! Where the fuck are you? Wait. Gimme a sec. I'll tell Scheffield. He's here." Her voice sounded further away as she addressed someone on the scene. "Detective Scheffield! Wait. Let me through." I heard scratching, as if the phone were being jostled. "Detective Sheffield. I have my C.I. on the phone right now at the transfer point. There are more girls, but you have to move right now." She must have had his attention because her mouth was back by the mic. "Okay, go!"

My first words were the address, followed by what information I had about the two vehicles. I paused for Mike to relay the address to Scheffield and for him to tell the other units so they could head to the warehouse.

"There's also two dead from a shootout." A lie of omission on my part to pave the way for keeping my name clean.

"Are you okay? Did you hurt anyone?"

"Yes, I'm fine. Nothing more therapy and alcohol can't take care of."

"But were you involved?" she asked with a tone that demanded an answer.

"I'll tell you all about it later. Everything." Another lie. "For now, help make sure the girls get safe, okay?"

There was a pause, a decidedly heavy one. "Okay," she finally said.

I could tell it wasn't okay. I understood. I wasn't sure if I wanted to tell her that I had killed someone. How do you have that conversation? I said nothing more about the dead bodies. That stuff could wait until I could craft the narrative a little better. We said goodbye with a promise to chat later.

I was alone again in the streets, my safe space. It was late, but there were still signs of life, mostly cars moving along the major cross streets. I heard sirens in the distance and wondered if they were heading toward the transfer point. The direction matched. The cops would have their hands full soon. Maybe another shootout. Maybe they'd get them all to go peacefully. Wasn't my problem anymore. I'd followed Lorelei's calls and avoided the rocks, but it had been pretty damn close, and I'd had to take another life to do it. It wasn't like squishing a bug, but I wouldn't lose any sleep over it. It had been a me-or-him situation, and I'd chosen him.

I don't even squish bugs, so perhaps that's a bad analogy. My mother was extraordinarily squeamish about that sort of thing, always raising a fuss whenever my father or older brothers killed a crawling or flying creature found in the house. She trained me from an early age to catch a moth or a spider and set it free outside. The habit stuck. The chickens in Idaho would eat up all the bugs in sight, but that didn't bother me in the least. Sometimes, I would catch an insect in the house to throw it to the girls—but I didn't kill it, so that didn't count.

Though there weren't many people walking the street as I made my way home, there were the ubiquitous campers in the dark corners and people sleeping in shadows: no families, as far as I saw, just individuals facing the world alone. Like me, they faced it in their own way, the best they knew how with what they had. I'm lucky that I had better resources. I stole and killed them to get them. Otherwise, where would I be? A burned-out cop in Kansas City, working the street and angry at everyone? That'd be great. I'd have been fired by now or done something regrettable.

Seagulls rested on the streetlights and building tops above. I smelled the salt and muck of the estuary. I was getting closer to home.

32

After a few hours of welcome sleep, I woke at 9 am to two texts and two animated, caffeinated voicemails from Mike. The messages were from earlier, near 5 and 6 am, probably as she cleared out the Tran scenes. The texts, much more recent, had links to two of her online articles about the two separate arrests. She had broken the hell out of these stories, and by being right on top of them and providing the anonymous source, she had an insight no other reporter could access. Other journalists had to wait for a police briefing that had yet to happen or run on what they could glean from the scene.

The articles contained even more information than I knew. She had spent her time well, as the first article dug into the Trans, their past crimes, their connection to the Binhs, who the other two girls from the garage may be, plus an exhaustive report of other murders and missing girls that had occurred in the past few years related to suspected sex trafficking of children in the area. The second article had more to do with the arrest of three suspects at the warehouse where twelve other girls were found. One must have gotten away. The names of those arrested and the two killed by gunfire hadn't been released yet, but it appeared the three arrested, along with their dead friend, were out of Stockton and part of a larger network. The article mentioned a dead security guard, but the name of the company and any relationship between it and the traffickers were absent.

Mike called again as I was finishing up the articles.

"You get any sleep?" I caught myself asking it with more care and familiarity than our short relationship afforded, forgetting she still probably wanted to know whether I was responsible for either of the dead bodies.

"No. None. I'm surviving on coffee and adrenaline, and both are wearing out. I wanted to check in with you before I crash for a few hours. Anything else I should know?"

"Yeah, but it can wait. Come over later if you can, and we'll chat. Xtra will be here soon. It'll be a reunion." I shocked myself with the invitation. I don't know where it came from.

A pause on her end. A thoughtful pause. A pause full of inner debate. "Sure, but I *gotta* crash for a few hours, then do some more work."

"Cool, but you'll be intrigued when I tell you what else happened. This time, *I* need *your* help."

"Cool, but are you gonna tell me about the dead guys?"

A text dinged in my ear. It was from Xtra, saying he'd be there in twenty minutes.

"Yeah. Can do. That was a text from Xtra. He'll be here soon. I'll let you go so I can get ready for him." It may have been true, but it was a convenient cop-out for me.

"Okay," she said softly.

The pause was on my end this time. A hopeful pause. "Alright. Call when you can."

I felt those awkward sensations again, and I wasn't sure I wanted them to happen. I wasn't in the best place in my life, and I had just killed someone. I wasn't ready to bear the emotional weight of someone else yet, regardless of how positive it might be, and I sure didn't feel worthy of anyone else's attention at the moment.

Putting that weight aside, I took the quickest shower possible and made myself presentable for my friend. Through the windows, it was a lovely day outside, so I sat on my stoop and waited. I was met by a beautifully bright sunshine, a light breeze, salt air, and an unexpected old veteran.

"Good morning, Young Sergeant," a smiling Marcus Williams said from across the street.

"Hello, Marcus," I said. "Here for the homecoming?"

"Yessir!" he said as a Silver Nissan rounded the corner. "When I asked you to help out a little, I knew you would, but holy shit. You struck gold!" He held up his right fist in salute, then used it to cover his heart in thanks. It made me smile. It made me feel like I did some good instead of wasting my time drinking.

The Lyft deposited a slowly moving Xtra and his backpack on the curb in front of my door.

"Good morning, Old Sergeant," I said, smiling. "Welcome home."

"And hello to you," he said back sheepishly. "You sure this is okay? Me hanging out for a bit?"

"Hell, yeah!" I said. "It'll be like a sleepover. We'll eat bad food, watch shitty movies, and complain about life and the world."

"I got nothin' to complain about," he said. "They got me on the good shit, so I'm feeling fine."

"Well, friend. The mayor and I have a story for you," I said. "C'mon in."

But Xtra didn't want much of a story. He'd only been out of the ICU for two days and was still pretty weak. The mayor and I gave him a brief rundown of all the trafficking arrests and how many murders of homeless people had potentially been solved. Throughout the four-minute story, we saw his energy wane, so we wrapped up quickly. I showed him his room and helped him settle in. He headed to bed and fell asleep right away.

"So, Young Sergeant," The mayor began, "all this trafficking stuff is well and good, but what are we gonna do about the other thing, the motherfucker out there killing dudes for fun?"

"You'll forgive me if I've been a little busy since we talked about that," I said with a small smile.

He waved as if to shoo me away. "I know. I know, but now that the field is cleared a little, we should see a better pattern from what's left unsolved."

"We can do that. Mike is coming over later, and we're gonna run through it all and see about a new problem."

"What new problem?"

"Not sure yet. You know a guy by the name of Oscar Braga or anything about Altru Security?"

The mayor knew nothing about Braga. He had heard of Altru and seen the vehicles around town, but that was it. Hopefully, Mike would be more helpful. Having a friend who does research and deep dives for a living could be beneficial. We said our goodbyes and promised to stay in touch.

A text from Mike woke me from a short nap. She said she'd come over and visit so we could catch up on the events of the previous night and morning. The sleep was golden, and I could have enjoyed another several hours without a single pang of guilt.

All the caffeine and adrenaline from the early morning must have dissipated from her system by now, but the few hours of sleep invigorated her. She spoke with fervor as she told me all about her long morning: her research of the Tran family's criminal background, the number of abducted children in the area, and their suspected use in trafficking operations, the murdered parents, as well as her interviews with other reporters needing background on what she already knew from her years of research. She was vibrant. Her hands flew as she spoke, her words rose and fell with dramatic inflection as she shared details of the morning, and her eyes stayed bright with the fire of excitement. I couldn't help but be a little mesmerized by how well she was versed in the topics of the underworld and how fervently she spoke about making sure the bad guys got put away. Even though I had faced down men with guns and stomped around in the dark to help make all this happen, she had worked on it for years, waiting for a break to tear down the curtains and bring light to the shadow world. My efforts seemed mild in comparison.

I talked through the events that occurred after I left her at the Trans' garage: learning about Braga, the surveillance, and highlighting Cooper's death. I may have skipped over the part where I killed a guy, the trafficker. We were getting along well, so I didn't want to risk admitting to causing a violent death so early in our relationship. Instead, I painted a picture where Cooper may have gotten off a few shots, but I'd let the police figure out the rest.

She listened, showing no emotion as I spoke. When I was done and had brought her up to the point when I'd called her, shut my trap, sat back, looked for her response, and waited. The machinery in her head was working. Anyone could see that.

Finally, she spoke. "Fuck those guys!" She said it sharply and with gusto. "They were all involved with murders of innocents and kidnappings of young children for use in the sex trade. I couldn't care less if they're dead and burning in hell."

While shocked at her response, the thought struck me that I still hadn't gotten around to asking her what "Survivor" meant in her bio, but I was getting a rough idea. It had something to do with her apathy toward the death of sex offenders.

"You're taking this rather well," I said.

"What's there to take? Bad guys are gone, and the streets are safer. I'm sorry for somebody's parents, but somebody's parents shouldn't have raised piece of shit humans. Fuck them. What have you found out about this Braga guy?"

The quick shift surprised me, and I needed a moment to adjust. My free time had been filled with sleeping and prepping for Xtra's visit instead of tracking him down, so I didn't have much to share about him yet.

She relished this new mystery as if she hadn't done enough already and got right to work on her laptop. Using the scant information I had gathered, Braga's name, company, and phone number, she came up with five news articles in business journals about the lucrative contracts the company had acquired in the past few years. Digging deeper into the subscription information sites she had used, she found even more: county tax records, military history, state DMV info, and a few court filings from his recent past. She found several recent photos of him and tracked down his current residence.

"What should we do about this?" I asked.

"Well, that's all up to you," she said. "At this point, all he's doing is having you watched, but we don't know why. Cooper said he wasn't part of the thing at the warehouse. What do you want to do about it?"

She had a point. We knew little, and there was nothing we could act on. The best thing to do was let it lie while we dug deeper into Braga. I'd keep an eye on the patrols to see if they'd replace Cooper and, if so, whether their patterns or rhythm told me anything, but at that moment, there was nothing to do about it.

"I have to get going," Mike said with a start. "I have another round of TV spots in a couple hours."

Time passed too quickly, and our "work" discussion took longer than I would have liked, leaving no room for anything more personal. As she recounted all that had transpired during her night and morning, she talked a mile a minute, her excitement invigorating and contagious. The scant sleep she'd had recharged her and gave her energy to spare. It was nice; I wanted more, but I understood.

Her next question surprised me almost as much as the change in her body language. She had been tense with excitement and energy, but as she was leaving my space, she stopped, and her shoulders softened.

She turned to ask, "Will you be up later?"

"Yes," I said too quickly. Not *maybe, we'll see,* or *how late?* An easy yes.

"Cool. Maybe we can have a drink and chat some more."

Cool indeed.

33

In the days following the big arrests, Mike Finney had become a minor celebrity on the news shows, thanks to all her appearances. A well-regarded *Atlantic* article won her the most attention on social media. She posted videos online of her interviews on local and national news shows about her role in notifying the police about the Trans and their hideaway, which was enough to make her meager mailing list explode from dozens to more than 500 paid subscribers. When a guest *LA Times* article released deeper details about the Trans and their connections in Sacramento, Stockton, and Long Beach, her followers jumped to over 1000. With each person paying five dollars a month, that meant a significant leap in earnings for a lowly reporter whose primary income came from a weekly paper that ended each quarter, scraping together barely enough advertising revenue to survive one more three-month effort.

Her newsletter began two years earlier to inform subscribers about the politics and economics of the unhoused community in the East Bay, with a strong focus on Oakland. Using the network she'd cultivated on X and on the ground, she learned about people, events, and crimes that would have escaped others' notice, turning them into compassionate and exciting stories that affected those involved. Sometimes, she secured vital services for the unhoused through her government and nonprofit connections. Once, she helped reunite a family whose children had been swept into the foster system. Her efforts didn't merely reunite the kids with their parents; Alameda County also found housing for the family. Her newsletter had weight, and now, finally, it was bearing fruit in the form of dollars, most of which she would put back into the community.

The relationship with Warren was something she didn't see coming, though she felt something rising within her over the past week of interviews and follow-up coffee dates. Their first intimate encounter was unplanned, happening after too much to drink at The Golden Door following another late-night television appearance a week after the Tran arrest. They were sitting at the bar, with Finney doing most of the talking. Warren just smiled and nodded at all the right times, his dark clouds parting to show bits of sun while she told stories from behind the scenes of the interviews. She shared more information with him about her research into the sprawling crime syndicates in other cities and outlined how they were connected. Sometimes the conversation lagged, and they fell into an awkward silence, staring at each other.

"What?" Warren would ask.

"What, what?" Mike would say with faux defiance as she looked away. She always looked back, though. She'd looked at him many times before, but why was it this, the first time she noticed his eye color was so odd? So bold. Greenish blue with a touch of gray. Gray hair at his temples and some in his beard stubble to match. The firm neck and jaw of a soldier, but with some of the softness of someone who was not as angry anymore.

Who is this man? she wondered. *How did he get hold of me? What the fuck am I doing here?*

Mike wasn't sure what sparked her flame for Warren, or where things were headed, but she liked it. He had almost single-handedly stopped a sex trafficking ring. That was both scary and exciting. There was a strong physical attraction, and he had an air of mystery about him that excited her. The ex-cop had some of the elements of a bad boy, yet without the toxic traits she had encountered in too many men. As dangerous as he was, he seemed—safe.

What was his life like a year ago? Five years ago? He's told me a little about his past romances. They all seem normal, a little sad. He seems a little sad.

She wanted him. She sensed he wanted her, but she knew he lacked the communication skills to say it or admit it to himself, so she'd have to make it happen. Finney leaned forward to within an inch of Warren's ear.

"I won't embarrass you in front of your friends, but I'd like to kiss you. Or maybe to have you kiss me, but somebody needs to kiss somebody."

Warren, mouth closed, swallowed and blinked. After a moment, he said, "We should go."

They went. Warren scooped up most of the cash left in front of him, leaving a healthy tip for Ma, and without saying their goodbyes to the crowd, they slipped off their barstools and exited. Once outside, alone, mere moments after the golden door of The Golden Door had shut, the two threw themselves into an embrace, followed by a soft kiss, an exploratory one. A kiss that asked the other if this was okay. Both apparently said it was, and they kissed again, more firmly this time and longer.

The walk home was wordless. Neither wanted to break the spell nor say anything to scare off the other. Mike carefully held Warren's pinky finger so she didn't float away into the air, or he didn't slink into the shadows where it was safer for him. Alone, surrounded by the whole world, their shoulders bumped. Mike wore her grin proudly while Warren kept silent, knowing better than to risk the moment by saying something stupid.

The first kiss in the bedroom was awkward, as was undressing and moving to the bed. There was more laughter than hot passion. Both lovers were out of practice, but willing to forgive the other as they took each step slowly. Most of the communication was nonverbal. There was an occasional "Is that okay?" or "Ouch!", but eventually, they figured it out and made the most of it—like people often do in these situations.

34

Filthy pieces of shit.

Braga was on-site at Hayward Medical Center's emergency room, gauging foot traffic and whether his team was adequately staffed for their needs. At least, that was the story he would tell if anyone asked him what he was up to. What he was really doing, though, was working himself up for another kill.

He had positioned himself in one of the many chairs in the emergency room's waiting area without announcing himself to the admission staff or his security team. He was dressed in his hunting gear: a dark hoodie and sweatpants, though this time he had an extra puffy coat and a knit beanie—camouflage to make the wolf look like a sheep.

He was surrounded by a sea of filth that, if removed from this world, would make it a better place, he thought. Braga had often thought the average member of the human populace was pretty sad, but the more members of the lowest of the low could be removed, the higher the median average would be. The more dreck culled from the shallow end of the gene pool, the better it would be for the rest of humanity.

There was one person, a black man of about forty-five years, sitting in a chair one row away from him, who received most of Braga's ire—though not all of it, as he had enough to spare. He was obese, perhaps 500 pounds, and his black hair hung in dreadlocks that had been allowed to grow untouched and unmanaged for who knew how many years. Though the collective human funk in the waiting room was rich and palpable, this man's personal brand was strong and distinct to the point of being unique and overwhelming. He was dressed in several layers, as if it were preferable to wear all his clothes rather than carry them. It all looked soiled beyond use. Dumped beside his plump ankles were two large, black garbage bags full of his possessions, or maybe garbage he'd gathered from the streets, given how appalling they smelled. Braga wasn't sure what the man was in the ER for, but he would make a wild guess that he didn't have insurance and that his care would come from a fund that might be better spent on a better class of people.

Another person, a crack-thin white man in his fifties with a scraggly hair-and-beard combination like a less well-kempt Ted Kaczynski, sat an aisle of chairs away. He wore the foam slippers given away at the county lockup and clothing apparently scrounged from underpasses and storm drains. He had the scent to match the look. His too-large slacks hung off his form and looked at constant risk of slipping off even while sitting. He reeked of feces. Hopefully, Braga thought, it was his own feces.

A loud disagreement at the admissions desk drew his attention away from Feces Man. A Central American woman, short, dark, overweight, and carrying one baby while corralling a toddler, was arguing with the admitting clerk in loud Spanish. The clerk didn't speak Spanish and was trying to find a co-worker who did. The woman, Braga thought, probably didn't have insurance or any means to pay for anything, yet she wanted someone to take care of her sick little brats. *Should have thought about that before you dragged them up from whatever shithole you came from.*

He'd seen enough. The level of security staffing was acceptable for the day, but he couldn't stomach these mongrels anymore. He slipped out a side door that lacked a camera and stepped into the crisp evening. He wasn't done immersing himself in the scum he could find tonight. At this point, he might have called it a night, gone home, relaxed, and thought of rainbows and puppies—but no. More anger and hatred seethed inside him.

For the past three years, he'd been getting by on a steady diet of kills on an intentionally irregular schedule, and that had been enough to keep his urges in check. A groove for him, but that groove was broken by his failed kill and all the heat brought down with the bust of the trafficking ring. Nine weeks since his last fix, the fat lady in Fruitvale. That kill had been easy but messy, necessitating a risky change of clothing in the alley before he got back inside his truck. Her stench stayed with him the entire drive home.

The plaza entrance to the medical center's ER was a buffet of sin, filth, and a disgusting variety of humans. There, two fat drunks sat fighting over who got to drink the remnants in a forty-ounce bottle of malt liquor. Closer, an old, bearded man who smelled of urine and wet blankets, looked at him with hands outstretched, begging for change. A little further on, a shape curled under blankets and a small tarp, making itself completely comfortable in the public space, as if in its living room.

He wasn't armed with any of his many confiscated weapons. Had he been, it would have taken all his willpower not to start eliminating this filth from the planet, from doing the world a favor right here and now. *Who wants these people to live? Their own families don't care about them enough to take them in. The shelters are already full of scummy people. They're overflowing. Who's going to miss a few?*

Braga walked on. While working, he let his limp take its natural form. While hunting, he hid it and dealt with the back pain, but tonight, in the hospital, he'd been in a different disguise. He was researching, so he wanted to be another character. He accentuated the stumble a little. His natural limp made his right knee and hip dip slightly to the right with every step. With a slight effort, he exacerbated that and made the effect look worse. For a brief moment, he felt sorry for himself, but then thought of his fallen Marines: Goyle, Earnhardt, Hansen, Salazar, and Guarino. He wondered what they would think about him cleaning the streets of filth. Had someone cleaned a particular street in Al-Sejar years ago, they might still be alive.

Enough limping for tonight. Time to get back into the game. He had parked his truck in a quiet residential area a few blocks northwest of downtown Hayward and prepared for a hunt. He'd left the coat and cap in the cab of his truck with the clothing he'd worn on the way to the medical center earlier in the night, wearing his special hunting shoes and taking only a mini-flashlight and a six-inch lock blade. He felt like getting dirty. He was thirsty and had seen enough filth tonight to know he needed to do something about it.

He knew the area well enough because of Altru's many contracts: the medical center, the university up on the hill, and a few industrial sites close to the water. Of course, Tennyson was only a few miles south, but the area wasn't the same as it had been three years prior. It would be hard to make a kill downtown, but he wanted to walk about a little to get a feel for the place, to let his senses soak in the different levels and layers and brands of filth the area had to offer. While there were commonalities among the people, each region had its own flavor. Downtown Hayward had none of the types of folks he'd seen in the RV or tent camps in Oakland or Berkeley. Sure, there were a few scattered tents here and there, but no built-up communities or large ethnic mixes as he'd seen elsewhere. A lower density of filth here seemed to embolden the individuals.

It was nearly 1:30 am as Braga approached downtown from the south. He had parked on the northern side but walked a large semicircle west of downtown, around the residential areas near the BART station, which brought him close to the library. He noticed the campers in the park's bushes and those who had made themselves comfortable in the doorways and under the eaves of the library. The bars were letting out, and the last few stragglers were returning to their cars and heading to their homes, homes the filth didn't have and hadn't earned.

Continuing east, Braga crossed Mission Boulevard and strolled through an alley, looking for movement. Nothing. On the other side, where the alley opened onto Main Street, he turned left and heard a commotion around the corner. The lights and sirens of a police car approached. Without altering his stride, he continued his walk north and crossed the street while unobtrusively spying on what turned out to be a disturbance or fight of some kind happening in front of one of the big nightclubs. In the distance, more sirens were coming. While the action at the club might keep the police busy and distracted while he hunted, it would also keep all the filth on their toes for a few hours. Downtown was burned. Braga decided to ditch this part of town, but getting a kill was still possible elsewhere.

Halfway up the block, he walked through an entrance to a brightly lit public parking lot. A few stragglers from the bars and clubs were leaving, while a few pieces of filth made it their home for the night—or at least their hangout for a while. The temporary residents laid cardboard out in the back-alley doorways of the closed pizza shop and yoga studio, moved their belongings in, and made the space their own.

Crossing back across Mission, he entered a shopping center's parking lot in the corner of downtown. He stayed close to the building on the lot's south side, but as he walked under the awnings, a single vehicle remained: a newish beige Dodge Charger. *That's a cop car.*

Braga saw no one inside the Charger, so he scanned the lot and the adjacent area for movement. Nothing. Leaving the safety of the dark, he approached the car parked under a light too bright for his liking, but like a moth, he had to go to it to confirm his concern.

He should have seen the extra antennae from a distance, but didn't until he got closer. It confirmed his guess. A laptop was mounted inside, and blue lights shone through the front grille. *Not good,* he thought. *Not good at all. Time to pull the plug and hunt another night.* If the other police activity at the nightclub wasn't enough, an unmarked vehicle meant there were detectives out there for some reason. Genuine fear struck him. He knew of the task force and that they did sweeps on an irregular basis. *Did I just walk into one?* He had to get out, and he had to do it now.

Without stopping his approach toward the Charger, he altered his path. Where he had been walking north across the lot, he made a slight right and planned to make another semi-circle around the northeastern part of downtown to get back to his truck. This meant returning to Mission the way he came, but before he made it out of the lot, he noticed the shuffling footsteps of a shapeless person entering the property from the far southwest side and heading for the Charger. Was it the missing detective?

Had they seen him yet? Braga didn't know, nor did he want to take the chance. Instead of risking being seen, he dipped under the awning between the Starbucks and the deli. Once in the dark corner, he turned and watched.

The lone person shuffled across the lot, headed toward a garbage can at a cart corral, made a modest effort to rifle through it, then headed to another garbage can at another corral. This one must have had better prospects, because the lump of a person stayed longer and dug deeper into the waste, looking for whatever this subhuman considered valuable inside a garbage can.

Not a cop. It was another piece of filth wandering the streets, but it was time to get out of the area. Braga waited as the shapeless one wandered off into the bushes to camp or do whatever it was going to do.

After a minute of waiting, he continued retracing his steps back toward the sidewalk along Mission and returned to B Street, away from the direction he was parked. He'd have to loop around a few blocks.

As he rounded a corner, an unmarked police car exited the lot across Mission and parked in the intersection with its blue lights flashing, the driver still inside. This prompted him to make a more obvious about-face than he wanted, but it couldn't be helped. He didn't want to walk by yet another cop or task force member.

Once again, he headed toward A Street through the shopping center's parking lot and turned left onto the big, well-lit avenue. He'd cross in a couple of blocks, wander through a few neighborhoods, and make his way back to his truck. On the A Street sidewalk, he noticed the shapeless person exit the bushes they had entered earlier and shuffle toward him. Either this was a piece of filth who went in there to shit, or a cop out on the streets looking for him or people like him. The next few seconds would tell.

Braga extended the blade of his knife in the uni-pocket in the front of his hoodie, keeping it concealed in his sleeve as the shapeless one shuffled toward him. The next minute would steel his nerves more than any time in his previous three years of hunting trips. *Was it a cop? Could I kill a cop? Would I kill a cop? Should I make the kill and run if it were a piece of filth? No. Too well-lit and exposed. Too many cops around. No. No killing of filth.*

Twenty feet. *Don't make eye contact. Use peripheral vision. Give a wide berth. I've got my hoodie up. My clothes are plain and indescribable, my limp isn't showing, and my hands are hidden.*

Ten feet. *Fuck.* He remembered too late. His shoes.

Eight feet. They made eye contact, and Braga saw the clean face, the sharp eyes—and the radio earpiece. *She's gonna see the shoes and figure it out. She's gonna say something and call for backup.*

Four feet. Braga lifted his head and pointed his whole face at her, distracting her attention from his hand.

35

Detective Sergeant Andrea Cozens parked her vehicle in the brightly lit shopping center lot on A Street near the supermarket entrance in the heart of Hayward's downtown. She was the last one out and about; all the other team members were already on their foot or vehicle patrols. She headed toward the main library and radioed to her team that she had begun. She wore a pair of dark, loose jeans, a dark blue hoodie, and a roomy black winter coat with plenty of pockets for her gear. The stylish ensemble was topped off with an old, knitted dark-green Tam o' Shanter she had found at a secondhand store. To the trained eye, she'd fail to pass for a professional homeless person, but from a distance, in the dark, she'd be just another slow-moving shape in the crisp night.

Eight officers from various departments, including Hayward PD, BART Police, BNSF Railroad Police, and county deputies, were on tonight's task force mission. For the past two years, the task force had been engaging in monthly patrols in different parts of the county, scouring the dark corners of assorted neighborhoods in attempts to stem the tide of violence against homeless communities. Few arrests were ever made in these sweeps, but the public relations value was fantastic, as was the real-time information gained about who was living where.

Tonight's assigned area: the downtown Hayward corridor between A and D Streets running southwest to northeast between 2nd Street and the Burlington Northern Santa Fe lines just short of 880. Here, a good portion of Hayward's professionally unhoused lived and operated. Since the massacre three years back, Tennyson Road has been less popular for transient citizens because of the institutionalized fear of what had happened. In addition to the memory of the killings, the city and county had added anti-homeless architecture and construction to the popular roosting spots in the Tennyson corridor to make it less friendly to that demographic: more and brighter lights, more fencing, and more concrete barriers to keep out potential wanderers or campers.

The homeless community in Hayward was different from those in the larger enclaves and camps in Oakland or San Francisco, with fewer families and more individuals affected by drugs and mental health issues. The population here needed occasional protection. But some were also responsible for low-level property crimes downtown, as well as most of the loitering and littering complaints from businesses and property owners.

The task force wasn't here tonight to work directly with the unhoused. They were here to set themselves up as potential victims. Though there hadn't been a killing that fit their profile since the Trans' arrest, for the past three years, every couple of months, an unhoused person would die a violent death that couldn't be explained as anything other than premeditated murder. The takedown of the Trans and their network cleared a solid 37% of the task force's open cases involving kidnapping and homicides. This still left a lot of unsolved murders, a lot of unanswered questions, and a lot of nervous people in the community. There may have been an active serial killer attacking the least cared-about segment of society, and it was barely on the media radar. *Hell, most cops don't give a shit, either,* Cozens thought.

The previous patrol in Oakland had been uneventful except for a fight the team had to break up before it became too serious, when two males had roughed up another guy rather thoroughly for his bottle of bourbon. The guy had looked in rough shape and was drunker than a skunk, but he'd live. She didn't want her team breaking cover for these people. They let the offenders go, and her teammates told her that the guy toddled off under his own power. The bottle of bourbon, sadly, was broken in the skirmish.

She had made it a priority for the team never to use the term "bum" out loud to describe any of the victims or members of the community they were working to protect. Vagrant, unhoused, houseless, homeless, unsettled, and destitute were all acceptable terms of use, but never "bum."

Fucking bums! Cozens thought to herself as she surveyed the crowd around her. While she and her team weren't about to allow any harm to come to them, if they could help it, that didn't mean she had to like them.

The assignment to the task force wasn't ideal, but it was better than riding a desk all day conducting background investigations on new hires. Before that, she had worked real cases, but that felt like forever ago, before her bad times. She had a couple more years until retirement and could ride this wave until then. Catching their suspect would be a bonus; it wouldn't hurt her career if they didn't. She and her team would do all that's expected of them. *It's all a PR move, anyway.* Each new murder or kidnapping had its own team of detectives working on it as best they could, so there was little the task force could do for any individual case.

But she was still a cop and a proud one, too. She had her mission and would do it whether she liked it or not, whether she liked this demographic or not. She enjoyed her core team and the stringers they picked up from other departments, who all came with high energy and enthusiasm. If she had to be out past midnight hunting a killer, she would do her best to find the killer.

The recently wrapped-up Tran case was another issue altogether. That was public service at its finest—if not too late for some of the parents. Girls were rescued, numerous open/unsolved cases were wiped off the board, and it allowed her team to more clearly see a pattern in their potential serial killer.

The Oakland Police Department had its hands full at the garage where the Trans had held the five girls. Despite Donald Vo and the Tran cousins saying nothing, there was ample evidence gathered from cell phones, computers, and scraps left by previous girls who had passed through the stash house on their way to who knew where. OPD continued with the homicide charges on all they could put together, but the FBI had taken over the trafficking angle.

Of the five girls found at the Trans's stash house, no living family was found for any of them, and they'd become wards of the State of California for now. *Who knows what would become of them,* but Cozens thought it sure beat what would have lain ahead of them otherwise.

Here, tonight, now, her view of humanity and her mission wasn't rosy. Six of her team were on foot patrol, and one of her two mobile units was in the public lot only a few hundred feet away. She took a stationary position, sitting on one of the landscaping retaining walls on B Street outside The Hall of Foam Lounge, a decent pub saddled with a location favored by derelicts and professional addicts who used the adjacent garbage dumpsters as forage pits and the many doorways as shelters. Her perch allowed her to watch the parade of all-stars stroll through the night. There were still revelers hopping from bar to bar, ignoring her because she looked too much like someone who should be ignored, but peppered within them were those she was here to protect— whether they deserved it or not. She had to remind herself that over the past three years, dozens of their number had been murdered, and no one had yet been held to account for it.

These were her people for the night. The old man stepping out the basement stairwell, tying up his pants like he had just taken a dump. The short black man moving from ashtray to ashtray looking for cigarettes with any life left in them, while checking the gutters for discarded gems. The two drunk warriors play-fighting loudly across the street in the public parking lot, yelling at each other about the Las Vegas Raiders. Yeah. These were her people. These and many more.

She got up and began walking again, this time going through the public parking lots and darker alleys. Her police gear was limited, but she had enough to keep her safe: cell phone, service weapon, pepper spray, expandable baton, flashlight, and, most importantly, her radio. This was in her coat pocket, but she wore an earpiece and a lapel microphone to keep the device out of sight. Cozens told her team she would camp on a park bench across the street from the city's new, shiny library.

The new building provided enough light to illuminate the park and most nearby areas in the underbrush. Not enough to see everything, but plenty to know she wasn't alone. Two other campers had already made hasty shelters in the bushes near her, one using a sleeping bag that looked to have had better days and the other a series of blankets and tarps, the latter strung from the branches using ropes and bungee cords. She kept her eyes out for other movements in the park, but didn't see any.

This part of Hayward had no bars or restaurants, so those walking the streets were either patrons returning to their cars or the houseless, high, or drunk off whatever they could get, however they could get it. There had been two recreational walkers mixed in. Those out for late-night strolls distinguished themselves by the briskness of their steps and carried flashlights or reflectors. She kept an eye out for anyone else who looked suspicious, anyone wandering out of place with no discernible reason or purpose, attracting attention by doing nothing other than walking.

With the bars now closed, any movement on the streets was noticeable. From her spot on the bench, Cozens listened to the other team members check in from various locations in their chosen areas: one along the train tracks, another at the BART station, one more in the business area east of Mission, and two others downtown, in alleys and doorways like hers. As the night progressed, they updated each other on their movements and where they'd stay static. If a person of interest came on someone's radar, a call would go out, and one of the radio cars, RoGo in the parlance of their team, would circle nearby and be ready to lend a hand. That had happened only twice tonight, and nothing came of either.

In one case, Agent Dave Terrel of the BNSF Railroad police had his eye on someone wandering the edges of the tracks with a flashlight, moving slowly while looking along where the railbed's gravel meets the dirt foundation. He called for one of the RoGos to stay close, but as the person neared, Terrel got a good look at the guy, an older black man searching for used bottles and cans to recycle. He wore what had become known as the "uniform," a dark hoodie, black pants, and black shoes. Sure, a relatively common wardrobe choice, but something to get excited about when combined with the location and situation.

The second instance was a young man looking to break into cars in the main parking lot by the movie theater. He was in the "uniform," but this wasn't enough to break cover. Instead, a call was made to dispatch, a patrol unit was sent in, and the team stayed away from the area. *Hell*, Cozens thought when she heard it play out on the radio, *the whole downtown area would probably be quiet with as much police coverage as we have.* In one of the bars downtown, minutes before closing, a drunken brawl had brewed up and spilled outside, necessitating three units from Hayward PD. They came with lights and sirens wailing, letting the whole area know they were there. After removing those involved in the fight, one unit stayed put to keep an eye on the patrons and hangers-on who remained. Since then, though, the night had been quiet.

Cozens headed northwest on Watkins Street and through the same lot she had parked earlier in the night, swinging near to ensure all her windows were intact. When she did this, movement caught her eye.

Across the lot, under a corner awning where a coffee shop met a deli, a man dressed in black entered the shadowed area. It was nothing, she was sure. Probably nothing. Well, maybe something. She'd seen people pop in and out of shadows all night long. She'd seen people dressed in black all night, many in hoodies. But this one had no logo. It was over a hundred feet away and only in view for an instant, but she was sure it was plain black. What also stood out was that the person wore it with the hood up and over their head. Not a sign of guilt, she thought, but not nothing.

The detective and task force leader was in plain view in the middle of the lot. Had she opened her car door or even gotten her keys out, she would have given away her identity as something other than a homeless drifter. Instead, hoping to salvage her cover, she kept walking toward a garbage can in the lot next to one of the shopping cart corrals. All the carts had been gathered and put inside for the night, and fortunately, the garbage had been taken out, so all she needed to do was make a quick, cursory glance inside the bin without digging through any old, warmed-up refuse. After spending enough time on what she hoped appeared to be an actual forage, she moved on from that can to another across the lot.

As she walked, she kept half an eye on the dark corner where the mystery person had gone, if anywhere. So far, he was staying put. This other can was stuffed with bags bursting with refuse, so whether she liked it or not, it gave her more time to rummage through it, ostensibly looking for treasure but still glancing occasionally toward the dark corner.

On the radio, Har Nanak in RoGo 2 said he was returning to the road after chatting with the HPD unit outside the action-filled pub from earlier. He was nearby, and the team was on a private channel so that they could be informal with each other.

"Nanak," Cozens whispered into her small lapel mic as she pressed the button attached to a wire tucked down her sleeve. "Stay in that main lot. Stay close. I have someone I'm keeping my eye on."

"I can do that. Let me turn around here on Main, and I'll park there," came the response from Nanak, the first Sikh detective in the county's history and the first to be allowed to wear his turban on duty. *A great detective, but it made him shit for undercover work,* Cozens had thought when she first met him.

If staying in the shadows and lurking was good for the stranger in the corner, Cozens could do the same thing. Adjacent to the front of the store, near the sidewalk, was a landscaped area with overgrown shrubs that provided concealment from the street and the lot. Provided no one else was already camping out there, it would let her do the same thing as the stranger: spy on the lot.

She was in luck. No one had yet occupied the shrubs. Once inside, she moved in deep enough to remain unseen from the parking lot, then turned around and focused her gaze on the darkest spot of the corner, hoping to find movement, hoping she hadn't missed his egress while she was turned away.

Time passed. The Hayward night scene moved along quietly and slowly. A few night zombies shuffled by in the distance, and further off, a train rattled through, but there wasn't any movement from the dark corner. Until there was.

The person decided that enough time had passed, and the nearby area was safe enough to move without any more eyes spying on him. Cozens assumed at this point it was a him until proven otherwise. He moved like a man, and it looked like he had a limp, but only sometimes. He stayed under the awning as he moved along the front to the sandwich shop, slipping around the corner and heading toward Main Street, back toward the heart of downtown and away from her. If she wanted to follow him, she'd have to break cover, literally and figuratively, and run across the lot to have a chance of catching up with him; the distance was so great. Instead, she had an idea, but it would require her to burn RoGo2.

"Nanak!" she said into her mic. "Put your blue light on right now and come out onto Mission. Park right at the intersection on B Street. Do it gently, but do it right now!"

Within ten seconds, blue police lights reflected off the tops and sides of buildings to the east. Ten seconds later, Nanak's vehicle came out of the lot and made a left, heading south on Mission Boulevard. She lost it soon after it turned, but based on where the blue lights reflected, he stopped where she asked.

"Okay," Nanak's voice came into her earpiece. "That was fun. Now what?"

"Stay there. Pretend to be looking south, but glance behind, too. You see anyone, or did you see anyone when you pulled out?"

"Yeah, there was someone on the opposite sidewalk. He's probably behind me now."

"Okay," Cozens said, relieved. "Stay there for a few. Let me know if you see him or if he passes you. I'll let you know more in a minute. It might be nothing. Dude just gave me the heebie-jeebies."

Sometimes, radio silence can reflect excitement and electricity. If the team leader got the heebie-jeebies, everyone's ears would perk up, and the whole team could feel the temperature rise.

As she hoped he would, the blue light made the stranger double back and retrace his steps into the supermarket parking lot. He walked a little faster than when he had departed, and this time, he looked as if he had a slight limp on his right side. No. Maybe not. He smoothed out his walk as he moved further into the lot. Still, this guy made her feel funny. Something was off.

She pressed the button. "Who is close by? RoGo1, where you at?"

"BART Station parking lot," Hayward Police Detective Carlton Stillman said. "I can head out to Grand and park by A Street.

A Street was the main east-west artery, the same one that ran alongside the landscaped area where Cozens was camped. From one end of town, it led to Interstate 580 and out to the valley, and from the other, it brought you to 880, the main artery on the east side of the bay and the main escape trail for most of Hayward's out-of-town troublemakers.

As the stranger quickly made his way, Cozens was now sure it was a man. She had to decide what to do. The man wasn't a suspect for anything, so there was no reason to roust or stop him, but she might be able to slow him down enough to get a good look and take his measure. Based on his trajectory, he was coming her way and about to turn left onto A Street after exiting the lot. She had to wait for him and prepare for his arrival.

She turned around and speed-walked along the side of the building until she reached the far end. Checking that the stranger hadn't yet made his left turn onto A Street, she exited the shrubbery, made her way to the sidewalk, and headed back toward where she expected the stranger to appear, taking on a beggarly shuffle as she had back in the lot. He turned up where and when she hoped.

He came around the corner onto the sidewalk, wearing the complete uniform: a black hoodie, oversized black sweatpants, and black sneakers. She couldn't tell if his T-shirt and socks were black, but if she had to make a guess, she would say yes. As she walked in the yellow gloom of the city's streetlights, something about the man's approaching shoes looked odd—a flap or something.

His body language changed when he turned the corner and came closer, not much, but enough to be noticeable. His shoulders tensed, and he put a pause in his stride. Stiffness. Though she couldn't determine his age, she could tell he wasn't young, nor was he old. He moved with some strength and litheness. Probably Caucasian, six feet, perhaps 200 pounds, but because of the loose clothing and hood pulled over his head, he was otherwise unidentifiable. He made an effort to avoid eye contact, while she made an effort to soak him in.

Those shoes, though. Cheap sneakers. Black, no logo, two Velcro straps, and cuts at the front that allowed the tips of his toes to hang out. They didn't look new, but they also didn't look like they'd been on the street for months, traded from bum to bum. *What's wrong with those shoes?*

As much effort as the stranger made not to look at her, she had to make an equal effort not to look at him. *The shoes. What's with the shoes?* When they found the original uniform in the recycling bin by the Korean butcher after the attack at Jack London Square, the shoes had no cuts or slits. They were similar, cheap black sneakers, but with laces, size 11. Other than the Velcro and the cuts, the uniform was the same. What else? At the crime scenes, some of the suspected killer's footprints were size 10. Others were 11, yet others still were size 12. The task force thought this meant they were looking for different people, but instead, it might have been something as simple as this. She bet these shoes were size ten, and this was their guy, but she put it all together too late to save her life.

As she drew even with the man, they made eye contact. She didn't see him withdraw the knife from his hoodie pocket. It was just there. It came from nowhere and into her throat too quickly to react to. Cozens felt the searing pain of the blade enter, twist, and leave just as quickly, slicing her trachea and cutting off her ability to breathe.

Her hands flew up to her throat in a weak effort to stem the bleeding and to somehow magically fix herself to breathe again. She didn't expect the pain to be so great. She didn't think fear and panic would strike so hard. She did expect more blood. Instead of a steady stream from her wound, it shot out as she coughed and choked, gasping for air, crimson gushing through her fingers and down over the pavement.

Falling to her knees and leaning forward, the blood continued flowing in earnest. She dropped her hands to her side, caught her fall, accepted her fate, and let gravity take her soon-to-be lifeless body to the ground.

36

Two feet. Withdrawing his left hand from the hoodie pocket, Braga brought the knife up in a swift strike to the cop's throat, twisting and wrenching it free in one motion.

Without hesitation, Braga took off in a sprint down the sidewalk, faster than he'd run in a while, and it made his limp show. He'd be hurting tomorrow; that didn't matter right now. When he spotted the flashing blue lights of yet another unmarked police car a few blocks ahead, pain tomorrow became an even less important detail. Escape was the only consideration now.

Even this late at night, there was traffic to contend with on A Street. When a small group of three cars approached, he ran in front of them, hoping to cause an accident that would slow potential pursuers and drain resources sent to the scene. As he weaved through the cars, he looked over his right shoulder to see if traffic was clear in the opposite lane. The formerly shapeless figure he now knew to be a female cop was sprawled on the concrete, clutching her throat in a futile effort to save her life. There was no way she could have called for backup, so they must have been watching. They must have been close. He had to move.

Making a right turn on Montgomery Avenue, a darkened road perpendicular to A Street, he lengthened his stride, which gave him extra speed but made his limp even more pronounced. Tomorrow, he would pay for that dearly. The turn gave the pursuing cops a new direction to radio in. As the cop car hadn't yet made the turn, he had a few seconds to act. Instead of going straight on Montgomery, he immediately headed toward a darkened area of a parking lot for a small medical building. The building faced A Street, but the lot opened onto Montgomery and the street to the west, Peralta Street.

He crouched in the darkest corner he found while the cop and vehicle passed by less than twenty-five feet away. The subterfuge wouldn't last. More cops would come. More radios and flashlights. Maybe even dogs. Braga left the temporary safety of the dark and continued his flight. He smelled what he wanted: metal and tar. The BART tracks lay on their overhead railways within a hundred feet, while two lanes of the BNSF rail lines ran parallel on the ground. A fence was erected on both sides to keep people out, but the urban wildlife still found a way. Tonight, he was the urban wildlife. Braga guessed that previous drifters had created trails. He was right. At the first place he checked, where the cyclone fence butted against a cinder block wall, someone had cut through the wires to create an accessway to the tracks that served as a superhighway for the homeless moving from town to town. It served him well tonight as a way to avoid the pursuing police cars, at least for a few minutes. Anyone on foot would still be able to hunt him, but first, they'd have to find the opening.

The gravel bed of the train rails would make enough noise should anyone else walk on it, so Braga wasn't worried about someone sneaking up on him. Conversely, this meant he'd be making plenty of noise if he wasn't careful. Slowing to a jog and staying on the part of the track bed where there was more dirt than gravel, Braga's eyes adjusted to the dark. He saw the outline of an occasional tent or camp along the sides of the throughway, but no signs of life within them. *How fun would it be to make a quick kill of one of these guys?* An entertaining yet intrusive thought. Exciting but impractical.

He was running as silently as possible, but the sounds of his footsteps and heavy breathing were too loud and would mask the wail of sirens or the footsteps of cops in pursuit. He stopped, waited, and listened. He needed to calm himself. He needed to gauge the world around him. His lower back was on fire. His lungs were bursting.

Creosote from the railroad ties overpowered all other scents. Hints of dirt and metal filled the air, too, but these were bare wisps of ghost scents compared to the strong smell of the preservative that kept the railroad ties from rotting. No other sounds were on the tracks ahead or behind, though sirens intensified from the nearby neighborhoods to the east.

His truck was only a few blocks away. He had to decide whether to take a longer, indirect route to avoid any eyes looking for him or make haste and get to his truck now before more vehicles arrived to help in the hunt. Braga's phone was in his truck, so he was unable to listen to the scanner app. The sooner he could get to that, the sooner he could check patrol movements. The task force would have been on a private channel, which was why he hadn't heard them while checking the scene, but by now, all units would be on the main channels, coordinating their hunt to find who they all hoped was the man behind the Tennyson Massacre. They weren't sure yet, but they were right, and Braga wouldn't make tonight his last free night.

Braga continued north along the track until the fence ended, and both sides opened onto the next street, Sunset Boulevard, a mixed-use area with homes, a few small businesses, apartment buildings, and a high school. All this guaranteed ample parking, plenty of vehicles to hide between, dark and shady spaces under trees for his truck to hide from the streetlights, and enough round-the-clock activity that vehicular movement by itself wasn't strange. It was another two blocks until Braga reached the street where he had parked. His truck was less than 200 feet away.

Braga grabbed the key fob secured to the underside of a wheel well. His car alarm was modified to turn off and unlock silently without turning on any lights. Same with the dome lights inside. His truck was dark, and the pine scent of his air freshener welcomed him. He tore off his clothes and washed himself with the baby wipes and alcohol gel as quickly as he could. Grabbing his alternative outfit, a simple white T-shirt, jeans, and sneakers, from the bag on the passenger seat, he dressed and stuffed the discarded hunting outfit inside the bag. *Damn! I should have tossed the knife. It's covered in cop blood.* He'd have to lose it along the way, and as soon as possible. Reaching under the seat for his phone, he opened the scanner app and tuned in to the Hayward police channel. Dressed and ready to go, he was wary of heading into a trap.

He had no idea how many units would be involved in the hunt, but with a downed cop, every patrolman in the area would respond. There would be at least four on duty in this part of Hayward tonight, plus the two extra unmarked cars he'd seen. Other units would come from the Alameda County Sheriff on patrol in San Lorenzo and Castro

Valley, the San Leandro Police, and the California Highway Patrol. This would worsen, so the sooner he got out, the better.

Listening to the traffic on the app for clues, he pulled his truck into the street. Three traffic stops were happening at that moment, each in various stages of progress, but their location hadn't been called. What he did know was that each car would likely be assisted by another patrol unit, which meant as many as six units would be tied up, the second unit providing backup or overwatch for the first, regardless of department. This meant he might have an easier time than he feared. *Good.* Fewer eyeballs looking in the dark corners for him. He drove with a larger cushion of comfort.

They couldn't pull him over without him giving a reason because no crime had been committed, so as long as he drove safely and sensibly, he'd be fine, even if he had police cars up his ass. The thing, though, was to avoid having police cars up his ass.

"Negative." A nameless officer said on the scanner app. "The driver was female and had her kid in the back. Truck was clean."

The cop repeated the rough address of the stop near downtown on Foothill. Since that one was clear, two more units were now on the road, looking for him. He had planned to head back to A Street to enter 880, but that was where the two newly free units were. It was a risky idea to begin with. Instead, he headed in the other direction on a minor road through the suburbs. He didn't see the blue lights until he turned the corner, and any deviation from his course would have looked suspicious. Braga looked at the scene and relaxed a little. On the opposite side of the street, a CHP cruiser had another extended-cab truck pulled over, with the driver standing outside. The man was wearing a black hoodie.

The truck was like mine. This wasn't a coincidence. They were looking for an extended-cab truck like his and a driver in a black hoodie or a sweater. The trooper conducting the stop didn't pay Braga any attention, but his backup did. The HPD officer eyeballed the truck and then stared directly at Braga. They maintained eye contact for three seconds as the cop calculated priorities. Then, with Braga not making the cut, the patrolman turned his attention back to covering the trooper and the driver at the nose of the patrol car.

With a bag of evidence and a bloody knife with him in the cab, he should have been scared, but it all happened too quickly for fear to take hold of him. He even waved at the Hayward cop when they made eye contact, which probably helped put the HPD officer at ease. That, and already being engaged with one stop, meant waving down another was too much work, especially when he no longer fit the profile and hadn't made any violations. *Let me just get the fuck outta here.* The quickest way was to go back through more cops, so he followed the minor feeder road through the neighborhood until a bigger street led to Interstate 238. That would take him around the heart of Hayward and onto the freeways, which would be the quicker way out of this mess. He'd take the long route home, following all the traffic rules and being the safest, most law-abiding driver any law enforcement officer had ever seen.

He recapped what they knew: that he wore dark hoodies and drove a truck. Unfortunately, the most damning detail was that they saw him running; they saw the limp. There was no way to hide that. He was convinced no one had gotten a good look at his face, though, so he could rest easy about this evening. While in action on his hunts, only one person had seen his face, and that was the man in Jack London Square who was now living in the produce market. If he could avoid this net of police cars, he would have to do something about the only witness who might point to him in court and say, "That's him, Your Honor. That's the man who attacked me!"

Braga pulled out his phone, which was an unsafe act while driving, but it seemed minor compared to having all his walls caving in.

"Hey! That job? Do it as soon as you can!"

37

Coffee choices were a point of contention for Mike and me in our growing relationship. Personally, I'm happy sipping whichever brand is on sale after it's run through a regular machine. On the other hand, she found this a savage habit and wouldn't spend another moment at my place without rectifying it. Yesterday, she brought a French press, an electric water kettle, and a pound of freshly ground premium coffee. I didn't think the change would take hold. I loved my sugary creamers, but appreciated the effort and fuss.

Within a short time, she had made my loft area her de facto office. I had great lighting for any quick social media video she needed to create, and faster broadband, too. In addition to the praise she had received in the media and from the public, she had also received her share of death threats from those who view the unhoused as garbage to be eliminated in any way possible. The threats came via email, social media, and voicemail, but it was prudent for her to spend more time in my secure place than in the easily accessible offices of *The East Bay Hub*. This suited me just fine. I enjoyed her company, and she seemed to enjoy mine. In the afterglow of all the excitement from the Tran arrests, we'd found some peace in the fact that she made a difference in the lives of a community that had been overlooked and preyed upon.

And me, because I finally did something of value other than drink all day and spend my dirty money.

I also had Xtra to attend to. The first two days were nothing but sleep for him, with an occasional few minutes of chatting and eating. After that, he was well enough to shower and walk around alone. He did his laundry and spent much of his time conversing with the mayor and us when he visited. My quiet home quickly became a modest hub for socializing and community activism. I kinda liked it. What I didn't like, what none of us liked, was that we still had a serial killer of unhoused people on the loose in the area.

We were stuck with the same, albeit detailed, information we had from before. Nothing new. What was new, for me at least, was the Braga wrinkle. After getting the name and his number from Cooper, Mike and I did what we could. I only learned the basics: Regional Manager for Altru Security, former Marine, lived in Oakland, no arrests, was in the news for booking lucrative contracts for his company, and occasionally made splashy arrests at his contract locations.

Could his interest have been as simple as keeping tabs on excitement in the area of his contracts? I lived five blocks from one of his sites, but until Xtra got attacked, their vehicles were never around. Now they pass or park nearby more often. In fact, I'd bet there was one parked down the road right now.

I woke earlier than usual because Mike said she was coming by for coffee. She was a little late, so I checked my phone to see if I had missed a call. There was a text a few minutes after 4:30 am.

> Cozens is dead. Call me when you
> get this.

Having no other information, I couldn't process it, so shock and surprise were my only options. I called her immediately. She answered after three rings.

"What happened?" I asked.

"Cozens got stabbed last night while on a task force sweep. They won't tell me too much officially, but one of the guys on the team says it was a dude she was looking at on the street. No one really knows what went down, but one of the team saw it happen from a couple hundred feet away. He says she got stabbed in the throat as she approached him, then he ran, and they lost him in the dark. They're going with the idea it was the Tennyson Killer." Mike spoke tersely as if she were relaying a report, which, I guess, she was. "I started getting all sorts of notifications about it around 3 am. I'm still in Hayward at the scene. There's a shitload of cops here."

"Well fuck!" I said heavily. "I'm sorry. I know you knew her well."

"Not that well. Just from crime scenes and interviews and such. Man! I saw her a few days ago at that garage. She was so fucking excited to get those guys."

"What can I do? Can I help in any way?" I was impotent here, but that seemed the right thing to say.

"No. I don't know. No. There's nothing to be done. I'm gonna wrap up here soon after I put out this last article. I've talked with a few cops off the record, and I have a good idea of the big picture. She paused, and in the silence, I felt a tone shift. "Hey, I don't think I'll be able to swing by this morning."

"I totally understand." I did, but I was selfishly disappointed.

She ended the call after telling me about her busy day ahead. I think she sensed my disappointment and tried to be kind.

I returned to bed for a few more hours. Upon waking, I was saddened anew by the loss of another cop, but even more, I was worried about the mental health of her workmates. I'd lost a few brother and sister cops, and it was always hell on me. I'd seen some older cops brush it off like it was nothing, but fuck those old dinosaurs. I'd never wanted to become so accustomed to that kind of loss that I felt nothing. I might have stayed in bed a while longer, but without Mike around, there was no point. Mike. It was odd for me to have a lover named Mike, but here we were. It felt natural. Mike. My lover, Mike. Mike, the friend of a dead cop.

I spent a few hours doing some chores and watching the news until I heard Xtra moving around in his kitchenette downstairs. I got dressed and joined him. He was in his "jammies," as he called them: hospital slippers, gray sweatpants, and a black t-shirt, his normal wear around the house. He'd been outside for brief walks more recently, now that he was more mobile. He mostly slept and spent time on the older laptop I'd lent him. I had wiped it clean, prepared it for a new user, set him up, and he was off. He quickly transferred all the accounts from his phone and the cloud and made it his own. Fine by me.

"Hey, Boss," he said as I descended the stairs. He raised his cup of tea as a salute. "You're lookin' good and refreshed."

"Feeling good and refreshed, friend," I said with more cheer than I felt. Then, dourly, "Did you know Detective Cozens? Cop from the task force?"

"I've heard the name, but I never met her. Why? What's up?"

"She got killed last night in Hayward on one of their patrols. Details are still a little muddy, but some are thinking it's your boy again."

X deflated and leaned back onto the sofa. "God damn!" he said softly. "I'm sorry to hear that, but now, maybe the cops will give a shit."

That was harsh but not incorrect. Wanting to change the subject, I asked, "When Mike had you look through those unsolved homicide cases the other day, you said none of the people were familiar. You were pretty high at the time from the pain pills. Since you're in a better state now, you wanna try again. I can share her Google stuff about all the unsolved cases that fit what we're looking for."

"Yeah. Don't know what good it'll do, but I can try again. Send it on over."

"I also wanna send you what I have on this guy from Altru Security. They're the ones who have been poking around here since your thing, and I can't figure out why. You know anything about them?"

"No. I mean, I seen the cars around town, but I never dealt with them in any way. What they want with you?"

"That's what I'd like to know. I know they're not here to keep us safe."

From my upstairs computer, I sent him the map Mike had shared with me and the folder on Braga and Altru. My hopes were low, but I figured it couldn't hurt to have another set of eyeballs going over the information. I was never a full-time detective in Kansas City, but I did my fair share of investigations in the military. The solution often lies within the facts you already know. It was a matter of correctly putting all the pieces together to create the best picture. Maybe Xtra could look at the pieces differently from the rest of us and see something no one else had. He'd gone back to sleep, but I had told him it'd be there waiting for him whenever he woke.

I had some free time since Mike was out working and Xtra was out for a while. I was hungry, and The Golden Door sounded good. My stomach churned happily at the thought of Spicy Green Bean Chicken and a few drinks.

The late summer evening was cool enough to need a coat. Lots of people wearing one, but having spent a few years in Idaho, I knew what real cold can feel like. This near-brisk evening didn't slow me down. It was pleasant, and I didn't have to worry about carrying a flashlight or bottle of booze with me tonight. I had no plans for wandering later.

A block away, I spotted an Altru patrol vehicle, another SUV parked around the corner from my home. Its driver, someone I hadn't seen before, stared at me, then looked away as if I wasn't there. Over the past few days, I had gotten the pattern down of when Cooper would be there and avoided coming or going out the front door during those times. It was silly sneaking in and out of my own place, but it messed up their surveillance. With Cooper dead, I had hoped the surveillance would stop. This new guy was a wildcard. I decided I should introduce myself.

I stepped off the curb and crossed the intersection to head directly toward him, but apparently, he didn't like that. He quickly started his engine and made an even quicker U-turn to avoid a conversation. I stood mid-street, stunned.

38

Warren had let Xtra use an older laptop at his warehouse. He made the most of it by syncing and updating his Google and Gmail accounts, so he could forgo the library or rely on his smartphone for everything. Now, he could really get some stuff done. He updated his VA profile to reflect his current medical status and asked Merritt Community Hospital to forward records of his most recent visit to the VA so his files would be complete and up to date.

Despite their estrangement, he emailed his ex-wife to update her on what happened to him. He made sure she spread the word that he was healthy and safe. Sandra. He remembered how they met. He remembered how her father hated him at first. He remembered their first time making love and how awkward it was. He remembered how much better they got at it. If anyone were around, they'd have seen Mister Xavier Travers wearing his biggest smile in days.

Sandra. He remembered the fights he had started. He remembered the pain he had caused. He remembered the drugs and addiction. He remembered all his lies. Xtra's smile had disappeared. He knew they were too far apart ever to make something happen again—but it was nice to think about. He was just happy he could communicate with her a little now that he was clean. That would have to be it.

Soon enough, he fell down the YouTube rabbit hole. Several rabbit holes, in fact: military history, nature programs, veterans' benefits, free training for veterans, technical training certificates, and, most interestingly, online yoga for veterans with trauma. A series of videos where veterans discussed their personal and medical issues and how yoga helped them work through their problems. One of the vets, an older Air Force Technical Sergeant, looked at the camera and said that yoga saved his life. His emotional and physical pain had teamed up with his addictions to create so much of a demon that the man almost chose death by suicide rather than continue with life for another day. *I gotta try that stuff.*

Finally, he opened the folder and map Warren had sent him. On the map, a pin marked each unsolved murder that fit the criteria for the suspected killer they were hoping to find. Most were clustered in the East Bay of Alameda County, with a few scattered across the greater Bay Area. Clicking a pin brought up a brief description of the victim and a few known facts about the case. A double-click took him to a view-only document that displayed information from the police report and other details.

Xtra only bothered to click on the pins in the areas he frequented. There were twelve pins, eleven murders in the territory he knew, plus one pin for his attack. He worked his way through them but didn't recognize any names or faces. That didn't mean he didn't care about them. They were strangers, but they were still his people, and he wanted to help catch the son of a bitch who killed them.

It had been a while since he'd spent so many days in one place, and he loved it. Yes, he was a little embarrassed about burdening

Warren, but his buddy seemed to enjoy his company, and Lord knows he needed someone around to keep his head up. *Hell, now he's got me and Mike with him.* Access to showers and hot water for tea made Xtra feel like he'd struck it rich. He got up to put on his electric kettle. Mike had brought one for him, too, when she found out he was a tea drinker. She also brought an assortment of teas he'd never heard of but was more than willing to try.

With hot tea in hand, Xtra sat back on the couch and looked again at the laptop, this time searching through the folder regarding Altru and Braga. There were note files and some images in there. The note files held links to articles about Braga and Altru that Xtra didn't bother to read, but he did click on the images. Many were the patrol vehicles parked in the neighborhood, which Warren had taken as a cause for concern. One of the image files was labeled "oscar.braga1/img." Xtra clicked to open it and almost dropped his mug.

He pointed and said out loud, "That's the motherfucker...," before remembering no one was there. There was no doubt. Same face. Same eyes. Xtra would know. They were locked together for only a few seconds, but it felt like an eternity in which Braga's blade had found a home in Xtra's gut.

His breathing quickened and grew shallow. His heart beat so fast and so hard that he felt it in his ears. He thought *that was why Altru was watching the place. They were watching it because of me.* He grabbed his phone and called the mayor.

39

The restaurant side of The Golden Door held a dozen patrons, all enjoying the best Chinese fare Oakland could muster. The bar was held down only by Ma, Fred, me, and Duke. Fine by me. I needed a few minutes of quietude to calm my mind.

The beer was good, but it didn't wash away my concern about the Altru driver. After his U-turn, I didn't head straight to the Door. Instead, I was shaken up and angry enough that I walked a few blocks through the neighborhood to calm my nerves and see whether the patrol SUV had moved to another area or left the neighborhood altogether. I saw nothing. He must have left.

"You heppy?" Ma asked.

"I'm sorry, Ma. What?"

"You heppy? With girl. I see you other night with girl. Look heppy."

"Yes, Ma. So far, very happy. She's nice."

"What her name?

"Mike. Her name is Mike."

"Mike! Aiya! Mike a boy's name. She definitely a girl, though."

"Yes, she is. Definitely a woman, Ma. A very nice one. Mike is short for Mikayla."

"She girlfriend? I don't want you to have girlfriend and be heppy. You heppy and drink less. I'll go out of business." She laughed.

"No, Ma. If I get happy, I'll still drink enough to keep you in business. You won't have to close your doors."

My spicy chicken arrived and was as perfect as I had hoped. Twice during the meal, I received notifications of movement at my front door, as if someone had rung my bell, but both times, the screen was clear. Odd, but not odd enough to delay my meal for long. Xtra was home. In fact, he should have been up and around by now. I would head back soon to see if he found anything helpful in the stuff I sent him.

For the walk home, I took an extra-long route to look for any more Altru vehicles lurking about. It still bothered me, even after a pleasant evening at the Door. A little more alcohol wouldn't hurt. Back at home, there was some whiskey left over from the night of Xtra's attack and some beer in the downstairs fridge. The classic jingle popped into my head. *From the land of clear blue water. Hamm's. The Beer Refreshing.*

I hadn't drunk that stuff for years until Duke brought it over the other night, a twelve-pack of sixteen-ounce cans. It was my father's beer of choice back in the day, and I had solid mental connections with hearing that jingle and the hot summer days in Missouri. One memory, although hazy, was simply of sitting on our porch listening to a rock station as my father mowed the lawn.

I recalled the late afternoon sweltering heat and being amazed that our grass could grow so quickly. I remembered getting impatient, wanting my father to finish mowing the lawn because I knew what would come next: he, my older brothers, and I would play football on the freshly mowed grass. It wasn't so much a football game as an excuse to run around and tackle each other. At the time, I didn't realize they were letting their little brother do so well. I naturally assumed I was the strongest 5-year-old ever.

Thoughts of my father and dead brothers were the last thing I needed now. I shook the images of them from my head and entered my six-digit code on the keypad. When I entered my home, I had only flipped on one light switch, the one that turned on the lights over the part of the front lower parking area that held my Honda, but I noticed the lights in Xtra's area were already on. I didn't think anything of it. Until I did.

40

In the seconds before the shooting began, I noticed a few things: First, I was in a perfect kill zone for the man on the stairs, straight in front of me. If I turned around and ran back to the front door, I'd be giving him, Stairs, a broad target on my back. Second, another man stood in the doorway to the lower bedroom, about to check inside. He was holding a flashlight, but may have had a handgun also—an unknown. Third, Xtra was lying in a growing pool of blood, probably his own, in the middle of the kitchenette–likely dead.

I did have some weapons upstairs, but I'd have to get through these two to grab them. Plenty of heavy tools were available in the garage, but they were all between the guy in the doorway, Doorway, and me. It'd be foolish to try to reach them as, most likely, I'd be dead before arriving. At this point, my only advantages were my knowledge of the layout and the fact that they were as stunned as I was. Movement would save me.

With a quick step to my left, I was out of the gun's kill zone before it was even pointed at me. The first bullet hit the door I had just come through. My beloved Honda would provide little cover, so it wasn't a long-term option. Instead, I moved around the back of the vehicle and quickly peeked through a window to learn their positions. Stairs had a good vantage point. He was a couple of steps up, giving him a broader view of my location. Doorway did what I hoped he would and moved toward my original position. That made him head in the opposite direction from where I was going. Two more shots from Stairs kept me moving.

The Cr-V is technically an SUV. Though it's neither tall nor long, it was good enough to provide cover for the few seconds I needed. Between the nose of the car and the beginning of the far hallway to the back exit was only ten feet. I was hoping Doorway would be in the crossfire of Stairs during those brief moments it took me to cover that distance.

With shattered glass spraying over me, I dashed for the mouth of the far hallway. I had another twelve feet to cover before making it to the door, but before slamming on the panic bar to throw it open, I reached down and grabbed the thirty-two-inch aluminum baseball bat I purchased on a whim at a thrift store. It leaned in the crevice of an exposed wall stud and was intended as a hasty security device should the need arise.

The need arose.

The two would need little time to regroup and follow me. My only escape from this point was a straight shot across the back courtyard, down a forty-five-foot narrow alleyway, and through another gate, the whole time being backlit and directly in front of anyone exiting the rear door of my place.

Instead, I slammed the door behind me and prepared for whoever came through first. I'd have to make swift calculations, but the thought struck me that a baseball bat is a shitty weapon against a gun and is limited in a brawl against anyone who knows what they're doing. I wouldn't be afraid of facing someone with a bat, so I focused on using it as a first-strike weapon against a surprised attacker. I had to make contingency plans for whether Stairs came through first with his gun or if Doorway did.

I didn't have time to smash the light inside above the door, but I did feel assured that the rest of the gravel and dirt courtyard was dark. They'd be coming in from the light. It's a tiny advantage, and I'd use it.

Doorway arrived at the door first and slowed his pursuit as he pushed through to the outside and gauged the landscape. His hands were empty, and that pause gave me what I needed. I was already wound up and ready for a half-swing. Seeing no gun and thinking he'd most likely cover his head when I swung, I aimed for his gut. It wasn't a home run swing, but it advanced the runners. I didn't have time for another wind-up, so after he doubled over, I slammed the heavy aluminum handle down against his temple. It wasn't enough to kill, but he'd remember to make wiser choices in the future.

By the time Doorway slumped into a pile in the threshold, Stairs had approached and switched the pistol, a banged-up SIG Sauer, to his left hand so he could better look around the corner. He may have seen his buddy on the ground, but he wasn't aware of how he got there. He slowed his approach, but he should have stopped altogether.

I pushed myself against the wall as tightly as possible with the bat coiled above, ready to strike. There were a few things in my favor: his passing from light to dark, the groggy body he'd have to step over while looking around the corner, and the fear of the unknown. The advantage was mine. Other than the gun.

Because he was backlit from inside, I knew exactly where he was in relation to the door and wall. The moment the gun barrel broke the frame, I struck downward. I was hoping to hit and break his hand, but I only hit the gun, dislodging it without an accidental discharge. To his credit, before the pistol even hit the ground, he surprised me with a swift right jab at my face. It didn't sting or stun, but it surprised me enough that I had to rock back to regain a defensive position. He looked down at the darkened ground for his weapon, and I attempted a toe kick to his inner thigh, which he blocked easily. The kick might not have hurt him, but I wanted him to give up on the gun. Instead, Stairs reached behind and brought out a knife, blade downward. Doorway's body was keeping the door open so that the hallway's light reached out to combine with the single bulb above the inside threshold. His knife looked simple enough, the kind you'd want if you needed to hurt someone, a Blackie Collins design or at least a copy. Knives were never a thing for me, but I knew enough that I didn't like them.

I'd never had proper training in offensive knife fights, but I had attended a course on knife defense. The instructor had been a retired Navy SEAL named Danny Shaw. At 5'7" and 155 pounds, one wouldn't think the logistics of his size would allow for the amount of ass-kicking he put out. By the end of the course, we all called him Daddy Shaw behind his back. The weekend had been full of wrist moves, falls, twists, and other defensive maneuvers one can do against an assailant with a blade, but the highlights came down to a few principles:

"When facing a dedicated and trained knife fighter, do everything possible to shoot the motherfucker."

"If he is trained in knife fighting and you are not, you will lose."

"If he is a poor knife fighter and you are good at defense, you have a strong chance of survival."

"Again, when facing a dedicated and trained knife fighter, do everything possible to shoot the motherfucker."

Those were the philosophical highlights, but there were technical ones, too. Mainly, in a fight, the hand will be the fastest-moving part of the body. The knife, being attached to it, means the blade is moving quickly, too. Don't fixate on grabbing the man's hand or wrist. Focus on avoiding it. Dodge it when you can, block or parry if possible. If you must present a target, let him cut the outside of your forearms. Lastly, anything can be a better weapon against a knife than no weapon at all. A baseball bat was imperfect, but it might be all I needed.

I supposed running was an option now that Stairs was without his gun and Doorway was down for the count, but I was mad now, and we were on my property. Perhaps in time, I'd second-guess my decision, but it felt like the right one in the heat of the moment.

Stairs twisted the knife to catch the light, his lips peeling back to reveal crooked teeth as he admired the shimmering steel.

I adjusted my grip on the bat, grasping it in both hands. "May I ask why?" I asked to stall and better gauge the situation.

"Yeah. You can ask," Stairs said.

I didn't answer on principle. He knew what the hell I meant, and I wasn't going to make him feel like I needed his permission, but I could tell he wanted to talk. I waited.

"The Boss just wanted your friend dead. You showed up, and now we have to kill you," Stairs finally said. He flipped his blade into an overhand grip, perhaps thinking it would look cool, but it worked better for me. We were about four feet apart, coiled, and ready to end this.

"Who's your boss, and how did I upset her?" I asked, not caring about the answer yet. In a few minutes, I'd beat the answers out of him.

"Look, man...," Stairs began, but his answer was interrupted when I used both hands to ram the length of the bat across his face. "You fucker!" he shouted as he primed his arm for a downward strike.

It's what I was hoping for. As he thrust downward with the blade, I trapped the knob at the base of the bat's handle in the corner between his right hand and the knife's edge. With both hands on the bat, I pushed it outwards and to my left, bringing his hand and the knife with me. In one motion, I dropped the bat, seized his right wrist with both hands, and pivoted on my left foot, continuing to spin my upper body the same way until my right shoulder met with his. The continued twist lifted his body off the ground as I held his arm tight. Physics and gravity did the rest.

When Stairs's back slammed against the ground, I pressed my heel into his armpit, pulled hard on his arm, and bent his wrist backward. This sharp angle made him drop the knife, placing his wrist and elbow at risk of snapping if he struggled. He moaned but was smart enough not to move. I had particular reason to add to his pain, and I was tempted, but there'd be time for that later.

I shifted my grip so my right hand held his splayed fingers up and out, keeping him pinned to the ground, and adjusted my feet. With a quick kick to his head, Stairs was out for a while, or at least stunned, like Doorway, in a pile on the ground. There wasn't enough time to gloat as my side exploded.

A third man was nearby, either in cellphone contact or close enough to hear the commotion. He didn't arrive in time to save his buddies, but he did get here in time to bust my kidney. The first strike stunned me, and I flew face-first into the wall, giving him easy access to land another blow to each side of my ribcage. A rib fractured with an audible crack.

He paused, and I glanced to my left in time to see a fist headed toward my face. It connected solidly enough, but the force threw me back toward the door because I had seen it coming and moved away. I had made a weak kick at Stairs earlier because I didn't want him to find the SIG Sauer he had dropped. He wasn't sure where it fell, but I knew, and I knew how to use it.

This would hurt.

I dove to the spot where the gun had been dropped, quickly grabbing it as the third guy approached. The force of his punch and the amount of follow-through had unbalanced him, which gave me an extra second to react, but he'd now closed that distance.

Safety off, I fired dead center into his chest. The three muzzle flashes revealed a different frozen picture of emotion as they lit up his face. First shot, surprise. Second shot, shock. Third shot, empty. Finally, as the picture show ended, his lifeless mass fell on top of me, reminding me of the damage he did to my ribs. As much as lying there with a dead man on top hurt, it was almost better than the pain from the effort of getting out from under the big guy. When I finally managed to heave myself out, I stood to survey the yard: one dead, two in fluctuating states of consciousness.

Taking the gun, I staggered inside and grabbed a roll of duct tape from the garage along with a vial of ammonia smelling salts from the first aid kit in the downstairs common room. I headed back outside to the courtyard and grabbed Doorway first, dragged him to a seated position against the wall, and taped his hands and feet together firmly. I did the same with Stairs before rousing him using the ammonia. Sniffing it myself to fight off the fatigue and dizziness, I felt my head clear a little, but it did nothing for the flames in my ribcage. Doorway wasn't unconscious, but the pain in his head made him want to stay quiet and unmoving.

Grabbing a patio chair, I slumped down and leaned closer toward them while shining the flashlight into the face of Stairs. "Okay," I began. "Again, let me ask—why?"

Stairs slowly stuttered out, "Wh... what?"

"No! Not *what*. Why?" I said. "Why did you kill Xtra?"

"He didn't say why," he said. "Guy said to come and kill old dude and anyone who got in the way. You, you got in the way."

"Okay," I said. "That doesn't make any fucking sense, but okay. What did Xtra do? Why kill him, and who wanted him dead? Who's the guy?"

"C'mon, man!" he complained. "I can't...,"

I fired, and a bullet struck the wall near his head, shattering loose pieces of brick against his face.

"Fuck! Okay!" he shouted. "Oscar Braga. He worked for him." Stairs nodded his head at his dead buddy. "We got hired by him. He knew more than I did, but Oscar Braga hired him, and we work for him."

I opened the wallets I had taken from their unconscious bodies when I moved them. Stairs was Tyler Greene. Neither the name nor the face was familiar. Same with the ID for the other guy, Doorway. James Sarafian. The dead guy was the only one smart enough to commit a crime without his wallet.

"What you gonna do?" Stairs asked. He was holding and moving his jaw, trying to decide if it was broken, dislocated, or just hurt to all hell.

"I'm going to kill you."

He couldn't see my face, so he was unable to gauge the level of my seriousness. Honestly, neither could I. My ribs hurt more than I'd care to admit, and the idea of dealing with their bodies didn't sound fun. I hurt now, but it would probably hurt more tomorrow and even more the day after.

"Not gonna lie, though," I said with the voice of pragmatism. "Your buddy fucked me up pretty good. I don't feel like dealing with three dead bodies right now."

My phone rang. During all the activities, the screen cracked, but it still worked. It was the mayor.

"Young Sergeant, you talk to Xtra?"

"No. He's dead. It was Braga, Oscar Braga from Altru Security. He had him killed. He's been watching my place because he wanted to kill X. He sent some guys over here to do it, and one of them talked. They killed Xtra, man. Right in my fucking house!"

I continued to tell him the rest about killing one of them and capturing two others. "Why the fuck would Braga want to kill Xtra, man? I don't get it, Marcus."

"I do, Young Sergeant. Braga is the guy what fucked him up the other night. He's the dude that's been killing all the other motherfuckers the past few years. X recognized him from the stuff you gave him, and he called me and left me a voicemail. I didn't get it until now."

Silence. The silence of sorrow and mental gymnastics. I weighed the idea of putting a bullet or two into Stairs.

The mayor finally spoke. "Don't tell anyone you spoke with me. Say you're in shock or something, and gimme as much time as possible before you call the cops."

I didn't want to know what he had in mind, but I knew exactly what he had in mind.

41

Marcus Williams didn't have cell service, but he did have a Google Voice account. With that came voicemail, which collected and held messages when the phone's owner was out of Wi-Fi range, as Williams often was. He knew all the Wi-Fi hotspots in the East Bay area, and he'd head to one when he needed to work or communicate with anyone. Many shelters and food centers had Wi-Fi because the street residents owned devices and kept in touch with the world that way. Such was the case with Williams.

He had long been clean and sober, and when he showed up to work a volunteer night shift at a shelter near downtown, his phone dinged with a new message. It was from Xtra.

"Hey, Brother. It's that Braga fucker Warren was asking about. He's the killer. He's the one that stabbed me, and he's gotta be the one that did all the rest, too. I saw him that night, and he's in the pictures Warren had me go through. He had his security dudes watching the building all this time. Young Sergeant is out for a bit, but I'll let him know when he gets back. How many of our people did he kill? Call me when you can."

He called Xtra back immediately but got nothing. He tried again. Still nothing. He called Warren and got him on the first ring.

"Young Sergeant, you talk to Xtra?"

"No. He's dead."

His decision to find and kill Braga was easy. He had the address from the information Mike shared. If Warren gave him a head start by not calling the police right away, and Braga was home, he could make it happen before the police were involved. He could take care of a killer who'd been wiping out his people for years. How much time would Warren give him? Braga's address was too far to walk, but it was just a few BART stops away. It was late, almost midnight, but trains were still running every fifteen minutes.

Williams moved with quickness. At the West Oakland BART station, he could board a train headed in the right direction and reach the Rockridge Station in four stops. A twelve-minute ride. If he timed it right and Warren gave him a head start, he could do it.

Braga's home was a former warehouse, recently renovated into a four-plex townhome with garages. Williams was impressed as it looked nicer than he expected. There was off-street parking for the owners and large picture windows facing a languid, urban street. Williams assumed, correctly, it turned out, that Braga saw his truck from his window and balcony. *Perfect! Probably alarmed, too.*

The streets were dark and empty of passers-by. It was time for the mayor to act. From the left sleeve of his coat, he slipped loose one of the two tools he brought with him, a fourteen-inch section of two-inch-thick lead pipe. It would be his multi-purpose tool for the night's festivities. After he checked that no one was around watching, he quickly and fiercely smashed the front windshield of Braga's truck. In response, as expected and hoped, the car alarm began wailing, and the lights on the front and back flashed.

An upstairs light flicked on, and Williams moved quickly to the side of Braga's garage, near the path to the front door. The light shone upon the treetops, and seconds later, the sound of busy, excited footsteps clapped from inside the residence. Braga was coming down the stairs, probably armed. No matter. This would only take a second. Williams drew the pipe back, ready to kill with the first blow if need be. Braga might pause before coming out, leading with his weapon. In that case, he'd smash the gun hand with the pipe, draw back, then beat his face with it. If Braga stepped out and stopped, Williams could brain him right there and then, ending all other considerations.

Williams waited to see how this played out.

42

Braga's cell phone sat silently on his kitchen counter. It shouldn't have been quiet, though. It should have dinged by now with a notification to say the job was done. *Did something go wrong? Did they get delayed? Are they fucking morons and forgot to tell me?*

How hard could this have been? One old man, one injured and drugged-up old man. Braga blamed himself for anything that might have gone wrong. He should have done this himself instead of having Alan and his crew do it. Then again, that's why he had someone else take care of it—he had a crew and could take care of it exactly when needed, whereas Braga lacked that kind of flexibility. He'd been working all day, and the trio needed to move soon after Warren left the apartment. Braga had been tied up when he got a message from his sentry saying Warren had departed. All he could do was tell Alan to move.

Still no text.

The living room where Braga sat was dark save for a dim glow bleeding from the single light above the stove. Right now, nothing else mattered: no TV, no radio, no scrolling his phone for pictures of pretty girls. He needed confirmation that the only witness to his crimes was dead. He hadn't eaten yet and wouldn't until he received word of the job.

A loud thud sounded outside, followed by a car alarm. His car alarm, Braga feared. He stood and ran to the front window overlooking the street to check on his truck. The windshield had been smashed, but no one appeared to be around. A neighbor's car had been vandalized a few weeks back, and Braga remembered being worried about his truck then. Now it had been targeted, and he was pissed.

He switched on the living room lights, threw on his sneakers, which had been sitting near his favorite chair, grabbed the gun he kept in the chair's side pocket, and swiped his keys from the kitchen counter as he headed down the stairs. At the bottom, he opened the door but surveyed the scene before running out. Using his key fob, he turned off the alarm, and the new silence was as stark as the noise had been. Feeling safe to proceed, Braga dashed out the door toward his truck.

He was tripped to the ground almost immediately, not seeing the black man standing flat around the corner of his garage wall waiting for him. He didn't see the pipe the man carried until the man used it.

Despite the surprise, Braga recovered quickly and, with his weapon, almost moved into a firing position on his back before the pipe crashed down, clubbing Braga's left forearm. The pistol, a Glock, now hung limply from his left index finger. A quick kick to the head stunned the killer, not enough to knock him out, but sufficient to part him from the firearm and make him temporarily compliant.

At some point during the confrontation, Braga's keys had flung across the asphalt. His attacker scooped them up, quickly followed by the discarded weapon. He placed the pipe into his waistband, then put the barrel of the gun firmly into Bragas into the back of his head. Williams grabbed the back of Braga's neck with his free hand and half-dragged, half-carried him inside and up the stairs, where he threw Braga back to the ground.

"Stay face down. Put your hands behind your back." From his coat pocket, the man pulled out a roll of duct tape. Braga was somewhere between stunned and too stubborn to comply, so he had to wrench Braga's hands behind his back before applying the tape. When that was done, he yanked Braga up to his knees and gave another command. "Cross your ankles," he said roughly.

"You're a fucking dead man!" Braga said, gaining his senses.

The stranger tugged out the lead pipe and struck his prisoner on the right trapezius, grazing his ear on the downstroke. Braga slumped to the floor, but his attacker grabbed him by the throat and forced him back up.

"I'm sorry. What was that, motherfucker?"

Nothing from Braga.

"I thought so. Now cross your fuckin' ankles."

Braga complied, but the movement enraged his shoulder again.

"You killed my friend. You killed my people."

Suspecting there was no way out of this, but through it, Braga leaned into the verbal and physical abuse. "Your people? You must be a fucking bum, too. Maybe you should have a better class of friends." The duct tape cut into his right wrist, but it was looser around his left.

Another blow. Another trapezius, the left. Again, Braga crumpled, and again, he was forced back up to a hunched position.

"Look," Braga said, "I'll give you 100K in cash. Take it, but leave my passport."

"Motherfucker, you ain't got that kind of money, not in cash anyways."

"Swear to God, I do. Drugs, too. I'm sure you'd want that."

"Drugs?" The man said it as if he were insulted. "Fuck that. The cash, is it here?"

"No. We have to go there. It's close, though."

"What? We gonna fuckin' Uber there or some shit? You remember I just smashed your windshield. You ain't afraid that might draw attention, or is that what you're hoping? Where is the money?"

"It's not here. We'd have to go there." Braga maintained eye contact as he worked the tape binding his wrists. It gave a slight bit each time he twisted his wrists against each other, creating an ever-growing gap between his hands.

The man stood silently for a moment, chewing on his bottom lip. "We don't have much time before the police show up. Not because of your alarm. You were nice enough to turn that off. No. Have you wondered why your three guys haven't checked in?"

Blankness washed over Braga's face, a blankness that said he was wondering why they hadn't checked in yet.

"Warren killed one and got another one to talk. He had a lot to say about you. That's how I found you, and that's why the police will be here in force in about, oh, I'd guess five minutes."

As shrunken as Braga was from the two strikes to his shoulders, he sank even further, but only briefly before his resolve returned. He straightened up as much as possible. "Then you've only got a few minutes to get me out of here if you want the money."

"No, fucker." A punch in the stomach. Hard. Hard enough to fold Braga back almost flat on his crossed ankles. "It means *you* only have a few minutes to tell me where it's at and to decide if you want to be alive or dead when the police get here!"

As soon as Braga bounced back up, the man punched him in the left kidney, sending him sideways. Sensing Braga was too stunned to move for a few minutes, he walked to the living room and grabbed a thick, cushioned pillow from the couch. A perfect silencer. Returning, he brought Braga back up to his knees and asked again.

"Where's the money?"

"It's in a warehouse. Oakland." Fear was in his voice. Not out-of-control fear, but close. He needed a little more time, a little more breath, and the right moment.

"Where? What's it called?"

"Take me there," Braga pleaded. "You'll need the keys on the table over there." He jerked his jaw toward a space behind the standing man.

He turned to look. It wasn't a big turn Braga hoped for, but it was enough. The pain from the gut punches hadn't been much, but the bashes to the traps still hurt like hell, as if his muscles had been flayed open. Despite the pain, Braga leaned back on his knees and sprang up toward his attacker, bypassing the gun and shouldering him as hard as he might. The man flew back, his right hand flying up, the pistol with it, and discharging a round past Braga's ear.

The man's head hit the floor with a solid thump, bouncing once before settling into place at a grotesque, unnatural angle. The Glock had flown out of his hand as he fell back. Braga focused all his remaining strength into his arms and shoulders in an excruciating effort to wriggle his way free. It wasn't easy. The tape didn't snap, and he had to vigorously work friction into it to make it more pliable and give him room to slip his hands free. The man stirred. He would clear his head and get up if he did nothing about it. The quick, solid kick to his face ended the fight, leaving the older man still. That wasn't safe enough for Braga.

With his wrists finally free, Braga grabbed the gun the man had dropped, kneeled near his head, and positioned the pillow over his face. Braga used it as a simple muffler to help soften the sound of the gun as the Glock officially ended the fight. Braga wanted more satisfaction from the kill, but didn't have time to enjoy it. The police. He only had time to grab his keys. He needed them. Another sixty seconds, and he'd be safe.

With keys in hand, he raced toward his garage, entered, and slapped the button on the wall that opened the door. A helmet sat on his motorcycle, and Braga placed it on his head in a practiced movement. He inserted the keys into the ignition, started the engine, and disappeared into the night.

43

Two of my ribs were cracked, my dear friend was dead, and once again, my home was a crime scene. Instead of being filled with long-dead women and girls, it was filled with freshly killed men. I don't think I had a preference. Neither had an upside, and I would need to send a cleaning team in before I could sleep peacefully there again. Knowing Braga was behind all this was small consolation because the whole thing had been staring me in the face, and I hadn't acted soon enough.

It was now up to the cops. After giving the mayor thirty minutes to do what he needed, I finally called the police. Now they knew who sent these guys, and they suspected the same person was behind the rest of the killings. This one arrest could wipe off three years' worth of unsolved homicides from their map. They needed to get to Braga before he figured out that something had gone wrong with his guys and their mission to kill Xtra. That's all assuming Williams didn't get to Braga before the police did.

While the paramedics tended to me at the scene, a patrolman took my initial statement before I was handed off to the lead detective. Usually, I wouldn't voluntarily talk to the police unless arrested, but since I did just kill a guy, they could have taken me to the station and done this the hard way. Everything in my story lined up, even the part about being at the Door before the incident began. I only left out the part about talking to Williams and the thirty-minute head start. They'd probably still refer me to the DA for formal charges, but no one thought I'd be arrested for anything tonight. After the interview, they asked me to stay in my loft, since it wasn't part of the crime scene and was technically a separate address. That was fine with me. That's where the coffee was, along with Xtra's laptop. I had swiped it from downstairs after calling the cops, initially grabbing it, thinking I'd want to show them all the information we had put together.

I'd be lying if I said I wasn't all flattered to hell that Mike seemed to drop everything to come to my place as soon as I told her what happened, not as a reporter but as a friend to Xtra and me. She'd be a reporter later, but for now, she was all mine to lean on and be comforted by. I had to let her up the side stairs to the loft to avoid the police tape.

The coroner had removed the bodies from my home after the crime scene team worked their voodoo. Mike and I were left alone with the reminders of death—bloodstains and the metallic scent of blood and spent ammunition. The mental damage, too, of course. We were stuck with that. She wanted to comfort me, but I wouldn't have it. We hadn't yet had a good chat about our expectations of gender roles, but I expected hers to be somewhat non-traditional. That was fine with me, but I also suspected that she wanted to comfort me despite her own loss.

This mess called for either action or heavy drinking, and since my actions were limited to calling a 24-hour crime scene cleaner, drinking was the best option. With Mike around, getting sloppy drunk didn't feel like a great choice, so I reached for my phone. A quick search turned up someone who'd come out the next day. They'd cost an arm and a leg, but it'd be worth it. There was no peace for me at my place with Xtra's blood lying about, let alone that of the filth from those who caused it.

I'd leave it to the mayor to tell their community. I sure as hell wouldn't post about it. Mike would be putting together a story soon. She probably already had something forming in her head, but she'd been too busy fussing over me to begin writing it. She must have been torn up about Xtra, but she kept moving and working to keep the bad thoughts from taking over. I could relate.

My phone rang. It was Detective Sergeant Khan, the lead investigator on my case. He had interviewed me earlier, and he was not pleased.

"Who did you tell about Braga?"

"What? No one! Why?"

"Warren, I'm going to ask you again, and you had better be telling me the fucking truth. Who else did you tell about Braga?"

"You guys were my first call after everything went down. Why? What happened?" Seeing how Williams called me, this wasn't exactly a lie.

"By the time we had a team in place, ready to go into Braga's home, he was already gone, and the mayor was dead. I know you know him."

The news didn't stun me, but it saddened me. Lorelei had brought another sailor to death on the rocks below her cliff. "Have your guys check his phone. Check Xtra's, too. I suspect he figured it out and told the mayor just before the guys came over to kill him." I said, knowing the cops would have taken it.

"Yeah? No shit, Warren. But right now, that's secondary to the bigger question of where the fuck Braga is! Warren, if I find out you leaked or somehow fucked this up, I'll have your ass." Khan abruptly ended the call.

He'd been loud enough on the phone that I didn't have to relay the news to Mike, and I saw her deflate before me. As crushed as she was by Xtra's passing, she was still willing and able to support me. She must have sensed my proximity to darkness and wanted to prevent me from slipping into it. The news of the mayor's passing crushed her. I didn't know the depth and length of their relationship, but the news caused her face to explode with tears and a wail of grief. Sadly, I was in my element, and she was crushed.

For a few minutes, I comforted her the best I could; I sat near her and then let her lie on the couch in shock and grief. But my mind stayed active with thoughts of what may have transpired. Xtra somehow figured out that Braga was the killer, probably by looking at the files I gave him, and he called the mayor. Before he could call me, the three guys showed up and killed him. That's what those notifications were at my door. Fuck!

Mike must have seen my wheels turning. "What's up with you?"

"I assume X figured out Braga was the guy who attacked him. I was out having dinner, and he needed to tell someone. He told Williams, and the mayor tried to do something about it." I skirted around telling her about my delay in calling the cops.

"And now they're both dead."

I paused, deflated by the reminder. "And now they're both dead."

"Now what?" she asked, "Just let the police do their thing?"

"Well, yeah. But you should do your thing, too. Perhaps you could put word out on your network to look out for him. Get a description out there and beat the bushes. Make it known that this is the guy suspected of killing all those people, as well as the mayor."

"What are you gonna do?"

"I'm gonna chat with security when he shows up."

Cooper was dead, but whoever had taken his shift the past couple of days had kept up a schedule similar to his, and I was hoping that pattern would hold. Despite the night's commotion and the police presence for the long hours afterward, I wanted the guy to be there.

I got a few hours of fitful rest, even with the crime scene team doing their thing downstairs. Mike stayed up to write her story about Xtra's murder, but chose not to visit the scene of the mayor's death. Maybe the killing of one friend was enough for the night. She eventually cuddled up next to me a few minutes after 4 am. It was nice to press against a warm body. In a way, I felt safer and warmer than I'd felt in a while. When my alarm roused me at 8 am, I was almost tempted to stay in bed rather than head outside to beat the shit out of a security guard. Through the windows, I saw that the new day's light had come. I was glad to see the bright shades of blue. They added some warmth to my soiled home. It didn't help my mood.

While I slept, the crime scene team finished their work and left. Mike must have let them out before she joined me in bed. They left a few papers on the downstairs counter, an inventory of all they had taken from the downstairs area. It didn't look like they tried too hard to clean up after themselves, but I'd deal with that later. I let Mike sleep a little longer while I went to extract some information the hard way.

Leaving out the back stairs to avoid the scene of carnage where, hours before, I had killed a man, I made an end run around my block to arrive at the back side, stopping to pick up a softball-sized chunk of concrete I found along the way. Before walking around any corner, I stopped and tried to spot a parked Altru vehicle. On the second try, I found one across the street and a block west of my place, facing east toward my building. I had to backtrack and skirt around another block to approach from behind him without being seen, but it was worth it.

Looking around the corner of a closed wholesaler's warehouse, I spotted the security car and the driver, waiting, watching. I hadn't taken enough time to dress properly for the event, wearing only sweatpants, sneakers, and a dark T-shirt. It was not the best attire to blend into the streets, but it was too late to change. The SUV was parked in front of a row of not-yet-opened businesses, but across the street and in my building, the produce warehouses were in their morning groove, with plenty of vehicles moving around the streets and alleys.

Waiting for a van to pass me heading east, I crossed the street after it, trying to stay within the driver's blind spots on the sidewalk. He was motionless in his vehicle. Asleep? No. He moved his head as if checking his cell phone, but returned his gaze to my building. It was time to start the interview.

I covered the last fifty feet to the car quickly and, setting my feet, heaved the concrete piece with all the strength my pained ribs could manage. The driver's window shattered, and before the glass stopped scattering, I reached through the opening with both hands and hauled the stunned driver out through the now clear frame, throwing him quickly and solidly to the ground. Sprawled out as he was, I gave him no chance to recover, though I could already tell he lacked the mental bandwidth to react. I brought one foot down on his gun hand and placed the other against his throat firmly enough that he was unable to catch the breath he had expelled after hitting the sidewalk. With his one free hand, he slapped pathetically at my heel.

"Do what I say, or I'll snap your fucking neck," I said softly but firmly. He debated for a few seconds but stopped slapping and relaxed. I took some pressure off his throat and moved his chin away from me using my toes. He was a righty, so I didn't have to reach across him to grab the pistol from his holster.

I checked for a round in the chamber and slid the safety off before kneeling and placing the barrel's point underneath his chin. His normally brown Latin skin was as pale as it could get, all blood having flushed from his face.

"When's the last time you communicated with Braga?" I asked.

After a few seconds of careful thought and consideration, all he could come up with was, "I don't know?" He was terrified, too terrified to speak sensibly. His eyes were too wide, his breathing was too shallow, and he looked scared enough to piss himself. I would have to back off. Fuck! I was hoping for some senseless violence.

"Okay, friend. Calm down. Everything is gonna be fine," I said while keeping the gun tight against his jawline. "Where's Braga?"

He took his first deep breath since we met and looked to be learning to speak for the first time, working his mouth and jaw as if he had just borrowed them. "Braga?"

"Yes, Braga. Where is he?"

"I don't know.

This had always been a long shot. There was only a slim chance that a stooge would know anything useful. What I didn't realize at the time was that I was being rope-a-doped. One of his knees shot up, slamming into my exposed stomach – inches away from the cracked ribs. Though not a direct hit, the pain was still sharp enough that it nearly made me piss myself. As my body lurched over his, his right hand shot up and grabbed my wrist–the one holding the pistol–and twisted it away. I had been balanced nicely on top of him, in control, but his attack sent me reeling face-first onto the concrete. My right arm was stretched out, my wrist locked in both his hands. Fucked, basically, unless I did something quickly.

He jumped up and used both hands to try to break the pistol from my grip, dragging my stomach across the ground and over broken glass on the way to his vehicle. Knowing it would hurt like hell, I twisted onto my right side and swung with my legs, sweeping his feet out from underneath him. He lost hold of the pistol barrel, and I rotated my gun hand in a way that loosed his grip entirely, giving me sole control of the pistol again.

We were both on the ground but too close to each other for my comfort. I gave him a solid kick to the midsection, stunning him and pushing me away. He doubled over, and I assumed a kneeling firing position. He recovered, saw the pistol pointing at him, and froze.

I hadn't experienced so much pain in a long time. Sharp stabs ran up and down my right side, and each breath made it worse. I made them short and controlled until I got my wind back.

Defeated, he leaned back against his car. "Can't be mad at me for trying," he groaned.

"Yes, I can," I said. If I didn't need information from him, I would have shot him; my pain and anger were so great. "Where can I find Braga?"

"I don't fucking know," he said, almost calmly now. "I've been trying to get hold of him for hours now. He said last night to come watch your place this morning before my other shift, so I did. I watched the cops come and go and tried to tell him, but didn't hear anything back. I was about to take off if I didn't hear from him." He shook his head and spat on the ground. "So, what happened last night? What was the big deal?"

My hand clenched around the gun. "He had my friend killed. May have killed another one himself. If you're working with him, that makes you an accomplice."

"No! Fuck that!" he said, leaning forward now. "I'm just sitting here and watching. That's all. I ain't got shit to do with any of that."

"No? You're covering Cooper's shift. He got killed. Did you stop and think about why?" I was painting a picture with colors I didn't have, but wanted to jar him a little. "Cooper was watching me until recently. That's why I knew someone would be here this morning." I tried to sound more confident in my story than I was. Between the pain in my side and the thin facts, I didn't have much going for me except the gun and the hope of inspiring fear of arrest or death in this guy. "What's your name?" I asked.

"Guerrero."

"Well, Guerrero. I don't care about you despite the knee to my sore ribs. I want Braga. Where would he go if he was in trouble?"

"Shit. I don't know him that well. He was my boss, and I helped him run some errands now and then. That's about it."

"Does he have another house or apartment in town?"

"Not that I know of. He'd sleep at some of the hospitals if he monitored an overnight or something."

"How about a buddy's place or a hideout?"

"What? Like a fuckin' Batcave? I have no idea."

"Fuck. Anything?"

"He's got a storage unit where he keeps some of his shit?"

"What kind of shit?

"I'm not sure. Never been inside. I only waited outside while he dropped stuff off and picked stuff up."

"Where is it?"

After Guerrero told me, the right thing to do would have been to call the police. I had a recent history of not always doing that. I had a bank account and a buried body in Idaho to prove it. There wasn't any room in this for me to fuck up. If I went to the storage area and killed or captured Braga, I'd get in trouble for interfering with an investigation, let alone killing someone.

I didn't see a way around this, so I had to hide behind Mike again as an anonymous source. When she called, I stayed close but kept my mouth shut.

"Khan," she said, sitting next to me on my couch, "I have it from a reliable source that Braga has a storage unit in West Oakland." She shared the address, and I was sure Khan got right to work on securing a warrant.

44

Prescott Storage was, aptly enough, in the South Prescott neighborhood of West Oakland, in the shadow of I-880. The brick building was built in the 1920s and underwent an earthquake retrofit in the 1970s, when steel beams and cinder-block support walls were added. This reduced the inside square footage by a few feet but helped it survive some of the substantial earthquakes the area had experienced over the last fifty years.

Braga's storage-for-Adderall deal with the owner, Lee April, afforded him anonymity and the largest storage space in the building. Some of the others were as big, but none were bigger. The owner also gave him 24-hour access, unlike the other tenants. Only a handful of his guys were aware this place existed, and none had ever been inside. There was no paper trail. It was safe. That safety was why he felt comfortable enough to grab a few hours of sleep on the cot he had stashed in the corner, though not before setting a brace on his forearm to protect it and taking a few painkillers. Thankfully, the arm wasn't broken, but it hurt like all hell.

Through the fog of pain, lack of sleep, and a still-pounding headache, he woke to sounds from the front of the building, but his groggy mind couldn't make sense of them yet. Sitting up on the cot, he felt searing pain in his shoulders and left forearm, making him regret moving. The fire and fog subsided, and the sounds became clearer. The office door opened and closed with a loud bang. He froze, except for his right hand moving to the handle of his pistol. *Is it April? What is he doing here at this hour?* Moving slowly toward the office, he stepped lightly. Braga peered through the glass door. The owner was sitting at his desk.

"What are you doing here so early?" Braga asked.

April stood up straight, obviously scared by the unexpected visitor. "You! You need to get the fuck outta here. The cops are looking for you. They're headed here now. Called me and told me to get my ass here and open up your unit for them. They got a warrant."

He pushed through the door and stepped closer. "Give me your keys."

"Why? You have your own."

"To slow them down. Give me your keys."

The owner handed them over slowly and warily, keeping eye contact with Braga and ensuring the desk stayed between them.

"This will slow them down, too." Braga extended his arm holding the pistol, and placed a round into April's forehead. The owner's body fell dead over the back of his chair.

Time was tight. He had to move quickly. Heading to the front door, he locked it again and secured the deadbolt. He moved back to his unit and grabbed what he needed: a shoulder duffel stuffed with as much cash as he could make fit, two guns with ammo, two sets of fake IDs, all the prepaid Visa cards, a scanner, some Adderall, a first aid kit, and a four-inch folding knife. That's all he had time for. Thinking he would likely encounter the police somewhere along the way, he took an extra minute to don a ballistic vest.

When he made a sweep to see if he had all he needed, he secured the safe, both doors, and both locks. He turned on the scanner and set it to the OPD channel, but heard nothing about his situation yet. Returning to the front door, he looked out the window to see if any new cars, marked or otherwise, had arrived. He couldn't take his motorcycle as the police knew about it. Rideshare cars weren't an option—his phone and credit cards were probably already being watched. He was tempted to take one of the other motorcycles. They were clean, but if the police were as close as he feared, they might block traffic around the building, and he'd be out of luck. No. The only way to slip out now was on foot. Using the owner's keys, he unlocked the rear door and exited into the cool Oakland morning, locking it from the outside as he left.

The police had a basic physical description but didn't know what he was wearing. He hadn't had a chance to change before leaving his house, so he was still wearing the same jeans, sneakers, and light T-shirt he'd worn when Williams attacked. Before leaving the storage unit, he grabbed a hunting hoodie and a ball cap. He wouldn't entirely blend into the streets, but neither would he stand out.

His only chance now, in the short term, was to make his old hunting grounds his hiding spot. Just for a while, just long enough to figure out a path away from this place. *Get out of the area and settle down. Make a master plan. Mexico would be a great place to start, but carrying cash would be dangerous. So, how to exchange it for something digital or electronic?* It was a problem for another time.

Before he was even 100 yards away from the storage building, the police units approached. Fast, too. There was nothing about them on the scanner app. They must have been using cell phones to communicate. Two patrol cars and an unmarked were headed to where he had recently departed, no doubt to meet the owner and serve the warrant. *The locked doors and dead body will slow them down for a bit, but they'll be on my ass soon enough. They've probably seen my motorcycle already.* Braga quickened his pace toward the underside of the freeway.

BART is out because of cameras and BART police patrols. The Greyhound bus terminal is at the BART station, so that's a no-go. Can't buy a plane ticket with cash anymore, and there would be eyes all over the airport. Can I call any of my guys, or am I burned?

He'd ignored the texts from Guerrero, worried none of his guys could be trusted now. Cooper's connection to Altru was obvious, and it was only a matter of time, Braga thought, before the police figured out that two of the three guys sent to Warren's place were Altru employees. *No, all my guys are burned. They're no good to me now.*

The ferry from Jack London Square to San Francisco was a viable option. It had no security, and no one would expect him on the other side. From there, where there would be less pressure, he could either lie low in the city or journey southward. Mexico would be fine for now, but a non-extradition country would be best; Laos or Cambodia would work. His money would go far, but getting out of Oakland was the first step. To do that, he first had to make it to the waterfront, to the small ferry dock—two miles with his worsening limp, an injured left forearm, and two tortured shoulders.

Above him on the interstate, the morning traffic was increasing, picking up in pace and volume. Behind, the police were out of their vehicles and banging at the door, trying their best to wake the dead owner. Ahead lay two miles of concrete, bums, filth, and urban ugliness he had to get through to make it to the next level of safety. Duffel bag slung across his damaged left shoulder, hands in pockets, and head down, he moved forward into the city.

A few unhoused people were up, shuffling around, and he wondered why they even bothered to wake so early. *They don't have jobs to get to.* There was electricity in the air that wasn't usually there, an energy he hadn't felt either on his hunts or patrols. He didn't like it.

Broken-down cars, vans, campers, and even mobile homes sat parked along most roads. Eyes spied on him as he passed, most people averting their gaze right away, but a few got a good, long look at the man walking through, surveying his face and overall size and shape.

45

Melissa "Milly" Avery had a good life compared to what she had been living, better than most people on the streets. It wouldn't be that way if she hadn't gotten clean after so many years of addiction to oxycodone and alcohol. She didn't like to think of all the things she did to get a pill or a bottle, but here she was now, with a van that mostly worked, a small camper trailer that wouldn't move but provided a good home, and a part-time job that supplied enough income to help her get by.

Her parking space was perfect! It was a block away from the shelter, where she could get a shower twice a week and use the bathroom as needed. As importantly, she was across the street and around the corner from a cafe. She didn't want their coffee, but she was close enough to get one bar of Wi-Fi on her phone. With the Wi-Fi, she attended online support groups, stayed in touch with her family on the East Coast, and, most importantly, kept up to date with the world through X and Bluesky.

She didn't need anything at the shelter yet, and she didn't work today, so she spent some time sitting in a folding lawn chair on the sidewalk, her patio, she called it, while checking the digital world. As soon as she logged into X, she received a notification that she had been tagged in a post. She felt a rush of endorphins because she was hardly ever tagged or mentioned. It made her feel special until she saw what it was.

> @sillymilly, look at this. Keep an eye out
>
> this morning.

Someone in her network had reposted something from @MiFiReports and tagged Melissa.

> Xtra and The Mayor are dead! The killer is
>
> on the loose in Oakland this morning. Oscar
>
> Braga. 43, 6', 210. Call 911 if you see him.
>
> #oscarbraga #tempesttost

The post included a picture—a media release photo from Altru after they secured another massive contract. It was a clear portrait of Braga.

She knew the mayor but not Xtra. Williams had helped her when the police were harassing her about her trailer. He got them to back off.

Movement across the street caught her eye—a man, forties, tall, well-built, a little stout.

Nah! Couldn't be him. He wasn't paying her or anyone any attention, just walking quickly, walking like he was trying to get away from something. On a whim, she called out.

"Hey, Oscar!"

The man paused, then slowly spun toward Milly. She glanced down at the photo, then back up at the man. It was him. He began crossing toward her. Then, seeing a cluster of cars approaching, he stopped. Instead, he took off in a fast walk to the west.

Milly trusted the police as much as the rest of the people on the streets, which wasn't much. She did something better than call them: she posted.

Just saw braga at 5th and brush st. He ran

toward JLSquare. #oscarbraga #tempesttost

Her post carried the original message about Braga. Anyone following the post or the #oscarbraga hashtag would be notified about the new post, as would the original poster, Finney.

Life on the streets had always been rough, but Milly had created the best life possible for herself. Her momentary encounter with this man, who, had there not been traffic to stop him, may have caused her serious harm. It made her rethink her place on the Oakland streets. Maybe it was time to go home—real home.

46

Braga had no clue who the woman calling his name was. He had been prepared to cross the street and kill her to shut her up, but the oncoming traffic made him slow down and realize the loss of time wasn't worth it. Getting to the ferry dock was the priority, and it was only ten blocks away.

A police car crossed two blocks ahead, and Braga quickly turned back, retracing his steps to the street behind him. It was the same distance to the docks, but along the quieter streets, he'd have less to hide behind and fewer people to blend in with. *If that patrol car is cruising the back streets, I may be fucked.*

On his side of the street, the only vehicle parked at this hour was a delivery van, its engine running, and the driver behind the wheel, watching his phone. With a look of shock, the driver lifted his gaze straight up and maintained eye contact with Braga until he passed the van. Without checking behind him, the driver's door opened and shut, and the patter of the driver's feet followed. Braga had to look back. He couldn't resist. When he did, he looked straight at the driver, staring back at him. *What the fuck is going on?* Knowing he'd been spotted, the driver froze, and Braga quickly sped up.

He couldn't keep up the pace for more than half a block. The injuries from the beating Williams gave him were too much to maintain such speed. He stopped and looked back to see the driver following him at a safe distance of 100 feet. Braga had no idea what interest this guy had in him, but if he stayed with him all the way to the ferry dock, he could easily tell the police, and they'd be waiting for him in San Francisco. He'd have to lose him—or kill him.

Running through the area would attract more attention than he wanted, and it hurt like hell. Even walking and breathing were becoming a problem. He turned another corner and waited, though he didn't have to wait long. The driver, a young, lean Hispanic kid, stuck his head around the bricks to find his target—but not far enough to see directly around from behind the pillar of the warehouse they were both skirting. Braga grabbed the smaller man and threw him against the cinder block wall.

"Why are you following me?"

With eyes wide and a voice an octave higher than what sounded natural, the driver said, "I wasn't foll...,"

Braga cut his words off with a punch to the man's soft stomach. "Tell me, or I'll kill you right fucking now." Braga brought up his four-inch lock blade and held the tip to the driver's eye.

"You're on X, right? You're the guy on X. Oscar Braga."

The news stunned Braga enough to release his grip on the man, and he stepped back. "What?" It was the best he could muster, but he regained his grip on the driver.

"There was a post this morning about you killing a couple of guys, and to look out for you. Someone else posted a minute ago that you were seen close by, and then I saw you."

"Did you post anything?" Braga snarled.

The kid glanced down and received another punch in the gut.

"Did. You. Post. Anything?"

"Yeah. A couple. Once when I saw you, and again, my location right before I turned the corner here."

Fuck!

Braga didn't have time to play with the man anymore. Raising the blade toward the driver, Braga plunged it quickly and deeply through the man's right eye, piercing his brain. The driver's light switch turned off instantly, and he fell to the ground as if his legs had been removed. Braga had chosen the eye and brain because of the quickness of death and the lack of blood, not mercy. Mercy was the last thing on his mind.

If the guy posted my location, the ferry dock is no good. There will be eyeballs everywhere. He didn't know the new plan, but the old plan was dead. Now, all he could do was run. But to where? There was one place possible, he thought—a place where he could get a car and handle a piece of old business. It was a risky move, but it would be oh-so-worth it.

47

Braga might as well have had a geo tracker on him for all the posts from the #tempesttost crowd. Since the original sighting at 5th and Brush Streets, two more reposts and a dozen more had been made. I saw them while scrolling on the couch, sipping my cuppa.

Mike was at my kitchen counter doing what she does best: writing. I wasn't sure what she was working on because she had a "don't fuck with me" air about her, saying nothing, leaning into her laptop, and striking the keys like she was trying to teach them a lesson. This was healthier for her than sitting with her sadness and doing nothing. Then again, what did I know about healthy grieving? My only experience with the loss of those close to me was my brothers and mother, and both of those events were a mess.

When my brothers died, my father, who came home for a rare extended stay, allowed me two days of crying. That was enough for a twelve-year-old boy. He wouldn't allow me anymore and snapped at me or gave me a chore anytime it looked like I might slip into what he called "melancholy."

My mother's passing happened when I was in Afghanistan. I was able to get bereavement leave, but didn't make it back in time for her funeral. The meeting with my father was as awkward as one might expect. We shook hands as was our norm and discussed the status of the family house, whether to sell it or not, as he only came back for intermittent visits. I hadn't returned home in years, so I told him I didn't care. I did, of course, but what could I do with the house of a dead woman while I was in the military? It was more sadness and confusion to stuff down inside me to go along with the grief and loss.

With Mike, a large part of me was relieved I didn't have to help her work through her feelings. I wouldn't know how to because I've never worked through mine properly. I've drank, and I've fought, and I've fucked all while saying "yes, sir" and "no, sir" while completing a mission. When my previous relationship with Laura fell apart, I let it. I was unwilling to face what needed to be done within me to make things right. Now, I might have been willing to bridge that gap, so perhaps a part of me was ready and willing to listen and help if she were prepared to reach out. Still, drinking, fighting, and fucking were easier to manage.

A notification dinged on my phone. Something at the front door? The image showed nothing. Maybe someone passed too close. I was on my couch, lost in my thoughts, when the notification returned me to the world. Another notification, and again, nothing and no one. The only other time that happened was the night Xtra got attacked. I wasn't going to ignore it again.

Sitting up and moving reminded me of my cracked ribs. Despite the tight bandages wrapped around my chest, the sting in my torso was more pain than I'd dealt with in a long time. As bad as it was, Guerrero's knee punch to my gut had made it twice as bad. Either the Acetaminophen hadn't kicked in yet, or this was about as much relief as I might expect. I let Mike continue with her work and went out my door to the upper landing. The lights above the lower living area were on, casting shadows over my Honda. I couldn't see beneath me, down the hallway I'd escaped through earlier, or the guest bedrooms, but there was no movement of any kind where I looked. Despite the wall that had been constructed to separate my place from Hub Produce, the din of the warehouse was still faintly audible: forklift engines, crates dropping onto the floor, and trucks backing in. Never enough to be a bother, but sufficient to cover any gentle noise that might have been inside my place.

Descending the steps, I saw more of the downstairs area but not the hallway. I'd check that out in a minute, but I wanted to ensure the door was secure first. Until now, I hadn't thought of checking my Honda for damage. Passing her, it appeared that four of the windows had been shot through, but I didn't yet see any rounds through the body. She was a mess, but it was only cosmetic damage.

As I was a few steps from the front door, Mike screamed out my name. When I turned, Braga rushed out from beneath the stairs, clutching a knife. Mike had followed me out of my space, curious where I was going, and was just in time to see Braga spring out from hiding.

He came hard at me with an underhand grip, knife point facing up. I assumed he would try to pin me against the wall and stab me multiple times in the gut, prison-style. Not the most effective, in my opinion, but it would put me on the ground where he could finish me off.

I pushed off hard to my left, avoided his charge, and let him pass. I had hoped his momentum would crash him through the door to the outside world, but no luck. He stopped and changed his hold on the knife, this time to a more sensible blade-down grip. He was giving off an odor of stress sweat, the electrical kind with an extra tinge of metal.

"I want your car keys, Warren," he said.

"You could have just asked." I noticed Mike had disappeared from the upper landing and hoped she was calling the police.

"Yeah, well, I also kinda want you dead. You're a pain in the ass."

"Sure," I said, trying to kill time, "and you were gonna use the knife so the neighbors wouldn't hear a gunshot and call the police. I'm sure you brought a gun, right?" I nodded toward the small duffel bag he had set near the front door and cursed myself for not noticing it sooner. "Very smart."

He wiped his forehead with the back of his sleeve.

I continued, killing time. "You could have carjacked someone, but that'd be a risk in daylight. They'd have a vehicle description. If you kill me and take my car, you'd at least have a head start." I had never shown Mike where I kept my pistols. A regret. That would have been handy right about now.

I was being too obvious. I should've kept my mouth shut and danced with him silently. He made a couple of quick feints with the knife, both of which caused him to grimace. *Is he injured? There's something wrong with his neck or shoulders.* That was my chance. With both strikes, he'd been slow to pull back. His next strike would be an opportunity.

He threw a quick left jab to my face. I saw it coming, but took the punch. He still held the blade, and I didn't want to avoid the punch only to move into the path of the knife. It hurt, but it looked like it hurt him, too. As he drew back for another jab, I went against training and grabbed his attacking wrist, only because it was moving more slowly than normal. Instead of some tricky maneuver, I kicked his shins to draw his attention away from the blade, then twisted to my right, pulling him toward me. This exposed his right shoulder, and I gave it a solid elbow after releasing his wrist. He grunted, doubled over, and dropped the knife, looking more stunned and pained than the modest blow warranted. I needed the break. My entire back was on fire from the ribs. It hurt far more than I expected, and every move made me regret not taking more painkillers.

I kicked the loose blade under the Honda and planted a knee solidly into his forehead. The fight was going my way, but I felt my steam leaving. If this came down to a grappling contest, I didn't know if I could win. Braga may be less than 100 percent, but he still seemed rugged and stout. I had to retreat and make it to my weapons before he could make it to his.

My hasty plan turned to shit before it started, as Braga's left hand knocked me straight across the jaw. I clearly hurt him, but I'm sure it hurt me more, and it made me lose my grip on his wrist, but I didn't worry. Instead, since my back was against the wall, I used it to push him away from me, my sides firing again. You'd think I'd get used to the pain, but each exertion felt like the tissue was tearing away from the bone. That wasn't the case. It was just the inflammation getting worse, but it hurt like a motherfucker!

Braga flew away from me and onto the hood of the Cr-V. I heard him grunt and exhale loudly. This was my chance to rush to my loft, where I kept my weapons. I turned and sprinted as best as my body would allow, a quick look back revealing what I feared: Braga was going for his bag and whatever firearms waited. It would be a close race between reaching my loft and getting a few rounds in my back.

The stairs I had climbed a thousand times were a painful obstacle, but I took them two at a time until I reached the top landing and the safety of my doorway.

"Warren!" Braga yelled from behind.

He wanted to slow me down or have me turn around, but I ignored him, continued toward my space, and slammed the door as two rounds landed near the handle. A good grouping from so far away, but I assumed he wouldn't stay where he was. He must have fired as he ran because several more bullets struck the door and walls. I figured I had no more than eight seconds before he was at my door.

Mike had frozen in place, unsure what was happening or what to do. I made the quick calculation to arm myself instead of grabbing her. Doing the latter would have left us vulnerable when he eventually kicked the door in. The immediate rush of adrenaline overrode some of the pain in my ribs, allowing me to jump over my couch. It still hurt like a motherfucker. I reached underneath, where I kept one of my favorite weapons, a Glock .40. There wouldn't be time for anything fancy. He'd come charging through the door, shooting, so careful aiming was hardly a priority.

Braga kicked the door in at the same moment I brought the weapon up level. I only had one hand holding the gun, so my aim would be shit. The door flew open, and as soon as it did, I let loose with three poorly aimed rounds. He never entirely broke through the frame when

322

the shots rang out, his hesitancy gifting me time to grip the weapon with both hands and assume a better shooting stance. Only then did I tell Mike to get down on the floor behind the kitchen island and call the police if she hadn't already. She had stayed frozen at the counter for the eternity of the event. I moved a few feet to my left into my bedroom, using the frame as partial concealment, even though the two layers of sheetrock were unlikely to stop any rounds he fired.

He must have known the police would be coming, so the smart move would be to flee. I had no proper cover but waited in a solid firing position, albeit slightly bent because of my ribs, for him to enter, if he ever did. Sure, he might be able to get in a lucky shot if he were to make a rush around the door frame, but the odds of that working out were slim. I wished I knew what his play was, what he thought he might get out of this now. If I could hold him in position long enough for the police to arrive, we'd be safe.

"Looking back," Braga said from around the corner, unseen, "I should have come myself and killed your friend. I'd have killed you then."

I said nothing, knowing he was baiting me. Any conversation would kill time for the police to arrive, but I didn't have it in me. I was in so much pain and probably more scared than I'd been in a while. It was more than my life in jeopardy here. Mike was in the kitchen, and I didn't care to think what would happen if I failed to stop Braga. The rocks underneath Lorelei's cliff were dangerously close. Her singing had stopped, yet the river's flow was in charge now, dragging me toward an inevitable doom.

"Was that other guy a friend of yours, too? I didn't catch his name, but he seemed like a real piece of street shit, just like Travers. He smelled like it anyways."

He planned to goad me into action, but why? To wait for me to get mad and yell something so he'd have a better chance when he rushed me? Why not just run away?

"I don't think I'm getting out of this, Warren. Cops are on their way, I'm pretty fucked up, and all the ways out look closed. You seem like a righteous motherfucker, so I wanna kill you before I go or get killed by the cops. Is that okay with you?"

My plan was simple: stay in a defensive posture until he gets tired of attacking or the police arrive. That plan, like many of mine, turned to shit when Braga sent three rounds into the loft space. From behind the island, Mike shrieked and tried to make herself even smaller.

"Who's your friend?"

The mere shift of his attention toward Mike brought a new set of emotions, not least a form of protective rage I'd never felt before. My feelings for Mike were new and tender, delicate little fiddleheads, green and needing time to grow and flourish.

Braga was far quicker than I expected, and three more rounds came into the loft space. This time, though, they seemed more intentionally sent in my direction, and immediately after, he dashed into the space before I could take proper aim. My three shots flew wide and high. He made it to the kitchen and landed with an audible grunt and thud on the far side, within feet of Mike, who was sitting in a tight ball with her back against the island, hands covering her ears.

I fired three more rounds dead center of the kitchen island, each recoil making my cracked ribs and bruised torso ache. There was grunting and sounds of apparent pain, but nothing that made me think Braga was out of action. In fact, quite the opposite occurred. Braga grabbed Mike by the throat and dragged her behind the island, screaming as she went.

"Well, she seems nice," Braga taunted from his temporary safe space.

My two brothers had died in a fiery mix of mechanical violence and teenage stupidity. My demigods were gone in the space of a few heartbeats, or however long it took for the car they were driving to come to rest. The Boone County-famous Warren brothers, along with two of their teammates, had been ripped from the world in an accident that was equal parts negligence, stupidity, and recklessness.

As a twelve-year-old boy freshly stunned by a monumental loss, the details at the time escaped me. I just knew they had died in an accident. What I only put together years after was that the boys, slightly buzzed after a football victory and a few beers, were joyriding along a county highway, weaving their way over and through the lines, heedless of concern for anything else in the world. The high they had from a victory over a rival pushed all good sense and self-preservation from their still unformed minds. Add in a trucker, high on a mix of tight schedules and amphetamines, taking a curve a little too wide and too fast, and you have four dead high school boys, three destroyed families, and a grieving county.

As absent and distant as my father had been, the frequency of his trips increased, as did their duration. He'd tell me his job as a consultant, contractor, or whatever euphemism he chose to hide what he actually did kept him away. Little me knew it was because his heart was broken, and he didn't have it in him to be a father anymore, even though he was still a father to a young boy who desperately needed one.

The deaths of Joey and Henry eventually killed my mother, too. The shock had taken its toll, but she limped by, dragging along a toxic mix of grief, depression, pill addiction, and alcoholism. Her "accidental" overdose ten years later took no one by surprise.

Naturally, the little emotionally abandoned child would become a soldier and police officer with a twelve-year-old's notion of saving others and hopefully preventing their violence-inspired journey of loss.

One of the lessons that the little boy grew to learn was that sometimes the violence brought into our lives needed to be countered with a superior amount and quality of violence to make the world safer for others.

I broke from my position and moved halfway to the kitchen, only ten feet away, leaving me open and vulnerable. At such close range, I wouldn't need much of a target; a shoulder or any part of his head would do. Instead, I got Mike, only her head at first, but then slowly more, and then Braga stood, hugging her tightly. He was done fighting, and it looked like he wanted a hostage to get out of there.

He and Mike stood to their full heights behind the island, with Braga keeping his body angled to the side, hiding his mass behind Mike's body. With his left arm, he had her held firmly at the waist, meshing her hips with his left one. The barrel of the pistol was buried under Mike's jaw, keeping her head forced back, his right eye barely sticking out from behind. Mike's eyes cried out for help, but she was silent as Braga inched her toward the door.

"This has been fun, but I should go. Your friend will stay with me for a while if that's okay with you."

There was nothing for me to say. The guy didn't know if he wanted to stay and kill me or not. Years of training and experience kept me locked into my firing stance despite my pain, my Glock waiting for its chance to speak and earn its keep. I needed an opportunity to capitalize on a mistake, and I hoped he didn't decide to go out in a blaze, taking Mike first. That seemed unlikely as his survival instinct was working again, and they continued their slow sideways shuffle toward the doorway, Braga taking great pains to stay behind Mike's lean frame. He knew I was waiting for a clear shot.

Ten more feet to the door.

"Why you so quiet, Warren? You seem the chatty type." He paused to take a quick peek behind to gauge his distance, but then returned his attention to me. "I won't hurt your girl if this all works out. I need some help getting outta here."

There was still nothing for me to say. From his position, Braga would be able to see the landing in front of the doorway and the stairs leading to it. If I were him, I wouldn't want to play this game walking backward downstairs. I needed one opportunity.

To her credit, Mike was a champ. She had overcome her initial shock and entered the mental territory of someone who'd been through some shit before. I still hadn't asked what "Survivor" meant in her Twitter bio. Her eyes were alive with activity, wide but less with fear and more with awareness. Whatever was about to happen, she wanted to see every bit of it.

Three feet from the door, Braga stopped to appraise my position, my lack of cover, with his single eye from behind Mike. He had seen the stairs and arrived at the same conclusion I had.

"Drop your weapon, Warren. Throw it on the couch. You get to stay here while your girl and I take off. I'll let you live. Just stay here."

I remained silent. He wasn't going to let me live. I wouldn't if I were him. He knew I couldn't stay here while he ran off with Mike. He had too much ground to cover to escape the building, and in that time, I'd be able to retrieve my weapon and try to make something bad happen to him. He also knew I'd shoot him the moment he gave me the opportunity. No, he had to kill me.

Keeping my body tight and ready, I began to lower my weapon, eyes locked on any movement of his gun. I needed him to point it at me before I could do anything. I relied on his need for haste, but I gambled poorly.

It seemed to take forever, but my gun's descent to my side eventually put Braga at ease. The barrel of his gun was still under Mike's chin. She was tense, both hands firmly grasping Braga's left forearm wrapped in front of her. Her eyes were wide with anticipation.

"Now toss it on the couch."

I had played this wrong. I saw a few signs of how I thought this would go, and I'd bet all my chips. I was now caught in the open with a weapon at my side and an armed assailant hidden behind a hostage, an assailant who needed me dead.

328

"Toss the fucking gun, Warren." Braga's voice carried fatigue and exasperation. Despite his superior position, he must have been tired of all this and simply wanted to be on his way after safely killing me.

I kept hold of the Glock, hoping the frustration would prompt him into a mistake or misstep. There was no noise in my almost-sterile white loft, and the commotion of the produce warehouse next door had ceased when the gunfire started. Mike's eyes bore through me, telling me something. Braga's rapid nasal breathing was the only sound as we waited for him to make what was going to happen happen. He gave a last solid breath, a sigh, really.

"Oh, fuck it," he said.

He untucked the gun barrel from Mike's jawline, which moved in an arc toward me. He did it too slowly, and within an instant of its removal from Mike, she tucked her chin toward her chest and rammed her head backward into Braga's teeth and nose, blood immediately spraying from his face. She ripped his left arm away from her midsection and sprinted back toward the kitchen, leaving her attacker stunned and exposed.

Again, I didn't have time to aim properly, but from only a few feet away, I'd hit him somewhere. Firing three quick rounds, I heard the punch of one bullet landing in his right shoulder and saw him spin in that direction. The second grazed the meat of his right bicep, and the third must have missed him altogether. The momentum from the spin took him through the doorway and out onto the landing, but as he ran, he raised his weapon toward Mike in the kitchen and fired three rapid rounds.

She shrieked as the bullets flew around her, one striking the nearby counter and sending up shards of marble, cutting her face. She reeled back and clutched her cheek that was spilling blood. I wanted to run to her, but first, I had to take care of Braga.

I could have shut and barricaded the door, hoping it would keep him out and that the police would arrive in time.

I could have sheltered in place.

I could have stayed inside the loft space and fired an occasional round at him, keeping his head down until the police came.

I could have let him run away, but that seemed the worst option.

Instead, I wanted to become the rocks that crashed upon the sailor.

I ran out of the loft. He was ten feet from the door, and I took the shot. From about thirty-five feet away, I sent two rounds into his running backside. Both landed true, one on his left shoulder and the other squarely between the shoulder blades. He fell forward, motionless, inches from his bag and the front door. I didn't want to take my eyes off him, but I had to check on Mike.

Her cuts were minor, as was the blood loss. It was one of those things that were scary as hell at the moment but left no serious physical damage. I confirmed she had called 911 and returned to the doorway to secure Braga's weapon.

He was breathing, barely, but he was alive. The shot that landed between his shoulder blades should have killed him, but he was wearing a vest I hadn't seen or felt in our fight. Knowing he had one wouldn't have changed anything, and besides, I wasn't a good enough marksman to land an intentional headshot from my position. I might have grabbed some rags or towels to help stop the bleeding as I did for Xtra, but I didn't have it in me to do anything other than secure his weapon and prop my door open for the police, who should be here any minute. I cleared both weapons, his and mine, set them on the hood of the Honda, and returned to Braga.

The pool of his blood had grown. That didn't upset me. It didn't upset me that I had to shoot someone. That was an easy decision. It didn't upset me to see the physical gore from the violence I had rendered. What upset me was that my home had been violated yet again, and this man was still alive. With Mike watching me and the police coming soon, I had no opportunity to end this with more violence. My only hope was that Braga would bleed out before help arrived for him. That would calm my world, and for that, I hated myself.

"Warren," I heard weakly from the floor beneath me. "Hey."

He wasn't going anywhere. The three wounds were bad enough to make him too weak to do anything, and I had sight of his hands. I sat beside him as he lay face down on the bloody concrete.

"Yeah?" I said.

His skin was white, and he licked his lips to moisten them so they wouldn't stick together. "Could you do me a solid and finish me off?" His voice was low and raspy but clear enough.

I said nothing. My stomach turned. He must have seen right through me.

"You know you want to," he persisted in a whisper. "Let's take care of all this the easy way. You understand, right?"

I understood, but I didn't want to tell him that. I wanted to stomp his skull in with my boot. I understood, but I wanted to stand on him to press all the air and blood out of his soiled flesh. I understood, but I wanted to drag him back up the stairs just so I could push him down them again.

Instead, I yelled up to Mike. "Could you grab me a bunch of towels from under the sink?"

She knew what I wanted them for and hesitated a moment, then, after wrestling with her own moral computations, did what I asked. Later, I'd ask what was going through her head during that moment of hesitation. She came and handed me the pile of multipurpose towels; the same kind I used to stop X's bleeding not so long ago. Now, I'd use them to help save the architect of his death. I hated myself for it and wondered whether this was an improvement in behavior. Then again, I thought, keeping him alive was probably the worst thing for him. That made me feel a little better.

I worked silently for a minute, placing rags where needed and tying others to hold them in place. Mike sat on the floor beside me, leaning against the wall, watching me work. When I was done, I joined her, and we both watched the now-passed-out Braga struggle with every breath.

We sat leaning against each other, having lots to say but not wanting to break the silence, the peace. Until I did.

"Survivor, huh?"

Outside, I heard the approaching sirens—the real ones.

48

Christmas seemed to come earlier every year, but really, it just came earlier than I wanted it to. After Halloween, the red and green decorations went up, and the ho-ho-ho-ing began. Thanksgiving be damned.

Everything in Jack London Square seemed to be festooned with holiday bunting. Everything except the seagulls. They were the same opportunists the year through, sitting on the handrails and bench backs, waiting for a handout to fill their bellies or the perfect wind to send them aloft like Santa's reindeer.

After several weeks of waiting, I finally received the news I'd been expecting and hoping for. My lawyer let me know the District Attorney wouldn't be pressing any manslaughter or assault charges against me. I hadn't expected them to, but the waiting had been wearing on me.

The killing of the intruder was judged to be in self-defense, my handgun was registered correctly, and there was a witness to the second event with Braga. The police simply couldn't ignore the fact that I had killed a guy—well, only one they were aware of, because I wasn't about to share any details about the trafficker I had shot after he killed Cooper.

After I was initially charged, I had to turn myself in. My attorney in Kansas City, Doc Bradley, had found a criminal defense attorney in Oakland, Arvid Newse. Though I was a guest of the city of Oakland for only about twenty-six hours, I got arraigned, and Newse had bail arranged. All in all, it went pretty smoothly for my first arrest. Newse assured me the DA's office was playing for the public so they would appear tough on crime, but no one expected the charges to stay.

He was correct, but the wait was interminable. We knew they'd take a few weeks to decide, so they had to let the investigations run their course. The previous week, we'd received word that the homicide investigation was complete and that a decision would be forthcoming. Newse told me he'd keep an ear to the ground to track the overall investigation, but I was a free man, not counting the time in the city lockup.

This morning, of my two regular cafes, I visited the one less regaled in Christmas adornments, the other looking as if my grandmother's attic full of decorations had erupted in the store. It was barely November, for chrissakes! I sat outside in the growing warmth, the temperature rising as the morning clouds faded. I expected Mike to arrive soon, but she'd been so busy lately that I wouldn't be surprised if she were late. She was still a ninja, but couldn't surprise me anymore if I focused on my surroundings instead of aimlessly letting my mind wander. Today, I saw her approaching a few blocks away on her bike.

"Hi!" she said, coming over to kiss me hello. I still wasn't used to the intimacy of such an act after several years of solitude, but I could get to enjoy it.

"How was the interview?" I asked. The producers of NBC's Dateline had approached her about involvement with a story they were running on Braga and his string of murders.

She pulled a face and shook her head. "It went well enough. They really want to put something out soon, but I feel they're making it too sensational, too tawdry. And it's all too late to help anyone. I tried to get them interested in a story about all the killings last year, but the mystery of the murders of the unhoused wasn't important enough back then. Now they want to make a big splashy piece. It's entertainment to them at this point."

"How much would they pay for your input on this entertainment?" I asked.

"We didn't get that far, but it'd have to be a stupid amount of money for me to get involved. Like crazy stupid. They just want sensationalism. Not to fix anything or help anyone."

I raised my mug as a salute. "Here's to crazy, stupid money."

"Even then, I'm not sure about the whole thing. It may take up more of my time than I'd like." She fell silent and looked away as if continuing her inner deliberations about jumping on board. After a few moments, she looked back. "What about you? How was your class this morning?"

Now it was my turn to look away. "It was fine," I lied—and she knew it. She knew I couldn't stay still or focused during my meditation sessions, and that thoughts and images of death kept visiting.

"Really?" She asked, knowing better than to believe me. She remained quiet, knowing the awkward silence would make me talk more to fill it.

"Okay, it sucked this morning," I said, giving in to her superior interrogation skills. "I can sit there and make it look like I'm calm, but my brain is still busy."

"Well, it's called a practice. Meditation practice. Stick with it."

I hated that phrase, but she was correct. I didn't like being left alone with my thoughts during practice, but I supposed that was the idea: to get away from them, to learn how to put them aside, and to focus on the breath. I still thought drinking did a better job of keeping my attention away from dark thoughts.

For a couple of weeks after the Braga thing, I spent most of my free time drinking, but I eventually noticed that while drunkenness may have kept the ghosts at bay, it also kept Mike away. She let me know that the drinking, by keeping all the bad thoughts from visiting, also made me a fraud. She was right, but for a while, I ignored it. I would have felt better being a fraud than having these extra memories visit me. Surprisingly, I didn't feel any remorse about killing the trafficker who tried to kill me. What did bother me was lying to Mike about it.

She was right that I was distant, silent, and drank too much, like I was with Laura at the end. I bottled up too much drama and trauma and kept it medicated with drinking. While the booze kept me temporarily safe, it also prevented any sunshine from entering the situation. I had a decision to make: stay the course to keep the bad thoughts from entering my brain and taking over, probably poisoning my relationship with Mike, or put the bottle down once in a while and find a way to deal with the visitors.

I had killed two people. A cop was dead, as were two of my friends. My home had once again been spoiled by evil and death. The purpose of my move here, like the previous time in Idaho, had been to avoid this misery. Instead, on both occasions, I fell right into its path, adding to all the reasons I quit the department and ran away. Could I run away again? Sure, but the same thing would happen. I'd get better for a while, but then something large or small would happen to make me want to return to drinking and avoidance. Not that I needed a reason. I was doing plenty of drinking here before the first dead body even arrived.

No, I had to accept the fact that alcohol, which was temporarily effective in helping with avoidance, wasn't a good tool for actually healing, for getting comfortable with the ghosts and their visits. Letting them visit and pass by was healthier. More difficult but healthier. She also finally told me all about her survivor story, and, in many ways, it put my history to shame. If she can become as strong and powerful as she's become after what she survived, I suppose I can put the damn bottle down once in a while.

So, between the meditation and online sobriety groups I visited, I managed to lessen my drinking. Harm reduction, they called it in the groups. I wasn't even sure I wanted to quit drinking altogether. I'd built up a small network of bar friends who kept my evenings at The Golden Door light and filled with conversation, but I supposed that not getting drunk every day was probably healthy for me.

I listened to Mike talk about her day and the other interview she had lined up for the evening, though barely. I was thinking about how to move forward through this mess and not merely avoid it, but then I caught myself.

"And how does that affect the Hub?" I asked. I listened well enough, even when mentally distracted, to follow enough of the conversation to jump in and ask a good question if I felt like I was losing focus.

"Like I said, it doesn't, other than being able to raise advertising rates. The exposure is great, but we aren't paid anything if another source uses our story."

Okay. Maybe I'm not that good at listening. She had just said that a moment ago.

"At this point, I'm making tons more from subscriptions than the Hub. They can't afford to give me a raise yet, so I'll continue with the TV spots and guest articles to help get more patrons." Mike had more to say, but she could tell I wasn't listening. "Your mind is elsewhere. What's up?"

What's up was things I couldn't tell her. What's up was how easily I'd killed Williamson when it suited me, and that I felt no remorse. What's up is that I really wanted to kill Braga and didn't, primarily because I didn't want to do it in front of her. I think it would have felt really good to finish him off, and letting him live was going to bother me.

I leaned back, embarrassed that she could read me.

"You thinking about selling your place and moving on?" she asked.

"Well, the thought crossed my mind."

"Crossed my mind, too. You moved out of your place in Idaho after you found all those bodies. I was wondering if you'd do the same here. It would be understandable." She looked down and away when she spoke the last sentence as if she was expecting me to want to move.

"Another thought that crossed my mind," I said, "is that wherever I move, something will probably happen to make me want to move away again. Maybe not dead bodies, but there will always be something, some type of trigger." I paused and looked directly at her. "I figure I'd stick around a while longer. Besides, you seem kinda cool."

"Kinda cool?" she said in mock anger. "I'm hella cool. You definitely should hang out with me more! Besides, I'm entering Sugar Mama territory with all these new subscriptions. Someone perpetually unemployed like you would do well to have me around."

We had never gotten around to the mystery of where my money came from or how much I had. If that ever came up, I'd run with the story that I took early retirement and invested the funds well. I wasn't sure I was ready to share how my income originated.

A smile crept upon my lips. "Well, that's an interesting idea: being a kept man, on-call at all times, waiting for Mama to need some attention. Whatever would I do in the meantime, between servicings?"

Mike blushed, not expecting me to make a colorful innuendo with her comment. She should know me better by now.

A silent pause. A pause brought on by the shared knowledge that deep down we were on the verge of an actual relationship, one with real feelings and depth, one where neither of us knew what came next. As real as it was, it was still one that I could fuck up in an instant if I weren't careful. I had fucked up so much already. I had killed again and held the secret away from her, creating a crack in our foundation before we even started.

I had followed Lorelei's voice, and I survived the rocks. The mayor and Xtra weren't so lucky. Williams played a dangerous game and came out the worse for it. X was in the wrong place at the wrong time and became a target. Mike, simply by being around me, was almost killed in the end.

Once again, I'd failed at avoiding conflict, and this time, even more people died. I tell myself I'd be happy having little or no connection to the broader world, to simply stick to my walking and drinking, but the world doesn't seem to want that. The universe must want me embroiled in some sort of conflict, to be cursed with demons and bad thoughts. No sooner do I make peace with one memory than another is created to visit me. Leaning away from or avoiding the bad things hasn't been terribly effective.

"So, what will you do between servicings?" Mike asked, half-teasing.

"I don't know. Maybe I'll get a job finally," I said, not meaning it.

"Want to invest in a mildly successful weekly newspaper?"

"Not what I had in mind."

I turned away, unsure where I was going with my words, and looked out over the bay. The water in the estuary danced with the breeze, pushing it from the west. On the railing nearest me, no more than fifteen feet away, sat an enormous gull, brilliant in its white and black. He looked me up and down as I did the same to him. Whatever problems or struggles he may have in his bird life didn't seem to weigh him down, and he proved it by taking off in flight.

The gull dove off the railing to catch air as he fell, but his wide, outstretched wings quickly found purchase, and he rose into the brightening day. He soared up and hovered over the water, seemingly motionless, letting the breeze hold him in place. When he spotted something of interest, or maybe when he felt like it, he dipped his wing and headed west, further into the bay, further out over the water. Maybe it was a friendlier land; maybe it was a safer territory. Or maybe it was just time to do so.

About the Author

Daniel D. Baumer is a U.S. Army veteran and former law enforcement officer. He is the author of *The Stone Harvest*, the first in the Karl Warren series. His stories are inspired by his life experiences and the people he has encountered in his many travels and adventures. Learn more about him at danieldbaumer.com.